The Feast

THE FEAST

by

MATTHEW G. REES

A WORK OF FICTION

LAST SUPPER PRESS

Author's Note

Have you ever wondered about the origins of a meal that you are eating or have consumed: the ingredients... the way they were cooked... the conduct, and perhaps the character, of the chef?

I suspect this is something that, on the whole, we try to confine to the very backs of our minds. For to consider the matter too closely risks opening what might – in certain cases – prove a very unpalatable can of worms.

However, it is the task of an author of dark fiction to confront such things. Hence the stories that follow in *The Feast*.

These tales were written over the course of two years in which I found myself returning, again and again, to what might be called their 'connective tissue': the dark side of dining.

It is – I feel – an area of age-old fascination (albeit a rather unsettling one).

On the cover of this volume, you will find an image of Vincenzo Campi's sixteenth century oil painting *The Ricotta Eaters* – chosen by me for its charming grotesqueness. Of particular note is the human skull that some consider detectable in the ricotta: a *memento mori*, a reminder of death, in a scene of careless indulgence.

Happily, I don't think I've suffered any of the misfortunes that unfold in the stories that follow. Nor do I know – for certain – of anyone who has. But I *have* wondered...

And – of course – there's a first time for everything, isn't there?

In closing, I should say that, as well as tales of the dark kind, readers of these stories will encounter narratives of a slightly lighter nature: the 'macabre-but-mirthful', as I think of them. Humour is sometimes the best conduit for the horrific, after all.

Finally, the stories in *The Feast* appear in this collection only and have not been published in journals elsewhere.

The collection was first published in 2021. One of the reasons for the 're-covering' has been to include feedback from readers who've partaken of the fare.

And now it only remains for me to wish you… bon appétit!

Matthew G. Rees
2022

For more about Matthew G. Rees visit
www.matthewgrees.com

Things sweet to taste prove in digestion sour.

William Shakespeare, *Richard II*

Stories

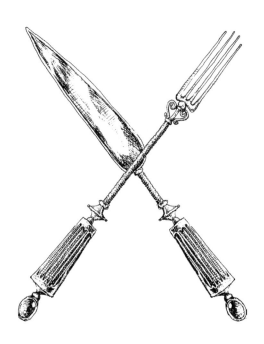

The Twilight Maiden

It was late and the sky was a cloak of indigo whose stars were beginning to twinkle when Giuseppe Dellucci arrived, finally, in the village of Collina Rossa.

The ancient stone towers of the hilltop settlement stood black and silent, radiating heat from the day's long sun no matter the hours that had passed since its orange orb had set. The scent of jasmine filled the night air, its white flowers luminously lovely on trellises, railings and the curlicued ironwork of balconies.

Since well before dusk, Dellucci had been climbing, rucksack on his back, into the dusty hills of that uncommonly quiet part of Tuscany, the train of the district having deposited him at a halt near a river whose quick, green water had lost all sound to his ears in the valley that now lay deep below and behind him.

Yet, as he entered Collina Rossa – the contours of its darkened houses suggesting properties of antiquity in the traditional stone-walled, clay-tiled Tuscan style – he felt not triumph of the kind he had expected, but something more curious: a sense within himself that its venerable walls and ways were listening... to his steps, his breath and even the beating of his heart... the isolated settlement seemingly wondering in its age-old foundations as to the identity of this advancing stranger of the evening, pondering the purpose he might have.

The narrow and curving streets were empty save occasionally for a woman, perhaps with a basket, disappearing into a dwelling, drawing a heavy, wooden door closed behind her, and cats, that looked silently from their ledges and steps in the gloom.

The small, airborne forms that Dellucci's eyes half-detected above him, he took from their flutters and darts to be bats rather than birds, while, in deserted and lamp-less squares, *i grilli* (crickets) chorused their strangely hypnotic night song.

The taverna *Vite Rossa* at last showed itself... in the corner of what appeared to be the village's main piazza: yellow light and conversation of a seemingly inconsequential kind emanating from a porch whose door stood ajar. Dellucci had, with difficulty, found the establishment's particulars in a guidebook of the old kind rather than on the internet (where the absence of any reference to the village had caused him to wonder if the settlement might be one of those that in parts of Italy had fallen into dereliction and abandonment).

As Dellucci now entered the inn, it did not fall silent in the way that writers of stories tend to concoct, but continued, as it apparently had been, its patrons talking, raising glasses and dining at tables of a small and simple kind. However, our traveller felt certain that his arrival had been 'noted', and that the taverna's entire clientele, while carrying on with their business, had either an eye or an ear fixed firmly on the stranger who now stood in their midst... to a woman and a man.

He announced himself to the landlord – a large, balding, big-bellied fellow with a walrus moustache, who stood behind the bar in an apron – enquiring thereafter as to the receipt of the letter that, in the absence of a telephone number or email address, he had written in request of a room: a communication to which the author had received no answer (Dellucci deciding to pursue his journey to Collina Rossa regardless).

After an initial expression of ignorance of the missive – in which Dellucci had described himself as a restaurateur in Rome with an interest in culinary research who would be undertaking a field trip in search of local 'finds' – the landlord, perhaps jogged by the traveller's production from a pocket in his linen jacket of an evidently well-stocked wallet, seemed to remember and, nodding and smiling, confirmed there was indeed a room at the inn and, with an outstretched arm, emerged from behind the bar to usher his most welcome guest to a table of his own.

On its cloth, the innkeeper briskly set down a bottle of chilled water, a bottle of red wine and glasses for each. Retreating into what Dellucci took to be a kitchen of some kind, the man, a short while later, reappeared with a fine-looking loaf of olive bread and a platter of pleasingly pungent cheeses. These Dellucci set about hungrily after his long journey and climb. However, he could not hide his disappointment at the absence from this supper of the specific delicacy that he had come in search of... namely, 'the maiden'. Or, to give the appellation that Dellucci had discovered a certain strand of cognoscenti had reserved for it through the ages, 'the twilight maiden': Collina Rossa's tomato of legend.

When the innkeeper – for whom a visit by a Roman restaurateur was clearly a rare thing – returned to Dellucci's table near the end of his repast, enquiring as to the acceptability of the meal, Dellucci replied that it had been wonderful, while adding (in what he hoped was both a casual and discreet way) that his one and only pity had been the absence from his plate of a tomato.

Agreeing vigorously, the innkeeper responded that the great shame was that there were no tomatoes available that evening, after which he quickly cleared away Dellucci's plates and the remnants of the cheeses.

Although Dellucci sought not to show it, the man's response puzzled him. For, all around, he could see diners who were variously cutting or sinking their teeth into tomatoes – specimens, he didn't doubt, of the precise variety of which he had come in search. Indeed, their preponderance was such, that it seemed to him as if he had arrived on the night of a festival devoted to the fruit.

Juice spilled from the mouths and dripped from the jaws of those seated near him – who ate in silence, save for their sucks and their chomps.

Dellucci sat sipping his wine as if untroubled by the sight of their faintly primitive feasting. But, *inside*, he was tantalised.

That night, as he lay on the covers of the bed in the attic room to which the landlord had shown him, Dellucci went over in his head the history of 'the twilight maiden', in so far as he knew it.

A 'great prelate' – there was uncertainty as to the figure's identity, but various cardinals and even popes had been speculated – had visited the village in a year that was lost in the mists of time, though perhaps the twelfth or thirteenth centuries. The visit to the village had been little more than a stop-over for the purpose of a night's rest for the members of the prelate's party – who were engaged on a tour of centres of far greater importance in the region – and for the provision of water and forage for their horses. But the consumption by the prelate of a tomato during his stay – most likely served with his evening meal – had overshadowed all other matters of that grand progress. For such was the tomato's texture and taste that (and here the chronicles that Dellucci had read in various libraries of medieval books in Bologna and Florence diverged) the prelate denounced it as 'unnaturally fine', 'tempting to distraction' and 'the most sinful of fruits' (to quote *The Histories of Alfredo of Foggia*). Or, on the other hand, if you believed *The World and its Events* by Sister Caterina of Piacenza, the tomato was truly 'the most delicious and wholesome of things', 'heavenly beyond words' and 'a great gift from Our Lord God'.

In a rare volume that Dellucci had been permitted to handle using gloves in one little-known library whose books were secured to its ancient shelves by iron chains, an illustration of tomatoes, with a rich and heavy ripeness, veritably groaning on their vine, occupied the margin beside Sister Caterina's eulogistic text. Awed at how the illustration had – for the best part of a millennium – survived with such… *allure*, Dellucci had noted the unusually deep colour of the tomatoes… more crimson than scarlet… and – holding his breath – had touched their images with his gloved fingertips.

In spite of the best efforts of Sister Caterina, the account of Alfredo of Foggia – stressing the 'forbidden' quality of the tomato – appeared to have held sway, seemingly leading (with other testimonies, mere fragments of which remained) to the tomato's suppression in an era that more or less coincided with the persecutions of the Inquisition. Certain faintly eccentric historical figures such as the horticulturalist Professor Giovanni Bassanelli, an improbable adviser to Mussolini (in the matter of diet), had made fleeting and at times quite cryptic references in their private papers and journals to the 'twilight maiden of Collina Rossa' (as an elite inner circle came to call it). Other than that, there was nothing… all official histories, heredities and genealogical trees of tomatoes stood quite bare of the strain. For eight hundred, perhaps a thousand years, the maiden had, it seemed, been banished. Proof of this being that he, Dellucci, a restaurateur in Rome – of two-and-a-half decades' longevity – would have known nothing of it… not even a seed… had it not been for the old and elegant gentleman who, having dined alone in Dellucci's trattoria one night and while leaving his tip, had asked his host if he knew of 'the twilight maiden', adding with a whisper and a squeeze to his arm, 'You *really* should try it', before putting on his black felt hat, collecting his malachite cane and strolling out into the busy Roman night.

Beyond the shutters of Dellucci's attic room at the taverna, the chorus of the crickets now steadily subsided. Free of the noise of scooters and cars that so often interrupted his sleep in Rome, his eyelids surrendered to a lovely lullaby of owls (whose downy forms he imagined peering from arrow loops and the ledges of haylofts).

Once only in the night did he awake – suddenly and to a sound that made his heart race. Beyond the village, in woods or perhaps the scrubby olive groves through which he had earlier passed, wolves howled an eerie nocturne at the moon.

In the morning, Dellucci showered and then breakfasted lightly on black coffee and warm rolls, with honey, brought up to his room by the landlord. Dellucci chose not to raise the matter of 'the maiden' with the man directly, sensing that the landlord (after the events of the previous evening) might have reason to be reticent about the fruit – pride; payment; perhaps a desire to keep the matter as a secret of the village, or even himself. A more roundabout approach with this rustic fellow might be best, felt Dellucci.

When the innkeeper asked Dellucci about his luncheon requirements, Dellucci responded that a plate of salami or prosciutto would be pleasing, supplemented by a nice local salad.

A short while later, he set about exploring the village.

As he strolled, Dellucci was surprised to find the streets and squares even quieter than they had been at the hour of his arrival. The shutters of houses and what he also took for shops were closed firmly against the sun.

When Dellucci tried the door of the church – which, like so many of the other buildings in the village, had an air of decay – he found that it was locked. A look of similar dereliction greeted him at the property whose peeling sign proclaimed it to be the post office.

He found some relief in the form of a fountain that sputtered in a small civic garden (itself otherwise composed of brittle weeds, rusted railings and seats whose wood was dry and rotten). Even so, Dellucci found the sound of the water not wholly comforting in those strangely still and silent surroundings.

Only once did Dellucci seem to detect human life: an old woman rocking in the shadowed interior of an ancient, mustard-hued house beside a lane where he walked. A breeze tugged the lace curtain of an unshuttered window from where the dark and serious eyes of her sallow and leathery face followed him as he passed, the slow back-and-forth of her chair giving out a steady creak.

Dellucci decided to look beyond the walls of the village for signs of life. It stood to reason, he said to himself, that the nurseries and plantations for the maiden would lie outside its ramparts, quite likely on those same slopes up which he had climbed.

Making his way to the settlement's limits, a strange thing occurred. As Delluci stepped through an archway of the perimeter, a shaft of blinding light besieged him. So bruising was its brilliance that he was forced to step back into the shade of the arch. He drew his sunglasses from a pocket in his jacket and, after a moment to compose himself, he stepped again into the light on the far side of the arch.

Once more, though, he was beaten back... and not only by the dazzling nature of the beam (never mind his dark lenses), but by its flame-like heat, which seemed to scald the skin of his face and his hands.

He retreated... all the way to the taverna, via twisting lanes and low passages whose shade and coolness came as a mercy, regardless – on occasion – of their dankness, sour smells and dead ends.

As he did so, he wondered – with creeping apprehension – about the strangeness of this citadel he had entered.

Yet, by the time he reached the step of the inn, he had dismissed such thoughts as being those of one who had grown soft in Rome, detached from Italy's true vine. Besides, he told himself, it had been noon. What was to be expected at such a time of day, and in a place like this, if not sunshine?

For a second, Dellucci brought to mind a remark made to him once by the worldly old patron of his restaurant... about mad dogs, Englishmen and the sun. The gentleman's voice had been sing-song, velvety. And his eyes… his eyes had… *laughed* (if such a thing could be said of them).

The *Vite Rossa* stood as still and as quiet as the rest of the village: the only sound being that of a couple of flies buzzing in the stuffy air of the shuttered bar.

Dellucci climbed the staircase to his room. As he did so, he passed a door from behind which came a sonorous snore he took to be that of the landlord.

Outside his own door, Dellucci found a towel covering a tray on which his lunch had been left, together with a note (from the innkeeper, he presumed). Please excuse his absence, the man had written, but the taverna was always quiet in the day… evening was the time when the *Vite Rossa* came to life.

Dellucci carried the tray into his room.

His luncheon proved a marvel of salami, prosciutto and focaccia, superior to that served in many a chi-chi establishment in Rome; the bread and meat being supplemented by a generous salad of spinach leaves, red and green peppers, sliced olives and shavings of truffle, all moistened with a dressing that made Dellucci's mouth water.

Although simple and peasantly, the meal was magnificent beyond words.

Yet, for Dellucci, one thing – *still* – was missing. To his dismay, his platter was again bereft of that which he most desired: the twilight maiden.

As he put down his knife and fork, Dellucci found himself wondering about something else: how such a repast, particularly the salad, could have been prepared by a figure who, although affable and helpful in almost every respect, was also, in his bear-like way, a little coarse and the possessor of two very meaty, hairy and clumsy-looking hands.

Having eaten, Dellucci decided, in the absence of any other activity in the village, to take a siesta.

He settled himself in an armchair in his room.

Shuttered against the glare of the sun, the room had a lovely, soft warmth that caused him to remember a woman he had once met in Naples when travelling, as a much younger man… how they had woken the next morning in her room above the bay.

As his eyelids now drooped, Dellucci's mind drifted to what he might do with the twilight maiden when that tantalising tomato was finally his: soups, sauces, salads, the finest physical specimens stuffed and presented on plates of their own.

He fell into a light and faintly feverish sleep, at times twitching, grinding his teeth and reaching out with a hand… as if to pluck at some evasive vine.

It was dark – and not merely due to the shutters of his room, but due to the darkness of nightfall – when Dellucci awoke; the time of day being a development that surprised and disconcerted him.

Anxiety – that he had passed nearly twenty-four hours in the village without so much as setting his hands… let alone his teeth and tongue… on the object of his mission – now began to gnaw at Dellucci. Faithful as many of his customers were, indulging his somewhat erratic closures of his trattoria in his rather eccentric pursuit of new pleasures for their palates, Dellucci began to wonder about the wisdom of what he had engaged upon. Perhaps the maiden was nothing but legend? A myth wildly exaggerated by medieval clerics and 'wise men' of the kind who would have you believe the world was flat and that the cure for any illness was to be sucked dry of your blood by a jar of black leeches. But had he not seen it… *there*… in the very bar below… stacked high on the plates of the natives… on only the previous night?

Yes, *tonight* would be the night, he told himself, as he put on a clean shirt for dinner: the night on which he would be inducted, the night on which the glories of the maiden would be revealed.

When Dellucci entered the bar, he saw that trade in the taverna was already good. In fact, he found himself envying the landlord for the level of his custom, wishing that such scenes could always be the picture in his own restaurant in Rome. His trattoria, although it had not impoverished him, had in no way made him rich, in spite of his years of toil. More to the point, Dellucci had come to feel that his business had aged him: cooking and serving often late into the night and then the early rises, before the sun was over St Peter's, for the freshest fish and vegetables that the markets might offer. On his climb to Collina Rossa, he had felt a tightness in his chest, a breathlessness, the hammer of his heart… and, on top of those tangible things, the sense that he had become… old… and alone.

Beaming a warm smile, the innkeeper hurried from behind the bar to tuck a chair under Dellucci as he seated himself at a table. Dellucci ordered some wine and, as the landlord turned away to fetch a bottle and a glass, Dellucci found on his table – and opened – a menu.

Turning its simple cover, Dellucci now saw – in letters that were no bigger than any other, but which, on account of their significance, leapt out at him – the words:

served with potatoes and a generous helping
of our local and very special strain of tomato
the twilight maiden

However, no sooner had his eyes glanced this than Dellucci found the menu being plucked from his hands by the innkeeper, who, depositing his wine and glass on the table, announced with an apology that the à la carte menu was unavailable that evening, while adding that he was optimistic nonetheless that his guest would enjoy the 'special dish' that was being prepared for him, if Dellucci would be kind enough to leave the matter to his host's discretion.

Taking this as a highly positive sign, Dellucci responded that he was indeed prepared to trust in the good taste of the landlord and would do so with the keenest anticipation. On hearing this answer, the landlord smiled and, uncorking the wine, filled his guest's glass.

When the *tagliatelle alla carbonara* came, it was indeed one of the finest versions of the dish that Dellucci had ever had: beautiful… creamy… cooked and presented to a standard he would himself have been proud to serve. It melted in his mouth.

Dellucci ate every last strand. Yet it was not what he had wanted or hoped for. And, as the landlord took away his empty plate with one hand, Dellucci saw that in his other – and destined for a different table – was a plate that fair groaned with tomatoes… tomatoes of a fineness he had never before seen… assembled without adornment, for their majesty needed nonesuch. Indubitably, before his very eyes and nose, *here* was the tomato of legend… the monarch of them all… the twilight maiden.

Dellucci wanted to cry out… to reach out, yet – knowing that he needed more than mere sight or taste of them… a chain of supply… seedlings, at the very least – somehow, with an intense effort (that was nothing less than torture), he both withheld his hand and bit his hungering tongue.

What *was* this game of cat and mouse? he wondered.

But he had seen the maiden now – there could be no other tomato with a look like that. The twilight maiden… She grew! She lived!

The landlord returned to Dellucci's table. Was there anything else he could offer him? the innkeeper asked, having deposited the tomatoes before a black-clad crone who to Dellucci looked to be about a thousand years old – and who was now setting about the fruit eagerly with her hen-claw hands and her horse-like teeth.

More wine, perhaps? the innkeeper suggested.

Dellucci assented.

When the man bustled back with a new bottle, Dellucci began. 'Tell me landlord,' he said, '… if you will humour my enquiry… why is it that – fine though the meals that you have served me have undoubtedly been – since my arrival in your village not a single tomato has crossed any of my plates?'

'A tomato?' the innkeeper said casually, whilst uncorking the wine, as if Dellucci had been referring to something of no special significance.

'Yes,' said Dellucci, trying not to sound too inquisitive '… a tomato. It is almost as if, for me… a visitor to this village, such a fruit is forbidden.' He forced what he hoped looked a good-natured grin.

'You have been unhappy with our hospitality?' the landlord asked, filling Dellucci's glass. 'The carbonara was cooked especially for you, signor,' he added, in a somewhat offended tone.

'My meals, as I said, have been a delight,' said Dellucci. 'But… last night – with my bread and cheese – no tomatoes. Today, the salad that came with my cold platter… no tomatoes. And, now again, this evening, a truly wonderful *tagliatelle*, but… once more… *no* tomatoes.'

'Forgive me for saying so, signor,' said the innkeeper, setting the wine bottle down on the table, 'but you seem to have quite a thing… for tomatoes.'

'Not one single specimen,' said Dellucci, still wearing his smile. 'And yet this district, this village in particular, has quite a reputation for a certain variety, does it not? And, pardon me if I seem to be forcing the point… but it has not escaped my attention that everyone in this restaurant seems to feast on them. Everyone, that is… but me.'

For a moment, never mind his great bulk, a distinct unease showed itself on the face of the landlord, who, with his walrus moustache, seemed to Dellucci like a boar that had been come upon in a forest and was now caught in a moment of indecision over whether to retreat from or charge at the hunter on its trail.

'Am I to be denied the twilight maiden?' Dellucci asked.

At this, the landlord's eyes seemed to dart to the doorway behind the bar, the one from which he both emerged with filled platters and disappeared with empty ones... as if it were *there*, behind its panels, that the answer might be found.

Observing this, Dellucci cursed himself for his stupidity in ever thinking that this lump of a man before him could possibly have created the meals he had been served.

Suddenly, Dellucci's self-restraint was overcome by passion, and he rose hotly from his table, determined to make for the kitchen and whatever was concealed behind that closed door.

Except that, no sooner had he risen from his seat, than he was back down in it... undone by the gelatinous nature of his knees, which seemed to have been stripped of all cartilage and bone. For the truth was that Dellucci – normally far too busy in his own restaurant to partake of the grape – had consumed not merely the first bottle that the landlord had brought, and the best of a glass from the one the innkeeper had newly uncorked, but the entirety of another – that Dellucci had wholly forgotten – in-between.

He slumped back in his chair, like a puppet bereft of its strings.

'A small grappa, perhaps?' the landlord now suggested (as if sensing the opportunity of a counterattack).

Dellucci, his mind as confused as his limbs – thanks to the strangeness of the village, the blinding brilliance of that morning's sun – acquiesced... and drank on.

In time, however, the beverages brought by the landlord grew bitter on Delllucci's tongue.

And, as he looked around the taverna at those who feasted, he grew angry and repulsed. One moment it was the piggishness of the patrons that offended him. The next it was their wolfishness that caused him to be alarmed.

Strangest of all were the faces that now showed themselves . . . of figures who seemed to have taken their seats silently, without even entering the inn or making salutations of any sort.

Among them was the wimpled head of a woman in holy orders who Dellucci realised could only be Sister Caterina of Piacenza, whose hagiography of the twilight maiden he knew almost by heart. Dellucci watched in awe as her slight figure feasted quietly on a great platter of the tomatoes – displaying, it seemed to him, all of the contentment and concentration of a big cat that had brought down some poor creature and was now devouring her prey in the peaceful shade of a tree. Juice and seeds streamed and spattered the half-moon of the white *guimpe* below her chin. Even more horrific, was the countenance of another: a tonsured cleric whose fleshy form Dellucci knew could only be that of Alfredo of Foggia – who in his manuscripts had denounced the maiden as if she were the seedling of Satan... yet was now gorging the self-same fruit as if his life depended upon it.

The sight of this inhuman gluttony sickened Dellucci.

Fuelled by an uncontrollable rage of both desire and disgust, he now rose, swept aside his table and staggered towards those diners engaged in their Dantesque debauchery.

On reaching them, though, words – and his knees – failed him, and, having swayed absurdly for a moment, he fell among them... to an almighty clatter of plates, a great chorus of coarse laughter and a huge, slurrying tumult of tomatoes from dishes of all kinds – soups, sauces, stews – that engulfed him on the taverna's floor.

The last thing of which Dellucci had any sense that night was his consciousness of being carried by the landlord, over his shoulder, like a hare that had been shot in the fields. Despite his drunkenness, Dellucci was struck by a singular sight: the strange, swinging gait of the landlord's left leg, as the latter lumbered him away to his place of rest.

It was the lusty crowing of a cockerel that caused Dellucci to awake: the bird's loud call having a sound that, to his ears, was part alarm bell, part dark delight (an avian equivalent of the sort of summons a barker might shout at the more dubious kind of travelling fair).

Dellucci found himself stirring not in his room at the *Vite Rossa* but in the cool and shady interior of a building that he took, from its odours and beams, to be some kind of barn.

As he rubbed his eyes with his fists, a crowd of faces closed over him.

Among their staring countenances, he recognised patrons from the inn. As he sat up and brushed straw from himself, their figures backed away.

Their retreat revealed the burly and aproned figure of the innkeeper, who was standing by a machine of an old-fashioned kind.

In a serious yet civil tone, the man began to speak.

'You came to Collina Rossa in search of the twilight maiden – a desire of the kind that we all understand. But I must warn you – it is my *duty* to warn you – that she and her seedlings are not bought cheaply: the twilight maiden is not some sort of scarlet woman of the docks or the streets. She requires a gift, a… *significant* gift, a… *sacrifice*, you might even say, of a more personal, a more… permanent kind.'

The innkeeper went on: 'We, Signor Dellucci, have all… given. For hundreds… *thousands* of years, the villagers of Collina Rossa have *given*… returning a part of themselves… *our*selves to the soil, *our* soil, of this hill – this red hill – on which we stand.'

The innkeeper gave a nod to the throng. At this, the villagers quietly began a series of partial disrobings that initially puzzled Dellucci but whose purpose soon became plain: removing hats, unbuttoning shirts, raising sleeves, lifting hems and unlacing boots… to show what they had given.

Finally, staring at Dellucci, the landlord drew up a leg of his own trousers and displayed his stout, wooden limb – so ancient and black that it might have been from the timber of the Ark.

With one paw, he now took hold of the handle on what Dellucci realised was a pulping machine of the traditional kind. With his other, he tossed to its mouth a handful of tomatoes that he took from a basket.

As they tumbled towards its iron gullet, a beam of light – that lanced the barn, as if from a knothole – fell upon the falling fruit… like some warrant from beyond the worlds of science and rational explanation: a sign that, *truly*, here was something unearthly, here was something without equal.

A murmur rose among the villagers, who stepped forward as one.

Dellucci heard the machine's handle grind.

'What will you give?' asked the landlord, as he turned it. 'What will *you* sacrifice?'

In the days that followed, Dellucci sensed not much more than one thing: a vague awareness of hands… fingers… moving tenderly upon him – in white gloves that seemed to be of the kind his memory told him his own hands had once worn in a library of books older than Italy.

Fleetingly, he seemed to see a manuscript upon which had been painted deep pools of a cochineal red. With this, he had the feeling that *he* had been impressed upon the pages of a chronicle, or inserted into an album or scrapbook.

In the kitchen of his restaurant, Giuseppe Dellucci can still slice, trim, stir, season, poach and grill, with a dexterity that exceeds the ability of most who would attempt those tasks. And, as the gracious host, his manner is much-loved by his many customers (who, to a man and a woman, it should be stated, were initially greatly taken aback by his loss).

In spite of his privation, his spirit is as lively as ever. As indeed, is his trattoria (which can be come upon, by those with a care to find it, beneath an awning of crimson in a simple back street not far from the Colosseum. Venture that way and you will in time hear its hubbub.).

If your visits should coincide, it could be that a certain elegant old gentleman will – with a squeeze of your arm – recommend a dish as (having dined) he departs for the evening.

With a flourish at those feasting (and by way of a hint at his worldliness), he may even add, 'When in Rome, do as the Romans...', the tap of his cane on the pavement thereafter being lost amid laughter, wineglasses meeting other wineglasses and cutlery keenly forking and spooning from platters and bowls.

Dellucci himself is likely to see you to your table, skilfully throwing over it a new white cloth, in place of one that has perhaps become stained.

And, occasionally, when the fancy takes him, he will, with his left arm – his only arm – lead from the kitchen his lady... into the aisle between the tables, where, to the delight of those assembled, the two of them shall dance.

THE END

Or… maybe not.

The twilight maiden, as I hope you have by now come to appreciate, reader, is a dark and mysterious thing.

And, in my role as its present-day chronicler, I feel more than a little obliged – perhaps in an echo of that rivalry between those arch scribblers Alfredo of Foggia and Sister Caterina of Piacenza – that I should advance a *different* denouement with which to close this story… an alternative last course for you to consider.

In this ending, the scenes… outwardly… are the same: Giuseppe Dellucci's busy restaurant in Rome, the awning of crimson over its windows, the worldly old man with the malachite cane, who might (should your visits coincide) squeeze your arm, flash an enigmatic smile and talk for a moment in a wine-flavoured whisper.

Your menu now, however, will be different in two respects.

In this offering, Dellucci has no lack of an arm. What has been taken… *severed* from him… is something hidden, something… lower-hanging. 'Things' with an *s*, I ought really to write, because we're talking in the plural here… a man's own fruits, to be clear: taken, pulpified, pressed, sunk into the dry soil of Collina Rossa, to be consumed by… the maiden.

Dellucci dances with his lady, nonetheless: her arms around him in the aisle of his restaurant, almost (some of a poetic disposition might think) in the manner of a vine.

He has her now, and yet, of course, he does not… and never shall. For that is the spell, the secret and the beauty, of the twilight maiden.

In these matters, I am no more than your servant… your *waiter*, dear reader. I am loath to dictate. An arm or 'sweetbreads'? I leave this choice of last course to your own admirable good taste.

A Table for Two in Moosetuckett

'Oh Norm, this place is *beautiful*,' said Andrea Lakowski.

'I thought you'd like it,' Norman Lakowski answered her, handing his jacket to the girl at the coat check.

'So much history!' his wife continued, as they waited at the Wait Here To Be Seated sign. 'Just *look* at the size of that moose head! How big is he!? D'you see his eyes? D'you think he's lookin' at us? Goodness! This place must be a hundred years old!'

'Well, it's a special occasion, so I figured we needed somewhere… special,' Lakowski responded.

'I'm surprised we haven't been here before,' his wife said.

'Well, things have… gotten in the way a little just lately. But anyway, here we are.'

A man – who appeared to be the manager, perhaps even the owner – made towards them. He wore an awkward-looking ginger toupee that drew their eyes in a way he seemed to register.

'Well, howdy folks,' he began, 'and welcome to the Moosetuckett Moose Hut, first opened way back in Nineteen Hundred and Thirteen and *o-fficially* listed in D.C. Dunleavy's *Log of North American Sites of Historic Interest* (competitively-priced souvenir copies available at our gifts counter). Let me show you to your table.'

The man moved them – a little too briskly for Andrea Lakowski's liking – to a booth that had the appearance of having been reserved.

'And may I say how nice it is to see you again sir,' their host continued as he set aside a cordon of red rope on two low brass pillars in order that the Lakowskis could be seated. He issued each of them with menus of a large, leather-look kind that had cords, tassels and an image of a moose in gold print to the covers.

Lakowski watched a little nervously as his wife took the inner bench of the booth (in the way that he knew she would). She disliked aisle-side seats for the way that she said they 'exposed' her. And these days there was a lot of her to be exposed.

She squeezed herself in, her stomach settling tight against the table's edge. Her breasts dumped themselves down on the tabletop, straining against her glitter-spangled white sweater in a way that reminded Lakowski of salamis in sleeves he'd once seen in the window of a deli store.

'What does *he* mean, "Nice to see you again"?' Andrea Lakowski asked as their host went off to his next meet-and-greet. 'Have *you* been here before, Norm? Without me?'

'Just the once,' Lakowski replied. 'Had to size-up the joint, didn't I? See it was fit and proper. For an occasion like tonight.'

Her eyes were already scouring the menu.

'Oh my! Oh, look at that! Oh, that just sounds so… But I can't. I can't!' she declared looking up at him. 'Not with my diet 'n' all.'

'Andrea,' he said, staring at her with a 'serious' look. 'I have some news for you on that. This is a special night – on that we're agreed – and I want *you* to enjoy yourself. *You've* earned it. *I've* earned it. You order what the hell you like.'

'Do you mean that, Norm? Really?' she asked.

'Wouldn't have said it, if I hadn't.'

'You know, Norman Lakowksi,' she said, placing a hand over his (he felt its warm film of sweat… never mind that their Ford outside had shown -5° on the dash), 'has anyone ever told you that, as well as being a devoted husband, you're a kind and generous man?'

'Can't say it's something I've heard too often in my life.'

'Well you *are* Norman Lakowski. You surely are. And tonight, when we get home, it could be that a certain Mrs Lakowski is going to be *pretty* generous with some portions of her own. Just tonight though – don't you go getting any wrong ideas. Tomorrow your Andie's going right back to her regime of being a good little girl.'

She lifted her hand from his and turned one of the plastic-bound pages of the Moose Hut's menu.

In the background, they heard the manager doing his thing at the Wait Here To Be Seated sign: 'Well, howdy folks and welcome to the Moosetuckett Moose Hut, first opened way back in…'

The Lakowskis both felt this repetition took a little shine off the specialness of their night but said nothing. Through the window behind them, a light snow was falling. The headlamps of vehicles were already casting beams on the highway beyond the parking lot. A neon sign in the form of an antlered moose head sent a red glow over the roofs and windshields of the parked automobiles and trucks.

A waitress arrived at their table and introduced herself as Bernice. She was young, and Norman Lakowski thought how – never mind her red-checked uniform – she had a nice figure and nice teeth.

His wife began to order.

After a while of writing, Bernice turned over a page of her pad and began on the next.

Finally, Andrea Lakowski – checking through her menu one last time – announced: 'Yep, I think that's it.'

She then looked up and said: 'Now, would you just be an angel and read that back – just to make sure there's nothing you've missed? This is a special night for my husband and me, and I just want to make sure that everything's perfect.'

Bernice read back the order, which was long.

Every so often, Andrea Lakowski interjected with a reminder or query, such as 'Remember, I want that *well* done' and 'Have you got that second order of fries?'. The rest of the time she just said 'Aha' and 'Ahum' as the young woman went through her list.

At the end of it, Andrea Lakowski said, 'Good, thank you, Bernice, I think everything's in order', and she gave the waitress a smile of the kind that her husband knew wasn't really a smile.

Bernice picked up their menus and made to turn from their table.

'Why hold on there, honey!' Andrea Lakowski called out. 'What about my husband here? You haven't taken *his* order. I surely hope you don't expect him to starve!'

Norman Lakowski saw the toupeed manager look over his shoulder from his position at the meet-and-greet.

'Sorry, I—' said Bernice.

'That's all right,' Lakowski broke in. 'Should've spoke up sooner. I'll just have the house burger and fries. That'll be fine for me.'

'Would you like relish with that?'

'Yes, some relish would be nice. Thank you, Bernice,' said Lakowski.

'Great! I'll bring y'all the dessert menus later,' said Bernice.

'Dessert menus?!' his wife now exclaimed. '*Slow* down, doll! We haven't picked our mains yet!'

She grabbed one of the leather-looks back from Bernice, in a way that made her husband feel embarrassed.

At the meet-and-greet, the manager was once more looking over his shoulder.

Norman Lakowski smiled at the girl.

'Oh,' said Bernice, and backed away from their table.

'That missy needs to get her act together,' Andrea Lakowski said now. 'This is our special night and I'm not gonna have *any*body spoil it for anything.' She adjusted awkwardly on her bench for a moment, then sank back in her belly-folds and jowls. 'Could do with buttonin'-up that blouse of hers, 'n' all. This is an eating establishment. Not a pick-up joint for little darlins like *her*. I may well be having words with Mr Wiggy-Top before we're done, if she doesn't watch her step, I tell you.'

Lakowski noticed over his wife's shoulder that, outside, the snow was getting heavier and beginning to silt the Moose Hut's window. He wondered what it would be like for driving afterwards but figured that he'd manage.

His attention returned to his wife, who at least seemed happy in the knowledge that her order was being attended to and was now staring around the restaurant.

'You know,' she began, 'I guess, going back, this place must have been some sort of a hang-out for trappers… beaver men, "frontier people". It really is very old.'

'Original timbers, I believe,' said her husband.

'That doesn't surprise me. It has a feeling, doesn't it? Can you feel it, Norm? I can feel it. But then I've always had a feeling for such things – you know that. Who knows what ghosts are haunting here? That moose head,' she continued, nodding. 'He sure is a big old boy. D'you think he's for real?'

'Guess he must have been,' said Lakowski, turning to look at the head, which was mounted in pride of place, above the Moose Hut's main counter. 'Leastways, one time.'

'And he isn't the only one with some history to be proud of, is he darlin?' Andrea Lakowski continued now. 'Twenty-five years!' she said. '*Twenty-five years* of wedded matrimony.'

'A special night for both of us,' Norman Lakowski responded. 'Silver stars all round.'

The manager appeared at their table and set down two bottles of cola whose caps he took off. 'Compliments of the house,' he announced. 'May I pour for the lady?'

'You certainly may,' said Andrea Lakowski.

'And I wish you a memorable evening here at the Moose Hut. Now, if you'll excuse me…' He gave a slight bow and made his way back to the meet-and-greet.

'Now *that's* what I call service,' said Andrea Lakowski. 'He seems kinda British, don't you think?'

'Well, you get what you pay for in this world,' her husband responded.

'You can say that twice. And tonight's *our* special night. In this special place. Thank you for bringing me, Norm.'

She sipped her cola. Some gas seemed to go up her nose. 'Ooh,' she said, and set down her glass. After a moment, she said: 'Norm, would you mind if I asked you something?'

Lakowski wasn't totally sure what her question would be, but he had a sense of the probable subject.

'Go ahead.'

'Well, we've been together a long time now and, well, I know I've gotten a little larger than I was, but – and answer me honestly – do you love me just as much as you always did?'

Her question, in more ways than one, puzzled Lakowski because – or so he thought – the fact that her father had forced the marriage upon him had surely never been in doubt. He had dated Ed Davidson's daughter no more than twice. Once at a movie drive-in when his wife-to-be had stuffed herself on popcorn and candy apples. The other time at the county fair when she had thrown up on the Ferris wheel. That Andrea Davidson was large – 'Just look at the size of her, boy, for Christ Sakes!' Davidson had said – was because she was… large… what some people politely called a 'big girl'… *not* because of anything he – Lakowski –

had done. In any event, his low sperm count – as later confirmed by a doctor – would have made pregnancy nigh-on impossible.

'Just as *much* as I always did, Mrs Lakowski,' he answered her, scarce missing a beat.

Bernice the waitress now brought out the first and second of his wife's starters, slipping Lakowski his burger and fries at the same time.

He watched as his wife dug into a mound of mayonnaise-smothered prawns, helping herself to a spoonful before Bernice had even set the plate to rest.

Soon she was into a chicken breast coated with yellow cheese.

'Oh, this is delicious, honey! Just delicious!' she said between chomps. 'How's your burger?'

'It's fine, just fine. Very nicely cooked.'

Lakowski was thin and had always been thin. He ate slowly, methodically (in the way that, over the years, he had noticed thin people generally did).

'You want one of these, honey?' his wife was now saying, in a second's break between stripping corn from a cob. 'They're *real* good!'

Her question afforded Lakowski an unwelcome glimpse of the churning pulp in her mouth. It made him think of the trash end of a garbage truck. He said nothing and let her eat on.

Bernice came back with more dishes, and, again, Lakowski thought how nice she looked. He wanted to tell her that her name was nice too but knew that he could not. So he simply gave her a smile when it seemed to him that his wife was unawares.

No sooner had Bernice removed the debris of the cobs than his wife was noisily sucking the meat from a set of crab's claws… followed by another set.

After that, Lakowski watched as she laid waste to a pile of ribs and a platter of potato wedges, and then a second portion of the chicken breast coated with cheese that Bernice apologised for not having brought out the first time.

Lakowski bit at his burger and picked at his fries, in his thin, insect-like way… steadily, methodically.

'Oh Norm. I'm so enjoying this. This is such a special night. Thank you God for letting me have such a wonderful man!'

When she had subsequently put away a burger bigger than the one he intended to be both his starter and his main, she pushed the litter of her plates, bowls and cutlery to his side of the table.

'Where *is* that girl?' she now snapped. 'We sure could do with some service round here. I'm not one to complain, Norm – you of all people know that – but, really, I may well have to have words with that manager – old beaver head – before we're done. A customer shouldn't oughtta be kept waiting. Leastways of all in a restaurant. I bet they don't have that problem in London, Norm. Paris, France, neither.'

When Bernice came to clear the table, Andrea Lakowski let out a loud belch.

Her husband saw that other of the Moose Hut's diners were looking their way. A grey-haired couple of senior years seemed to call the manager to their table.

Lakowski tried not to catch their eye. He felt like whispering something to Bernice, by way of apology, as she cleared his wife's junk, but judged it best not to.

Andrea Lakowski's nose was already back in the pages of the Moose Hut's menu. It was, Lakowski had noticed before now, the only part of her that had not tripled or quadrupled in size over the years… so that it now seemed absurdly small for her stature. A child's nose, in fact.

'Oh, *that* sounds nice,' she said now, commenting on something that had caught her eye.

She looked up for a moment, and Lakowksi thought about how her eyes had grown so very small and sunken, in the pale, puffed-out doughball of her face. He wondered how she even saw.

'I hope this doesn't sound stupid,' she began, 'but do you think that, back in the day, trappers and all those "frontier people" would have eaten what we're eating now?'

For a moment, Lakowski wondered if she had ever gone to school. She had not been at *his* school, he knew that. Her father had been a farmhand or woodsman of some kind. He remembered him in dirty denim dungarees on the porch of their shack. Lazy eye, bad teeth… a mouth of chewed tobacco. Strictly no interest in his daughter as soon as she was wed.

'I think that's a fair question,' Lakowski answered her. 'My expectation is that they ate pretty much the same ingredients as we're eating now. Only they ate them kinda different from how we presently go about things.'

He liked the sound of this answer… the depth it seemed to have – but saw that his wife wasn't listening.

'If you're still okay with your burger, sugar, you won't mind if I go ahead and order a couple of small things… just to keep me occupied… while you're eating that burger of yours? It's quite a large burger that you have there, Norm.'

'Course not,' he answered her. 'This is a special night. We both know that. You go ahead.'

'Thank you, Norman Lakowski,' she said. 'Thank you for being my husband.'

Bernice came back and took her order.

As Lakowski had come to expect, his wife's idea of 'a couple of small things' was anything but.

Bernice again went over onto a second page of her pad as his wife requested steamed lobster tails, deep-fried medallions of turkey breast and – finally – steak… eighteen ounces – 'Make sure they're well done, missy' – served on the T-bone, with eggs, fries and mayonnaise on the side.

After the waitress went, Andrea Lakowski announced her need of 'the little girls' room'.

Lakowski watched nervously as his wife slowly rocked herself along the bench opposite him. He found himself thinking of a sealion they'd seen on TV at a water park someplace… sliding on its tail-flipper or whatever it might have been… along the edge of the pool.

The table's edge dug into her.

'These tables sure are a tight fit,' she complained. 'They oughtta give a lady a little more room. That's something *else* I may be taking up with Mr Ginger Top, *I* can tell you, before he has our cash.'

'Is there enough room there?' Lakowski asked.

'Yeah. Just,' she snapped.

As she lifted herself, he thought again about their fateful date at the county fair – where her father claimed he – Lakowski – had 'done the deed' with his daughter.

Lakowski remembered (as his wife now finally rose, awkwardly, to her feet from the bench seat) a balloon in which it had been possible to go for rides. You didn't take off properly, in point of fact: a rope tethering it to the ground saw to that. But you were airborne, all the same. He hadn't joined the line for the basket, fearing that – even then – the weight of the girl tagging along with him, who he sort-of knew (but didn't *want* to know) was his wife-to-be, would have seen them refused ('excess baggage'). Besides, he wasn't sure how she'd have climbed in the basket, anyhow.

Later at the fair, after she'd stuffed hotdogs, brownies, potato chips and all sorts of gunk as they'd wandered the stalls, the bar on the car of the Ferris wheel had only just locked shut over her belly. Looking at the sundry splatter marks now visible on his wife's sweater-front as she wobbled then steadied herself on the floor of the Moose Hut, Lakowski was reminded of the way she had vomited in their car on the Ferris wheel – not to mention on the heads and legs of the couples who'd had the misfortune to be in the cars below theirs on the ride.

He remembered how snot and sweat had slathered her pudgy white face, glistening in the evening sun.

The exchange that followed the scene on the wheel came back to him.

'For Christ's Sake, Andie!'

'I can't help it. It was somethin' I ate.'

'Jesus. It wasn't *some*thing, Andie. It was *every*thing you ate.'

'And what in Hell's name exactly do you mean by that?'

'Well, you just—'

'And watch your mouth, Norman Lakowski!'

'*My* mouth?'

'If my Daddy ever caught you talkin' to me like that, your life wouldn't be worth the livin'! Takin' Our Lord's name in vain! How *ever* were you brought up?'

He had dropped her at the top of the trail to her place, watched her waddle off down the dirt track.

Two weeks later her father began raising hell about how his daughter had been 'de-flowered'.

Now, as she found her footing on the floor of the Moose Hut, Lakowski said: 'Well don't be long in that ladies' room, honey. We don't want your food getting cold.'

'Don't you worry about me,' she replied, stepping away, huffily. 'I'll be right back. Which is more than can be said for that young woman who's supposed to be waitin' on us. *My...* has she some learnin' to do!'

Lakowski watched the snow thicken on the roofs of the autos and trucks in the lot.

Bernice came back to clear some last items of his wife's litter and wipe over the tabletop.

He wanted to say sorry for picking the place... for picking her night, but judged it best to let it lie.

His wife's return was heralded by heavy breaths and a light but perceptible vibration of the cutlery and glassware that lay on the table.

'And not a damn thing laid!' she said, squeezing herself back into the bench seat.

Lakowski wasn't sure if he was imagining it, but the table – which was, he knew from his previous visit, bolted (and maybe even welded) to the floor – seemed to move.

He wondered if the thing might come loose.

'Might have known!' his wife continued. 'Well, I'm sorry, Norm – you *know* I'm not one to make a fuss – but we're entitled to better service than this. This is a special night for us. And that Bernadette, or whoever she is, she's messin' us around. I'll be having words with the management here when we're through. You see if I don't. Reckon we're due some of our dollars back.'

Bernice brought out his wife's lobster tails and the deep-fried medallions of turkey.

'Well,' said his wife, 'it sure is nice to see some food round here – at last.'

Lakowski continued with his burger. Experience had taught him that when his wife was in such a mood the best thing to do was let her blow herself out. He winced a little as she set aside her knife and fork and shoved the fried turkey cuts in some tortilla wraps coated with a barbecue sauce she'd asked for on the side.

He heard the unspoken disgust in the steps of the grey-haired couple who had earlier called over the manager and who were now on their way to the exit having settled their check.

Even out in the lot, as the wipers worked snow from the windshield of their Buick, he felt the glower of their faces.

If you only knew… he thought to himself. *If you only knew.*

He fed his throat with a single fry.

Bernice now brought out his wife's steak. It put him in mind of an elevated plateau he had once seen in a magazine in the waiting room of a dental surgery. He watched with genuine interest as, progressively, his wife reduced it on her plate. The disappearance of its mass caused him to think about various changes that certain experts he'd seen on TV were claiming were happening to the planet. Soon she had a hold of the T-bone in her hands and was gnawing at what little meat remained.

Having stripped it clean, she set it down and let out a belch, smaller than before, for which – to his surprise – she apologised.

'You enjoyed that,' said Lakowski.

'I did,' she said.

'Ate everything on your plate.'

'Waste not. Want not,' she said. 'That's what the Good Book tells us, I do believe.'

I'm glad.'

'Thank you, Norm. You know…' she belched again '… this is proving – how do they call it? – "a night to remember". A special night.'

'And now,' said Lakowski, pushing away his own plate, on which a third or more of his burger remained, '… dessert.'

'I can't believe it,' his wife said. 'Seems like we only just got here. I can't believe that it's that time already.'

She reached over and took what was left of his burger and began biting into the bun.

'All good things have to come to an end… but not before dessert,' said Lakowski.

'I like the way you say that, Norm. I think that could be how you won me, you know. Your way with words. A woman likes a thing like that. It can help make up for ways that a man falls short… in other areas.'

'So what'll it be?' asked Lakowski, who didn't want their conversation to head any further down the road he thought his wife might well be wanting to take it. 'I have it under advisement that they do a pretty mean ice cream here.'

She took a fistful of fries that had gone cold on his plate, shoved them in her jaws.

'Well, I don't know,' she said, giving him another eyeful of her mouth-mash. 'I'm feeling kinda full. A lady knows her limit.'

'Surely a little one won't hurt?' he said. 'That's all *I'm* thinking of having. But I'd feel kinda awkward, sitting here, eating one on my own. I think I'll skip it, too.'

'Oh you mustn't—'

'No really, it's fine,' he said.

'Tell you what,' she said, 'I'll join you – just for a little one.'

'You will?'

'Yes,' she said.

'In that case, I *will* have a little one after all.'

Bernice came to the table and ran through the ice creams the Moose Hut had, describing precisely how they came and supplying details of their sauces, cream-toppings and syrups, in a way that Lakowski found impressive.

'I'll have the Moose Hut Mint Mountain Choc-Chip with molasses and whipped cream on the side,' said his wife when Bernice had finished. 'And make sure that the cream is *whipped*. I've no care for that runny stuff. Turns my stomach.'

Bernice looked to Lakowski. 'And for the gentle—'

'Hold on there, girl! Not so fast!' his wife broke in. 'I also fancy one of those – what did you call it? – raspberry…'

'Raspberry Rocket?'

'Yeah. I'll have one of them too. Every woman's entitled to a Raspberry Rocket once in a while. Can't go without *all* your life. No matter what some husbands might think,' she muttered.

'I'll take a scoop of vanilla and a wafer,' said Lakowski. 'Thank you, Bernice.'

As Bernice brought out her ices, Lakowski watched his wife engage in a sort-of squirm of delight in her seat. He had heard or read somewhere of such a thing as a 'sugar rush' and sensed that this was what – in avalanche form – was about to hit her. The *squirm* seemed about all Andrea was able to manage, and Lakowski wondered, once again, about the tightness of the table, its 'proximity' – to use a word he had heard deployed by Dexter Grady, deputy manager at his depot – to her chest and her seat.

Nervous that the night was coming to its end, he toyed with his ball of vanilla as it melted on his plate. He watched as his wife went through the lime-green tower of the Moose Hut's Mint Mountain.

In one way, he thought, her efficiency – as an eating machine – was admirable. No wrecking-ball rig could demolish anything half as quick.

She raised up the tall, fluted glass where the ice cream had been and drained the last of its brown-green slush into her mouth.

For a moment, she took the glass away from her lips and held it aloft (as if in imitation of men in bars in England – who, so Lakowski understood, drank what he had heard were called 'yards of ale').

Having worked her tongue over some last sugary slicks, she set down her empty trophy with a thunk, and drew the back of a hand over her wet, green moustache.

Lakowski became aware of the eyes of other diners, a number of whom – having finished their meals – were now leaving to a series of thank yous from the manager: 'We hope you enjoyed your evening at the Moose Hut… Come back and see us again soon.' For several moments, a small boy stared at Lakowski and at Andrea, till he was snatched away by his mother.

As people headed out to the lot, which was in near darkness now, snow blew in through the Moose Hut's front door.

The manager came over to their table with one of those inquiries – 'Well how y'all doing here?' – that Lakowski knew meant 'Hurry up and get on with whatever it is you're still at'.

To his relief, his wife seemed too occupied with her second ice – the Raspberry Rocket – to offer up any complaints.

Lakowski watched as, for some moments, the manager stared at her... transfixed in what seemed like disbelief – as Andrea's spoon gouged craters in the vanishing Rocket.

'Well, I'll just, um...' the manager said eventually and made off to the counter area where he checked various items of paperwork with Bernice and certain of the other waitresses who were there.

In other parts of the Moose Hut, chairs were being upturned onto tables and lights were going out.

His wife consumed the last remnants of the Rocket in the same manner that she had the Mint Mountain, this time pawing a pink moustache from her face.

'Well,' she announced, finally, 'I am *done*.'

With this declaration, Lakowski knew the moment... the fateful moment of departure... the ending of this long and special night, had arrived.

'Well, I'm just going to settle the check and have a word with the manager,' he said, rising from his seat.

'Yeah. You do that Norm. You have a word with him about that waitress – that Bernadette or whatever she calls herself – if he ever wants to see our trade again. And *don't* go givin' any tip. Somethin' wrong with your ice cream, hon?' she called after him, referring to the collapsed scoop of vanilla left on his plate.

'No, I'm done, too. But have it if you want it.'

'I think I will,' she said. 'Sin to let food go to waste.'

Behind him, Lakowski heard the rattle of a spoon as she dumped his dish down on her side of the table and set to work on what he had left.

'I need to get outta here, I tell you! You'll have to *move* this table!' Andrea Lakowski said.

'Well, I'm sorry ma'am, but I *can't*. This restaurant is a site of historic interest,' the Moose Hut's manager responded. 'That table's been screwed down there since Pearl Harbor.'

'Pearl Harbor? What the hell has Pearl Harbor got to do with this?'

'I'll thank you to mind your language, ma'am. This is a family establishment.'

'Coulda fooled me – with the way your alleycat waitresses go round… flashing their tits and ass!'

'Ma'am I'm—'

'Move this table! *Now*!'

'That table's moving *nowhere* ma'am, without official authority from the mayor's office. And the mayor's office won't be open until nine a.m.. And until such time as I have authority to do so otherwise, that table's staying right where it is. I'm sorry ma'am, but that's the law.'

'But I can't move, dammit! This is impossible! You're outta line, mister! *Way* out! Where *is* my husband?'

'He's gone, ma'am – like I told you.'

'You just wait till he hears of this!'

She paused for a moment.

'What do you mean "Gone"?'

'Left… so it seems.'

'B-b-but what about the check?'

'Paid it before he walked out.'

With this remark, the wind – it seemed to the manager – suddenly went out of her. She deflated… in the manner of someone stuck in quicksand whose efforts to escape had achieved nothing but exhaustion and deeper entrapment.

She sank back. 'I have to get out… I need the bathroom,' she said, more quietly now.

'Ma'am, if you can just stay there and hold on… till the morning.'

'Till the morning!?'

'… when I can get to the mayor's office. Meantime, I'll get you some coffee and cream. Maybe I can rustle up a cookie or two. Would you like that?'

'Yes… thank you. That would be… nice. You wouldn't happen to be British, would you? I was saying to my husband that, to me, you sounded kinda British. I expect he'll be back soon. He must have gone for something. That's what must have happened. This was our special night, you know. Our night to remember. He arranged everything.'

She noticed then that the dining room was in darkness save for the scarlet glow that invaded it from the neon sign of the moose head that, for the moment, still burned in the lot outside… also the lights of a refrigerator unit near the counter, in which various cheesecakes and gateaux were displayed.

In the quiet gloom, the moose head, on its timbers above the counter, seemed to her to grow huge and monstrous.

In his Ford, on the snowy highway, Lakowski wondered how long it would be till he hit the State line.

Although telling himself it was impossible, he seemed to hear – above the sound of his wipers and the forward motion of the Ford – a long and terrible bellow that, for several moments, echoed through the forests that flanked the road.

The red tail lights of his auto grew distant in the deepening dark.

Two small scoops of Raspberry Rocket.

The Catch

If ever there was anything ordinary about the fish with which Henri Gagneux hoped to secure a place at the side of the widow Estelle Lecuyer (and perhaps admittance to the chambers of what seemed her very chilly heart), it was surely in those moments of his presentation to her of his catch, unwrapping it from its papers with great ceremony on the table of her parlour where – to her not insignificant displeasure – he had placed it.

'What is it?' asked the widow Lecuyer, in her customary haughty manner.

'It is a fish,' Gagneux replied, as if entranced by the glory of his offering.

'I can see that. What do you take me for? Some kind of imbecile? What *kind* of a fish?' the widow asked sharply.

'A… carp, I think, madame,' said its conqueror, his attention distracted by a silver candlestick that stood on the lace of the tabletop (the best of his own being made merely of brass).

'Hah! A *bony* fish!' said Madame Lecuyer. 'I ought to have known! Where did you get it?'

'In the Lac Saint Luc,' Gagneux answered. 'I caught it with my own two hands.'

'That I can believe,' said the widow. 'No one else would have bothered.'

'Do you wish me to take it back?' asked Gagneux.

'And do *what* with it?' asked Lecuyer. 'It is dead… is it not?'

'Why, yes.'

'In which case, I might as well keep it. The bony old thing…'

And she wrapped the carp back in the paper from which Gagneux had unfolded it – the fish seeming to study them both as she drew Gagneux's scruffy sheets over the fixed, black pupil of its large and golden-edged eye.

As she took the fish to a pantry, rustling in her black gown, Madame Lecuyer cursed to herself the old fool Gagneux and the latest of his absurd trophies – all part of his ridiculous attempt to court her, as if he were himself some kind of 'catch'.

For his part, Gagneux was certain that, never mind his humble stock and the *froideur* for which the widow was famous, he had now moved an important step nearer her table and, with it, her bed (in spite of the advanced years of each of them) and – most important of all – her fortune. The latter had long been the talk of the small southern village of Saint Luc ('Luke' in English), especially since the death, some ten years earlier, of her husband – a bank official well known in Paris – who was referred to locally as 'Number Four'.

'I'll see myself out,' Gagneux called after her.

'Good!' the widow called back, who – as careful with her money as she knew Gagneux to be keen for it – locked the carp in her cool pantry with an old and long-shanked key.

Henri Gagneux's satisfaction with his gift was short-lived. For no sooner had he passed out of the gates to her house on his bicycle than he collapsed over its handlebars, careered into a ditch and died.

Such was the strange suddenness of his passing that a magistrate from the nearest town was ordered to conduct an inquiry into the matter.

Gagneux's attempts to woo Madame Lecuyer were well known in Saint Luc. And although he was considered a fool (albeit possessed of a devious streak) lacking a single cent to his name, his death caused him to be seen in a sympathetic light, particularly when set against the continuing long life of the widow, who was widely disliked for her fortune and her perceived lack of charity. Some spoke of the old lady (who seldom strayed from her manor house and grounds) as being a witch, who had struck Gagneux dead with a spell. Unflattering references were made to the many husbands she had had.

In due course, a hearing was convened in the village at which intelligence was presented to the magistrate about the unusual fineness of the fish that Gagneux had caught. No one had actually seen the fish – these testimonies to its quality arising from accounts Gagneux had himself given to various locals while riding through the village on his bicycle (with the fish wrapped in the wicker basket to its front). Thinking it would in some way count against Madame Lecuyer, there was unanimous agreement among these 'witnesses' that the fish – in reality, a plain and mediocre thing – was both handsome and grand.

'It was a fish like no other,' a blind woman said, in the hush of the court. 'Truly, it's scales shone,' she added, to a rising murmur, '… like the armour of Louis Quinze.'

In spite of these assertions, no demands were made by the magistrate for the production of the fish, the gentleman ruling that it was reasonable to presume that it had already been eaten – a statement that increased the villagers' ire to the point that the justice had to use his hammer to silence cries in the courtroom about the fineness of the fish, its boneless beauty, its great weight and remarkable grace.

Conscious of Madame Lecuyer's fortune, family history and important connections through her late husbands, the gentleman also deemed it unnecessary to call the widow to give evidence to his inquiry: a fact that further caused the villagers of Saint Luc to seethe.

He duly declared that Henri Gagneux, 'a man no longer young', had died through a failure of his internal organs as a result of the exertions of catching an unusually large fish from the Lac Saint Luc. Unfortunate as the matter was, there could be little doubt that the creature had taken his heart, the magistrate pronounced.

He then hurried from the hearing as fast as he could, praying he would never have to set foot in the village again.

And that, it seemed, was the end of that.

Except that. when Madame Lecuyer unlocked her pantry with her heavy key, on the day after the one on which Henri Gagneux had brought it to her, the fish was no longer there.

Somehow – rejuvenated – it had arisen.

Initially, Madame Lecuyer was unsettled by the disappearance of the fish. The papers in which Gagneux had wrapped it were still where she felt sure she had set it down, on the shelf in her pantry. Had someone – or some*thing*, perhaps – taken it? Was there another occupant in that large mansion of hers, where she – not unlike a ghost – had lived alone for ten years?

For all of that first day of the carp's disappearance, Lecuyer investigated the mansion's shuttered rooms, its cobwebbed attics and its damp cellars.

Outwardly, she was steely enough in these explorations. But in her step and in her hand, now afflicted with an unfamiliar slight tremor, there was a nervousness of a kind she had not known since her wedding night to the very first of her husbands, some sixty years before.

She snatched dust cloths from furniture and pulled open closet doors, fearing what she might find. She discovered nothing, however, beyond empty armchairs, stopped clocks and stuffed animals in glass cases, not to mention rails of her old dresses, ballgowns and furs.

In those unused parts of the house that were without electricity, she continued her search with a candelabra of flames, as the light of that long, strange day withered and died.

But nothing unusual revealed itself to the widow, who eventually retired to her parlour, where Henri Gagneux had first – or so she thought – brought his fish.

There, she sat awake all night, too agitated for sleep.

As the dawn's first light fingered its way through the gaps in her shutters, Estelle Lecuyer began to wonder if Gagneux had ever actually brought the fish. She found herself thinking that the papers on the shelf in the pantry might have been from another of his 'trophies'. She remembered the battered cock pheasant that looked as if it had been run over by a bus. On seeing a maggot crawl from its beak, she had slung out the shabby thing. Maybe the wrapping paper belonged to the bird? Maybe there had never been a fish?

In time, these thoughts reassured her and, with warm sunlight entering her parlour, playing pleasingly upon her wrinkled face and leathery hands, she fell asleep.

It was some six or seven days later – the hearing in the village having concluded in uproar – that Madame Lecuyer found herself witness to an occurrence that caused her to reconsider her thoughts.

She was darning an old woollen stocking in a room blessed with a view of her grounds, of which she was fond, when a strange sound caused her to pause and hold steady her needle and wool. Regardless of her years, there was nothing wrong with the widow's hearing. She could detect the drop of a pinecone anywhere in her park and the tick of a clock in any far room of her house.

The sound that she heard now was at times a kind of slapping and at others a kind of dragging, or squirming.

Casting her eyes about the room, Madame Lecuyer eventually lowered them to the floor.

There, to her horror, she saw the form of a fish. One, moreover, that was flicking and pulling its way towards her, across the flagstones of her sewing room.

And not just any fish but, indubitably – for there could only be one with such an awful dark eye – the carp of Henri Gagneux.

Lecuyer leapt from her chair with a scream.

Her sewing box flew from her knees, showering the room with a great spray of needles, pins, ribbons and reels that the widow had been saving for years.

For a moment, the fish seemed to halt, as if surprised by the items that now streamed and rolled around it. But, after only a few seconds, it advanced again… jaws agape, propelling itself by the fins of its belly and its flanks.

Although aghast, the widow Lecuyer was – let it be said, if it were not already understood – a *femme formidable*, and, seizing a knitting needle from the scattered contents of her upturned sewing box, she now took up arms against the horrible carp.

The fish seemed to register her 'spear' – the sharp point of her raised needle sparking in the sunlight of the room – and, apparently having second thoughts about its advances on the widow, promptly turned tail.

Madame Lecuyer now made after it, screaming: 'Be off with you! Out of my house! You bony beast!'

But the carp proved too fast for her, slipping between a crack in her skirting boards, as if between the weeds at the bottom of Lac Saint Luc, and into the old and dark fabric of her house.

After some initial trauma on her part, in which she sat up awake in her parlour at night, spurning the pillows and sheets of her four-poster bed, the widow's world went undisturbed for several days, and she resumed her usual round of tasks and activities: polishing candlesticks, beating hearthrugs and pickling vegetables and fruit from her garden. Once more, she rationalised that the carp could not really have been there: its appearance that day in the sewing room a trick of her mind or some confection of the light. Entirely unaware, by dint of her reclusive existence, of both the fate of Henri Gagneux and the hearing in the village, and also her refusal to take a local newspaper (let alone an apparatus such as a television or something as alien as the internet), she determined that next time he called with some 'token' she would make clear to him that she had had enough of his silliness and he was no longer to enter her house.

It was in this more composed frame of mind that Madame Lecuyer seated herself one ensuing morning at the grand piano in the mansion's music room. Playing the instrument was perhaps the distraction in which she took her chief pleasure, leaving the doors of the old house open so that its notes might carry through its many chambers. Although for years lacking the attention of a tuner, its keys still possessed a pitch that was pleasingly melodious, never mind the arthritic weave in the fingers of elderly Estelle Lecuyer.

That morning, however, having seated herself and lifted its lid, her hands fell upon not the keys of the piano, but something different entirely – something scaly, and damp. Looking down, she saw – to her horror – the carp... stretched out... on its side... on the keys.

She screamed as the fish – once again, it was, indubitably, the carp that Henri Gagneux had brought her – lifted its head to her, as if delighted by this tickle to its tummy of her fingertips, its jaws parting in a satisfied grin.

The widow sprang from the piano stool and slammed down the lid. Retreating to the room's doorway, she stood gasping for breath. After several moments, the thought struck her that the carp was in fact now cornered and she hastened to her kitchen for something with which to carry out its despatch.

Returning to the music room with a long-handled broom, she now lifted the piano's lid with the bristled end of her weapon. And, in almost the same instant, she brought the broom crashing down on the keys.

A grotesque chord sounded from the grand – followed by another and another of the ear-splitting same – as the widow swung again and again at its keys, an awful vibration all the while consuming the room which threw photographs in their frames from the mantelpiece and sent vases and ornaments crashing to the floor from the tops of tables and shelves.

Eventually, her arms shaking and weak, Estelle Lecuyer stopped, and rested on the broom-handle.

Her heart racing and her face flushed, she stared at the keyboard of the grand piano, on which she now saw… nothing at all – as if the carp had never been there.

In the days that followed, the carp continued to appear. At times it would be in her bathtub – either before, or, even worse, *after* she had entered the water… causing her to leap out in a way that belied her years. Before she was able to act against it, the cunning creature had a way of pulling with its jaws on the chain that drew out the plug, and then disappearing down the hole despite its disproportionate girth. By the time the widow was able to hurl a jar of bath salts, or the brush with which she scrubbed her back, the fish would be gone (bar an impudent last flick of its tail).

At other times, the widow would wake from a nap having somehow sensed the presence of the fish in her parlour – discovering it *there* on her hearthrug, in front of her evening fire, lying on its side like a dog. Invariably, by the time she had taken hold of a poker, the fish had scuttled behind a heavy bookcase or up and into the mahogany housing of an old grandfather clock.

An even more startling thing now occurred. The appearance of the carp – till then an undistinguished specimen whose only distinction had been its lack of distinction – began to change.

To the disbelief of Estelle Lecuyer, who feared that she must be turning mad, the creature – while remaining fish-like in many respects – grew first a moustache, then began at times to wear spectacles, and took to dressing – over its gills, at least – in a shirt that lacked a collar. In short (and in so far as a fish could do such a thing), it began to resemble Henri Gagneux – even appearing in what seemed his own black beret.

The widow now decided that come what may she would have to catch the fish and put an end to this torment, once and for all. For, if she did not, someone like the postman or a priest seeking money for some cause (there were seldom any other callers to her house beyond Henri Gagneux) might knock at her door and find a gibbering wreck fit only for the nearest asylum.

So it was that, vowing she would evict the intruder even if it was the last thing that she did, the widow Lecuyer resolved to set a trap for her fish.

When, in her sewing room one morning, she saw a blackbird drawing a large and juicy worm from her lawn, she raced outside, beat off the bird, bent to the grass and tugged out the worm with her hands. With a great grin of satisfaction, she then hurried back with it indoors.

There, with her crooked fingers, she impaled the wriggling thing on a sharp needle that she tied to a ball of grey wool. Having composed herself, she then began to drag her bait through the rooms of the old house.

Only once did the widow catch sight of something that *might* have been the carp: a not very mouse-like eye peering from a hole in the skirting of the room that had been her last husband's study. She trailed the worm back and forth in front of the hole while proclaiming its tastiness and loveliness. But the awful black eye merely receded into the hole's dark depths. Oh, that fish was a wily one, all right.

Later that day, wondering what to do, the widow wandered the grounds of her mansion contemplating how she might put an end to the beastly business of the carp, fearing that if she did not do so it would drive her from her home, cause her to lose her mind and put an end to *her*. As she walked, she glanced – with a sense of foreboding – at the manor's lichened walls, its sun-bleached shutters and its old, chipped slates.

Suddenly, she heard the ringing of the church bell in the village. Walking to the railings that separated her property from the lane that passed it, she saw a youth on a bicycle.

Aware that it was not a Sunday, she called to him, 'Boy! For whom does the bell toll?'

'Henri Gagneux,' he answered, without stopping.

'Gagneux!?' exclaimed the widow.

'Today is the day of his funeral. They are burying him at last.'

'Henri Gagneux is dead?'

'Of course, why else would they be burying him?'

And, with that, the lad disappeared down the lane.

Madame Lecuyer retreated to her house, entering it quietly and holding her breath.

The carp's spurning of the worm – she was certain now that the awful eye could only have belonged to it – together with this news of the death of her would-be suitor, convinced her that the fish was nothing less than his awful reincarnation. Penniless as he was and born of the peasantry, Gagnneux had always had a taste for the finer things in life, she knew. Evidence of this had been his greedy glances at her silver… his horrible habit of running his coarse hands over her ornaments and furniture. A mere worm from the garden would have been insufficient temptation for a sly fox like Gagneux.

Clearly, she would have to tempt him with something else.

When Lecuyer lay on her bed that night, it was not in her usual plain chemise, buttoned to the collar and stiff with starch, as had been her way for almost all of the previous ten years. The apparel in which she was now attired could hardly have been more different.

Her white and bony legs lay sheathed in dark stockings of the finest Parisian silk. This hosiery – a gift from Husband Number Two, or possibly Number Three – she had recovered after a diligent search through many a drawer. True, the stockings clung to her more loosely now, with wrinkled ridges rising at her knees, in ways that had not been the case when – rather firmer in calf and thigh – she had first worn them... a lifetime ago. Even so, she was not displeased. Around her upper half, she wore a negligee whose blood-red satin revealed her breastbone in a diamond of pale skin that plunged almost to her bellybutton. Her grey hair, meanwhile, rather than being tied in a tail or scraped back and pinned in its usual bun, was spread, thinly, at her shoulders and on her pillow.

And that was not all that the old widow wore. Her face, she had also adorned... painting it (albeit, on account of the arthritis in her fingers, not quite with the dexterity of her younger days), so that her narrow grey lips now sported a rather clownish smile, and, on her cheeks, two rough circles of rouge that lay rather heavily daubed.

This scene of seduction was completed by the odour of a hoarded perfume well past its prime and the silvery light of Saint Luc's moon... shining through her deliberately *un*shuttered window.

'Henri Gagneux!' she called out, in a stage whisper of the kind that as a young woman she had once employed in certain rather burlesque Paris reviews. 'Are you there, *mon chèr*? Can you hear me, Henri?'

The still and dark house issued no response to this apparent summons to her bed. So she repeated it, huskily.

'Come… come to your mama, my little one… my beau. Permit me to tickle that… *tummy* of yours. Your lady is lying here, waiting.'

And this time, with her acutely fine ears, she heard in some distant downstairs part of the house the sound of a knock and a scrape, as if the leg of a table had been caught, and, thereafter, the sound of a slither of a kind that might be heard from the belly of a viper over newly-fallen leaves in a rain-dampened glade.

The noise caused her to remember – with a shiver – the scene in her sewing room. But, albeit with a faint quaver in her throat, she continued to call out into the darkness from that place where the moon shone upon her.

'Henri? My angel… is that you?'

And now she heard a bump and a struggle, and the same sound over and again – this noise emanating, so it seemed to her, from the staircase of the house, indicating that her suitor, if it were he, was climbing her steps.

'Oh yes! Yes… pretty one. That's it! Keep coming! Keep coming to your mummy. She has a treat – the treat of all treats! – for you.'

And now she heard a steady, rhythmic slap and heave from the landing beyond her bedchamber, punctuated, so it seemed to her, by the odd gasp and wheeze.

'That's it! That's it! My little fish!' the old widow beckoned from her bed. 'Oh, you are so big and strong! Come to me! Come to me now in my chamber! I am here! I am waiting!'

And with that, lying flat on her back, she parted – in their slack, black and wrinkled stockings – her old, white and bony limbs.

Finally, her night-caller was at her door. And – all need for entreaties now redundant – she listened, without speaking, to the sound of a repeated crawl and thud across the carpet of her floor.

Suddenly, all fell silent, and the widow Lecuyer, holding her breath on her bedspread, strained her ears to the calm that had come over her house. It was then that perhaps the most terrible sound of all – a dreadful thump, thump, thump – like the report of a rubber-headed mallet – began at the end of her bed.

At this noise, the widow lifted her head from her pillow and peered over the tops of her stockinged toes into the gloom, calling out in a quiet voice and with some hesitation, 'Henri Gagneux? Is that you?'

And in that very same moment, propelled by its pectoral fins and with jaws agape, her Lancelot, her Don Juan, her Mister Darcy, appeared above the oak board at the end of her bed – the moonlight falling on her suitor's scaly head and awful black eyes.

Horror and revulsion surged through her.

Yet she called the creature on, even so.

'Ah, at last. My pretty thing,' she said softly, as it fell over the board and onto the bed. 'Come… come now. Come to your Juliet.'

Steadily now, with flicks of its tail, the creature advanced in the channel between the widow's dark-stockinged legs. On and on it came, rocking and open-mouthed, towards the harbour of her chalky thighs.

'That's it. That's it, my lovely,' whispered the widow Lecuyer, as the creature neared her with its snout.

'You have a hunger, don't you? My little thing! As I have also, let me tell you. A hunger… for *this*!'

Whereupon, just as the awful thing was about to 'dock', the canny widow Lecuyer – with an angry shriek – drew down on it from a bedside table three of her hairnets stitched into one with which she now bagged the frightful carp.

Leaping from her bed with her catch, she now flew from her chamber for the kitchen of the house, as fast as her feet would carry her.

There she filled her largest pan with water from a tap and quickly placed it on her old-fashioned stove, lighting inside it a pile of dry timber.

As steam rose in her kitchen, like autumn mist over Lac Saint Luc, she took hold of the captured creature and flung it into her cauldron: its bubbling water spilling over, with a great, serpent-like hiss.

At the moment of its immersion, the creature – as if determined not to be denied in its desire to haunt her – performed one further trick: its black eyes and gaping jaws giving way to the pained features of Henri Gagneux, as if it were really he, Madame Lecuyer's would-be *beau*, who was being boiled – whilst begging for mercy – in the pan's scalding water.

Madame Lecuyer stepped back in horror at this sight of his agonised face – before, in the next instant, stepping forward swiftly with a heavy lid that she brought down determinedly over the pan and whatever it was – fish, man or both – that thrashed and boiled within.

'Monster! I have you! I have you at last!' she cried.

Later that morning, as a lush orange sun beamed through her windows, Madame Lecuyer – fancying herself still quite the showgirl she once was – finally dined on her carp.

'I have you now, you fiend!' she cackled, forking its grey flesh to her mouth.

Her drool and the carp's moist juices spilled greasily from her.

The shiny secretions streamed her heavily rouged lower lip and powdered chin, and dripped – in the manner of blood mingled with water… or sweat – in oily, pink blotches on her plate.

'You mangy thing! You dog!' she exclaimed as she devoured the fish. 'You who had the cheek to think you would have your way with *me*... Estelle Lecuyer! Look at you now – you ruin! – as I pick at your bones! What are you? Nothing! The evidence is here before us both – in the form of your skeleton, that I – with these gums – have sucked clean. You who would have tupped me! Well, I have had *you*, Monsieur Cock Carp. I have had *you*. Look and see!'

Soon there was scarce a shred of it left.

Except, that was, for the carp's head. And, in particular, its awful dark eye which, in spite of her crowing belligerence, stared up at her *still*, in a way she disliked.

'Pah!' she said eventually, pushing away her plate, with an attempted disdainful flourish.

Finally, she threw the last scraps of the fish onto the wood fire of her stove and listened as the flames consumed them, with hisses and spits.

A long time passed before anyone in the village of Saint Luc felt themselves troubled by the non-appearance of the widow Estelle Lecuyer. The relative isolation of her house, standing in its own large grounds beyond their settlement, together with the sharpness of her tongue (it had always been her way to warn passers-by to keep from the fruit trees of her park) and the oft-repeated tales of her sinister conduct and meanness with money, all saw to that.

In time, however, certain of the locals began to remark that it had been a while since anyone had, in the way to which they had been accustomed, seen her stern form staring out from a widow of her property, or been snapped at fiercely by her bustling black figure from inside the railings of her park. So it was, that, eventually – out of curiosity perhaps, rather than concern for her well-being – a gendarme was summoned from the nearest town.

The officer was later to report that, on entering the heavily-shuttered house, his first and striking impression was of a noxious smell – like that of rotten fish.

Proceeding with a handkerchief over his nose and mouth, he made his way through the warm and malodorous darkness of the ground floor, eventually climbing its stairs to the storey above.

Scenting the smell to be at its strongest behind one particular door, the officer – partial in his private life to pungent cheese and known to his fellows as a two-legged *Chien de Saint-Hubert* (Bloodhound) with a nose for the strangest things – took hold of the door handle in question… and turned it.

The same magistrate who had overseen the hearing into the sudden passing of Henri Gagneux now arrived – cursing his luck – once again in the village of Saint Luc: this time for the purpose of inquiring into the death of the widow Estelle Lecuyer.

The hall in the village that served as the courtroom was full to overflowing.

For days, rumours had spread (like those fires that in unlucky summers sometimes strike that dry corner of southern France), the gossip gripping not only little Saint Luc but crackling through the whole district and beyond.

The widow, it was asserted, had died horribly – choking to her death on an object that had become lodged in her throat.

Initially, this was said to be a fishbone – a cruel, spiked thing – that had become stuck in her craw.

But, quite quickly, others – who declared themselves better-informed, by virtue of family connections in the police department and the profession of undertaker – claimed that the object was something else entirely: a 'part' that was altogether bone*less*, in fact.

These same figures whispered knowingly of garments in which the widow had been found on her deathbed: a black cape, scarlet stockings and precious little else.

'I saw that fish on which she feasted,' the blind woman who had spoken at the inquest into the death of Henri Gagneux now declared. 'On its head were the horns of the Devil, and, for fins, the most awful, cloven hooves. Truly, I have never witnessed such evil,' she told the hushed and dreadful court.

Puzzled by what the villagers expected from him, the justice recorded a finding whose equivalent in English law would be termed 'misadventure'.

One consequence of what has become known as *L'affaire du poisson et Madame Lecuyer* is that, to this day, fish is a dish that can seldom be found – even on a Friday – by travellers who have the fortune to happen upon that otherwise observant small parish.

The hire of a rod in that idyllic spot is a wholly impossible thing.

Fungal

Nebelstadt
(Mist Town)

Our city is damp… damp with an enveloping, vaporous mist that moistens the black cassocks of its priests, slimes the smooth cobbles of its squares, and coats the necks and faces of its citizens with an oily film that glistens in such scant, leaden, gloom-filled light as our cloud-congealed skies permit.

This… climate… of dripping lintels, matted hair, mildew and mould spores – some product of latitude or longitude (I know not which) and our location on what was once a great and wild marsh – prevails for nine-tenths of our year. The exception being those weeks of high summer when swarms of mosquitoes descend on our canal-side streets and courtyards, in search of the flesh of those who are foolish enough to either attempt their sweated sleep *un*shrouded or to dine *al fresco*, without some lit coil or cigarette smoking thinly in their defence.

Some say the effects of the ceaseless drizzle run deep… much deeper than mere surface irritation and the necessity of regular baths and changes of clothes: that the wet air is corrosive: rotting chests (both wooden and human) and not simply rusting the rings of fingers but loosening them (even those of the wedding kind); an unguent not merely of the body but – so to speak – of morals and the mind.

Dissolution… disintegration… is something on which I feel qualified to comment. The starting point of the story that follows is a passage from my decline and…Well, I'll leave you to judge whether the appropriate next word is *fall*. You might think some other word more fitting.

Now, though, to begin…

It was at the point of my near exhaustion of the fortune my family had left me that I developed the habit of wandering the back streets of a certain quarter of our city that was – and is still – given over to merchants in old books, maps and what might be called 'curiosities' of a kind.

In its narrow lanes and small, half-hidden squares, I sought out distractions of a more affordable and (I hoped) edifying nature than those offered by the opium dens (their latter-day equivalents, I mean), gaming tables and other dubious houses of the night that had been my milieu till then.

One late afternoon, while wandering that district, my eyes alighted on a window that seemed new to me. It apprehended me by reason of its strangeness, having nothing in it bar a simple sign adhered to the inside of its glass, which read

SELF-SUFFICIENCY

Enquire within

Conscious of the diminishing nature of my funds and not entirely unsympathetic to the clamour that we all must do more to help Mother Nature, I was more than a little intrigued.

The season was now our mosquito one and the day's setting sun was a yellow-red yolk in the gaps between the buildings behind me, its broken beams dispensing strange flashes and pools of light to dance on the glass of the window before me. Beyond, the shop's interior seemed in darkness.

Always an easily tempted soul, I pushed open the door and went in.

The jangle of an old-style bell heralded my entrance – repeating its ring as I stowed the door – instinct told me to do so *softly* – in its jamb.

The interior was empty save for the dull sheen of a glass case across the far end of the room.

I walked towards it and waited.

The daylight was fading, and the shop seemed without any kind of bulb. The waist-high case – as far as I could make out – contained nothing.

I drummed its top with my fingers, glancing about me at the drab, unadorned walls of the premises.

Eventually, I let out a cough.

'Yes, yes – I heard you the first time!' came an irritated voice – that of a man who seemed elderly – from some concealed quarters at the rear. Other sounds – that might have been from the re-arrangement of boxes – quickly followed from where the proprietor – if that's who he was – seemed to be.

For a moment, I turned away to look back at the street and the buildings that now loomed blackly in the row opposite. I was struck by the earthy smell that the shop seemed to possess. Aromatically, it was as if I had stepped down a level to some kind of cellar, though I knew that I had not.

My ears now detected a shuffle of feet behind me, and I sensed a figure draw near.

A curtain of glass beads billowed outwards and gave way – with a gentle clatter – to the form of an elderly man. I use the word 'form' because there was so very little of him in the dim light that I was able to discern. His face was strangely featureless, the whole of his being having the same drabness as the premises in which we stood.

'I've come about the sign,' I said.

'Of course you have,' he responded. 'Why else would you? There's nothing but that here!'

As he spoke, the room's odd odour increased. It was as if a certain fungal dampness clung to him, in the way of woodsmoke on an old, roving Romany, or the lingering reek of livestock on a shepherd or farmer's skin. Unless I was mistaken, the smell seemed to issue from his mouth.

The room, I noticed, grew colder. I remembered – briefly – the pleasing warmth of the day's sun that I had felt only moments previously (though the interval strangely seemed a great deal longer).

'Yes,' I began rather circuitously, 'I was wondering if—'

'Self-sufficiency!' the man interrupted. 'Do you want it or not?'

Interested but sensing that some caution might not go amiss, I replied: 'I… *might*. The proof shall be in the eating of the pudding, of course,' I added, attempting a smile.

'Very well,' said the man, for whom pleasantries clearly held no interest. He bent to the glass case and, in the murky light, drew out an object that in my earlier inspection I had overlooked.

This, he now placed, with some care, on the counter.

'A mushroom?' I said.

'If you will,' he replied.

'The source of self-sufficiency?'

'Yes.'

I tried, for a moment (and failed), to make sense of his shadowed face. I began to turn on my heel; a smile (possibly of a condescending kind) passed over my lips.

'You're not interested then?' he continued.

'No – if it's all the same…' I said, heading for the door while wondering how I could have submitted myself to the overtures of such a crank. 'I'll just—'

'Go back to your "digs"… and your debts… your pointless so-called studies, your soulless rooms…'

I stopped.

He continued: '…your drug habit, your… syphilis.'

I turned.

'How do you… Who *are* you?' I asked.

'Never mind that,' he said. 'Do you want it or not? Self-sufficiency?'

I stepped back to the counter, albeit somewhat uncertainly.

'Is this an *Alice in Wonderland* thing?' I asked. 'Is that what this is all about?' I adopted a faux friendly tone, judging this wise with someone who seemed to know so much of me. 'I've tried all sorts in my past, I admit,' I continued. 'But my palate has grown rather jaded. I'm a *recovering* consumer now.'

'Is that so?' he remarked.

'What would you have me do with your… specimen?'

'Why, *eat* it of course!'

'As the way to… self-sufficiency?'

'That is correct.'

'Just the one?'

'One will be enough.'

'And after that,' I said, thinking of what he seemed to know about me, 'you and I shall be… friends?'

'For ever, I don't doubt,' he replied, as brusquely as before.

'Very well then. I shall take and eat this… body.'

He began to wrap the growth – we didn't get into the specifics of exactly what the *thing* was – with some paper and string.

'*How* shall I eat it?' I asked, deciding it best that I continue to humour him.

'Any way you like – as long as you do,' he said, tying a final knot and handing me the small package. As he did so, I noticed in the gloom the strange nature of his fingers, which were ugly – somehow oddly knobbly *and* fleshy, at the same time.

'One of my "five a day",' I said.

'Something like that.'

'What do I owe?'

'Nothing,' he replied.

'Nothing?'

'I think of it as all being for the glory of the garden,' said the man.

'The garden? Whose garden?' I asked.

'Oh, never mind that,' he said. 'Just a turn of phrase.'

Puzzled, I placed the package in my coat pocket and turned to leave.

This time the man said nothing to stop me.

I drew open the door, to the same jangle as before, and turned back to where the man had been. 'Glad to have made your acquaintance,' I said, before realising that the room was empty.

The glass beads of the curtain swayed and glinted in the little that was left of the light.

I have never wholly lost my appetite for the thrill that accompanies the turn of a playing card… the rattle and bounce of the little white ball in the lovely spin of the roulette wheel. Falling back into the welcoming arms of our city's demi-monde, I forgot – for a while – the strange 'shop' of the antiquarian quarter, the old man and his 'gift'.

It nestled – still wrapped – in a corner of my coat pocket until, one early morning, after another night of indulgence, my fingers fell upon its paper and string as I strolled back to my rooms.

Hungry after my nocturnal exertions, I decided to fry some bacon on my stove.

Remembering the package in my coat pocket, I retrieved it.

The mushroom… toadstool… fungus – whatever it was – that lay inside, now looked rather limp, like an umbrella broken and bedraggled after a particularly turbulent rainstorm. The pearl-grey nature of its stem was, it struck me, somewhat finger-like.

Even so, I tossed it into the pan with my rashers, and made some coffee while my breakfast cooked.

I admit that when I came to eat, I did so with a degree of trepidation. Remembering the strangeness of the old man and his shop, I toyed with the curious growth for a while. However, I brought to mind just a few of the many foolish things that I'd done in my life… and – suddenly – speared my fork into its upper stem and cap, and… ate.

Although rather fleshy and lacking firmness in my mouth, the taste was better than I had expected, possibly enhanced by the smoked nature of the bacon I ate with it.

Having breakfasted, I fell asleep, as the city came to life.

Given my lifestyle of many years, I had grown accustomed to awaking in a state of general seediness and fatigue. However, when I rose that afternoon, I felt considerably refreshed. I remembered a strange sensation from my sleep, along with something that I had seen in my dreams: an umbrella… *not* battered and sodden but altogether different – pushing upwards, opening gracefully, in a kaleidoscope of colours. Not so much an 'umbrella', in fact, as a 'parasol'.

Three or four days later, I noticed the first growth.

I was making my way over a footbridge on the S— Canal when I had a feeling of something awkward, protruding from my ankle joint, catching itself against the upper edge of my left shoe. Later, sitting on a taxi-boat, I discreetly pressed it with my hand.

I initially thought it must be some kind of bunion and was surprised when, beneath my ankle sock, my fingers came up against something not hard but a substance that seemed fleshy and pliant.

Back at my rooms, I inspected it with some apprehension.

The louche nature of my life had accustomed me to occasional inflammations of a personal kind, normally dealt with for a fee by one of the private physicians on G— Street.

But this… *growth*, resembled nothing of that kind.

Nor did it seem some weal of skin or spur of bone.

Above all, strange as this may sound, it seemed… *alive* – and, before my very eyes, extending.

Although I'd done little if any academic work for weeks, I felt tired and sickly. Telling myself that this 'thing' protruding from me was in all likelihood a mere passing swelling of the kind that would be dismissed by any doctor… the product of nothing more sinister than the build-up of some natural bodily fluid… I resolved to think no more of it and went to bed.

In the morning, I observed that the stem had grown a cap. I was flustered, I confess – yet also… fascinated.

In the days that followed I felt not the least bit unwell. Absurd as it sounds, it seemed as if I had acquired a not unfriendly companion, like some kind of small rodent or even a tomato plant for my window sill. The other growths came gradually. One from my right ear, another from my left nostril. And then – perhaps assisted by a change in the weather and time of year (autumn with its cooler temperatures and dankness was now upon us) – the rest revealed themselves, growing upon me, thickly and fast. A forest swarmed my torso, groves climbed my neck, plantations raised themselves on my thighs and calves. Others, that were ugly and jungular, reared themselves in my armpits and – if you must know – the regions of my groin and my arse.

Needless to say, by now I had made the connection with the man in the shop and understood his meaning when he spoke of self-sufficiency and… gardens.

I harvested myself. Partly from necessity (owing to the sheer profusion of my fungi), partly from curiosity and a strange hunger – that grew inside me, as I ate.

I cut my stems – perhaps half a dozen at a time – with a kitchen knife, sawing through the 'trunks' so that a slight, visible stump remained. My 'fruit' I then fried, or boiled, and ate with a chop, or piece of liver. There were, however, more than sufficient of these growths for me to eat as a main course, and this I did, perhaps with some garlic or olive oil, and bread, toasted and buttered.

No sooner had I cut myself than my 'orchards' grew back: a ceaseless, self-sufficient supply.

The taste? The taste was not at all unpleasant. It seemed to speak of my body in younger, happier times (when money – and all that went with it – had been easy). On occasion, I imagined the chatter of pretentious wine-tasters and food critics: 'Ah yes, I'm getting hints of a very dangerous liaison…', 'Oh this is *definitely* seared with the afterburn of something very ill-advised…', 'Pleasing notes of a high-octane night when all was gambled… and lost'.

For the most part, my face was spared. A growth would sometimes surprise me when I went to shave. These I would cut *out* rather than *off*, leaving my features a little pocked, though not intolerably.

Relations of the kind to which I was accustomed with the opposite sex remained possible provided I sought them *between* harvests: when my body was 'fallow', so to speak, its crop 'gathered-in'.

Having grown used to my condition, my curiosity grew as to whether my state was unique, or something that I shared. I returned to that old, bookish quarter more than once in search of that singular shop and its keeper, but I found no trace of it – or him.

Short of funds and in need of something to do, I looked-in one evening on a lecture at the university. Professor P—, a pompous timeserver, was preaching about an issue of no interest in a once-a-year lecture (thank God it was as rare as that!) of the kind he was obliged to deliver in order to justify his (wretched) tenure, which his ancient grey fangs held on to as if they were those of a sabre tooth tiger.

I was attempting to stifle a yawn, wondering how I might best achieve my escape from the sparse audience in the auditorium, when my attention was seized by the useless old bumbler in a way that he had surely never intended.

From the cuff of his right sleeve, what seemed a growth – one of the kind that had taken root on me – showed itself as he chalked something dull on a board. My eyes caught sight of its cap and stem, before it concealed itself and drew back into the drapes of his shabby black gown.

Instead of leaving, I remained.

I engaged the old booby afterwards, thanking him for what I said had been a compelling address.

Unaccustomed to such interest – those who'd been dotted about the hall had left rapidly after the faintest applause – the doddering fool rambled on for a while, as I feigned all ears.

My real interest lay not in his theories and words (which were feeble and tedious) but in the caps that seemed to be squeezing themselves above the buttoned collar of his shirt, like saplings, or perhaps pistons that had been reduced to a peculiar slow motion.

His vanity stoked, he said to me, finally, 'Why don't you come to my rooms tomorrow evening, and dine?'

'Love to,' I replied.

When, as arranged, I called at his chambers, our ancient academic proved a reluctant dining companion. He feigned puzzlement when, after a second glass of claret, I asked him about the secrets that his body concealed.

I raked a blade across his front, then – to his astonishment – drew its small serrations over him again, this time in the opposite direction.

Like some drug mule caught at a border-crossing, his bounty stood exposed.

A veritable rainforest showed itself, there, on his chest.

By this time, keen as I was to know – in more detail – those that I myself nursed (for the record: Destroying Angel, Cryptic Bonnet and Dead Moll's Fingers), I had grown familiar – via various books and encyclopaedias – with the mushrooms, toadstools and fungi of this world. (I adopted the English nomenclature: the tongue of Shakespeare seemed to me somehow best suited to the varieties I encountered.)

Many of Professor P—'s specimens were of the kind that might perhaps have been expected on a figure who was a rather unappealing example of later life: Drab Tooth, Humpback, Bald Knight and Wet Rot (also, the slender stems and slight hoods of Funeral Bell).

Yet his slack stomach, rounded shoulders and puny limbs also held certain specimens whose discovery – on such an awful old fart – pleased me greatly: Golden Navel and Pink Disco, to name but two.

(Almost) needless to say, I set to work on the gibbering old gibbon – harvesting what took my fancy… and lighting his stove.

Anticipating that his 'fruits' might be on the tough side, I'd wisely – as it turned out – armed myself with some tarragon and garlic, which I now added to the oil warming in the pan. He made a grab for its handle, but I beat him back, till he cowered in a corner by the side of some books.

Weary of his continuing whinges, I decided to take matters in hand – and stripped him there and then of his entire crop.

What was left of him – arms, legs and so forth – I bagged for future use, reasoning – from experience – that a fixture like him, who the university had found so impossible to uproot, would also be a hardy perennial in the culinary sense (albeit always in need of some seasoning).

'Yes,' I thought to myself as – eventually – I dined, 'hints of soiled mackintosh, mothed tweed and old sock. Unpleasant notes of stale pipe tobacco, too. More pepper, garlic, spices – any *damned* thing! – next time,' I noted, as – rather grimly – I chewed.

I suppose that biologically I had by now acquired a taste for such things (even the most poisonous – to whose toxins I, in time, grew immune), which was why – apart from the moderate 'thrill' of it – I had bothered with such an awful old specimen as Professor P—. If one had been a patron of a *boucher chevalin*, he would surely have ranked as the roughest horsemeat on the rack: all teeth, hooves and ribs (and certainly no brain). I had, by this time, partaken – fried, roasted, steamed, casseroled, marinated and bread-crumbed – in probably half the staff in four of the university's faculties. Quite a figure! Along the way, a goodly number of Twisted Deceivers, Powdery Piggybacks, Snakeskin Grisettes, Greasy Brackets, Bilious Boletes and Mire Navels – the varieties will come as little surprise to any familiar with such septic and self-absorbed institutions.

Temptation of a more welcome kind came one morning as I opened a letter that – to my surprise – had been slipped under my door. The prettiness of the paper, its scent and the neatness of the writing all suggested a woman's hand. As I read on, the author said she had been present at the speech given by that pompous ass (*my* words, not hers) Professor P—. She had noted at the time, she said, my interests in those matters about which he had discoursed – and she wondered now if we might meet for the furtherance of her research.

I was intrigued.

I remembered how a young woman had sat on a bench in the lecture hall: the moonlight playing on her hair rather beautifully through a window… as if she had strayed ethereally from a fairy ring in a field or wood.

But was she really after my thoughts… or did she perhaps have something *else* in mind? By that time,

I knew all too well that the filamentous fungi of Europe included a stubby, curve-capped strain *Boletus pseudoregius*… put plainly, The Pretender.

After some contemplation, I decided to agree to my correspondent's request: to join her 'for supper'. But I would be careful – *v-e-r-y* careful – lest *she* should have ideas of plunging her knife and fork into *me*.

On the appointed evening, a cold fog hung over the canals of our city, fingering its way through the empty lanes and unfurling in long, thick clouds that filled the silent squares. I was nervous and – as someone who for so much of his life had been neglectful of his health – possibly even feverous. The city's perpetual wetness, and my own perspiration, moistened my cheeks and neck, as I made my way to her address.

In my mind, the dampness seemed like a saliva: the city's very *drool*, emanating from its old churches, warehouses and shuttered markets, which appeared to watch and listen as I passed.

Nausea began its awful gavotte in my gullet. In my stomach, grey water shifted greasily, as if I had become some sort of human adjunct to our labyrinthine canals.

I heard but could not see (on account of the shrouding fog) heavy barges and the slow thud of their engines, pushing low waves of water to the dripping sides of wharfs. Their progress caused me to imagine great marine creatures… whales, repeating some pilgrimage of ancient memory – crossing our city, as they perhaps once had, before its construction: disciplined, purposeful herds, unknown to the rest of us, in the ebony depths of the night.

Finally, I came to what I took to be my correspondent's door.

It was an old – *venerable* – portal, dark save for small clumps (in the corners of its panelling) of brilliant jewel-green moss, illuminated by the soft light of a lantern.

It had the look of an entry that no one had opened for years.

I tapped, thinking there must be another entrance. My hostess greeted me, even so.

I was immediately struck by her loveliness. And for a moment we stared at each other, without speaking.

Finally, she invited me in.

Her rooms were lit with candles, the chambers being large, high-ceilinged and almost empty, save for their shelves of books and an occasional chair. There were so very many books – piles… *towers*… of them – that the house seemed more a library than a place of human habitation.

She poured wine and we talked – in a rambling way – about Shakespeare, Balzac and Goethe, our conversation conducted for the most in a manner that was light, even playful.

For our supper, she served the largest cap of fungus that I had ever seen.

It had been baked to a crust which she cut through with a knife… as my eyes followed. Her choice of dish, I felt, could have been no coincidence.

I ate and continued to drink politely, determined to give nothing away (in more than one respect).

She replenished my glass frequently and liberally, and – though remaining on my guard – I sensed my earlier anxieties slipping from me.

Strangely, my head contrived to feel both light and heavy, as if my own 'cap', so to speak, had grown burdensome to my 'stem'.

Gradually, I grew aware that I was hearing her read poetry – which may or may not have been her own. In my languid state, I seemed to detect the words 'truffle' and 'hunt'.

With their enunciation, I was suddenly aware of her being on top of me.

Her hands worked their way quickly along my shirtfront, loosening its buttons.

Casting aside the cotton, she clawed for my treasure – my Angels, my Fingers, my Bonnets – that she knew – I could tell – were upon me.

But the truth was this: that I – in the days before – had dined on myself so heartily that nothing, save some pitiful stems and ugly stumps, remained. I was unfruitful, like a forest that had been bombarded in a battle then stripped of its smashed timber for the campfires of its belligerents.

Amazed at my greed, she froze.

And, before she could do anything, I was at her.

She tried to fight me, but – thanks to my feasting – I was too strong.

In an instant, I was ripping and gnawing.

My hands and mouth seized at her body's glorious banquet: Mealy Oysters, Forest Lamb, Marsh Honey, Tongues of Fire, Jewelled Araminta, Candelabra Coral and Fishnet Bolete.

Sometimes my feasts have ended awfully: my body retching and my mind racked by weird and disturbing hallucinations brought on by excesses of psilocybin in the growths that I have eaten. More than once, I have seen myself hanging – stalk-like – from the corner of the grinding maw of a great monster of the kind that might have been conjured by Hieronymus Bosch.

But *this* banquet…

It was transport to the gloriously transcendental… to the heavens themselves.

Oh, how I gorged!

She was… divine!!

The groves of academe have not been my only hunting ground. The Law and the Civil Service – great hidden plantations of the cobwebbed and the dank – have been sources of sustenance. The Church also, of course. My nose for these things once led me to dine on a priest in his confession booth (having scented his secret garden through his window of wire mesh). 'My daily bread, Father, if you please,' I said, as I drew open his curtain. Beneath his vestments: Chicken of the Woods, Golden Fleece, Milking Bonnet, Plums and Custard, and – to finish – the squat, black balls of King Alfred's Cakes.

Accountants, however, I now shun, owing to the sourness of their crops: Bitter Beech, Drab Bonnet and Gristly Domecap (tolerable only if very carefully cooked). Likewise, park-keepers (who I have found to be nurseries to a man of Redleg Toughshank – scarce worth the eating, as its name suggests). Tram conductors I abhor (carriers – invariably – of Stinking Parachute and Flea's Ear). Ditto waiters (I've yet to meet one who hasn't brought me *Hebeloma crustuliniforme* – 'Poison Pie', to the unlatined). The same for tooth-pullers and most medical men (always – in my unhappy experience – reliable for Rancid Bonnet). Perhaps the worst are writers, stewing whey-faced in their sunless garrets: the stalks, scabs, puffs and gills of sundry Rusts, Rashes, Leeches, Poxes and Shadows are theirs, strewn over pale skeletons that are barely worth the picking.

Yes, my happiest harvests have undoubtedly been at the university, where, one day soon, even the dullest members of its senate will surely wake up to their losses of staff: eaten away, it might be said – under their very noses.

I have the feeling that, eventually, a student – a very *eccentric* student... eager to study, if such a condition can be believed – will ask questions. And the senate – that bunch of dribbling dodderers – will suddenly realise it has a whole forest of vacancies to fill.

And I shall then step from the shadows to take the chair of my choosing... having – forgive my little joke – already (in one sense, at least) taken the pick of their seats.

Sometimes… at night… I have the sense of being at the centre of a great fairy ring (not of elves and pixies, but of the mushroom kind).

In the darkness, I feel the stalks and gills of its circle brush against me… like the tightening of a noose.

The call has come: a summons to sup with the senate – at the very highest of high tables – whose members clearly have plans for me.

On what shall we dine? I wonder: Devil's Tooth? Bloody Milkcap? Icicle Spine?

How should I dress? Dinner jacket – or tails?

I question the caller at the other end of the telephone.

'Come as you are,' he responds, keenly. 'That will be quite sufficient.'

Unless mistaken, I hear a crystal dinner bell… tinkling down the line.

The Heritage Vegetable

Beneath her bouffant helmet of salon-curled silver hair, Audrey Britton was seldom less than busy. Busy with this, busy with that. Church bazaars, coffee mornings, jumble sales, notices for the parish newsletter. Busier than ever since the passing of her husband Arthur. She considered herself a stalwart supporter of anything that was for the good of the local community in Titchmore Green.

So when a new family arrived in the village, taking over a property and selling boxes of vegetables grown on its parcel of land, Audrey felt it her duty to get involved and lend them her aid.

She filled-in the flyer that came through her letterbox at The Thrushes, placing an order for a 'mixed' box of vegetables to be delivered there fortnightly.

Doing so, she reflected on how there would have once been no need. Her husband Arthur had been such a keen gardener. After his retirement from the planning department at Mulverhampton, and their subsequent move from the conurbation to 'the country', village life – the *traditional* English life – at Titchmore Green had given his own 'innings' – as he liked to call it – a whole new lease. And how he'd *loved* his garden… until, of course, his heart attack… and 'sudden death' (in the pathologist's words) – amid the banks of his potato plants. For a moment, Audrey now caught sight of him, in her mind's eye: slumped over the wooden handle of his earth-embedded fork. His Maris Pipers, she remembered: his pride and joy.

Glancing through the kitchen window at her bird table, where some tits were swinging from a string of nuts, Audrey saw – behind it – the near-wilderness (to her sensibilities, anyway) that Arthur's vegetable plot had become. She sensed her eyes moistening, a slight shortness of breath. She tried to think of something that might cheer her. Suddenly, she remembered the 'secret' she and Arthur had shared: his carrot... the cheeky one he'd brought in to her, from the garden, that day. 'Look at this, Aud. Look what I've gone and grown!' he'd quipped.

Well, it *was* a strange thing... a sort of three-into-one... all grown together... that looked like nothing so much as a gentleman's...

They'd had a chuckle... there, in the kitchen... and after a few minutes he'd gone back to his gardening: hoeing and drilling and sucking on his pipe.

And that, she' d thought, had been the end of that – till two weeks following, on a Sunday night, when the pair of them had been sitting in the living room, watching TV.

'Look, Aud!' Arthur had called out, all excited.

And, raising her eyes from her knitting (a winter scarf for her nephew Nigel), she'd seen it – Arthur's carrot – live... on national TV. Not the actual carrot, but a polaroid photo he'd – unbeknown to her – taken and sent in, to the show (which had been famous – in its day – for that sort of thing).

'And we're grateful to Mr Walter Pennyfeather, of Crewe, for forwarding us a picture of this um, specimen,' said the presenter, who couldn't keep a straight face.

Well, the studio audience were in stitches, of course.

In his armchair, Arthur had simply winked at her.

And then... how the two of them had sat there and laughed!

Twenty million people saw it, to be sure... that carrot. That was how many tuned-in to shows like that, back then. Half the population – at least. She'd heard neighbours talking about it in the village shop. And at the post office. 'Did you see that carrot?' she'd heard them chuckle.

But the funniest thing – the *strangest* thing – was that nobody knew that it was Arthur's carrot.

To this day, it was her secret.

When the vegetable box came, Audrey (who'd found it in the front porch, with an invoice) was a tad disappointed... on more than one count.

First, and most obviously, was the somewhat shabby state of the vegetables therein. Since Arthur's passing, she'd been getting her veg from the supermarket in town (on the same day she went in for her fortnightly appointment to have her hair done). The supermarket veg was always so very clean. Yes, she remembered how Arthur's crops would be 'on the soily side' when he brought them in from the garden, but she'd always been able to give them a brisk wash under the kitchen taps: get them looking shipshape. *These* vegetables, however – the ones in the box – were – there was no other word for it – *dirty*. Earth... mud... *loam*... clung to them. What was more, it had dried out, so that its grey-brown lumps... and crusts... and grains... and smears, were *caked* on. True, she would soon have these unwelcome coatings off with a scrubbing brush and a good soaking, she thought to herself. But even so...

Her second disappointment lay in the nature of the vegetables, hardly any of which she recognised. While she thought some of them *might* have been carrots and even a cauliflower, they definitely weren't – to her eyes – cauli-like or carroty in colour, instead being strange greens... and purples... and pinks.

And there was something *else* – particularly when it came to the rather puzzling, long and curved – almost horn-shaped – items of produce in the box, with their 'hairs' and their knobbles, that... uneased her. After scrubbing them under the cold tap, she wondered – with a shudder – if she would ever be able to put them in her mouth.

She looked again at the invoice note and decided to telephone the supplier.

'Hello, this is Audrey Britton, The Thrushes, speaking,' she began. 'To whom am I speaking, please?'

'This is Noah,' said the voice at the other end. 'Can I help?'

Slightly thrown for a second by the respondent's name – which seemed to her an oddly old one for a voice that seemed to be that of a fairly young man – Audrey nevertheless gathered her thoughts and ploughed on.

'It's about my vegetable box. I just wondered if I could have some more *traditional* fare.'

'I'm sorry?'

'*Traditional* vegetables,' Audrey repeated, stressing the adjective in what she felt was a firm but polite way… in order to drive home her point. 'Haricots verts, petits pois – if you have them – carrots that come in orange?'

'Just a moment, please. I'll look up your order. What did you say your name was again?'

'Audrey Britton, The Thrushes,' Audrey repeated, not wholly liking this need to identify herself. 'I'm quite well known in Titchmore Green.'

'Okay… let me have a look. Right, I can see,' the voice came back after a moment. 'A. Britton. One medium box. Artichoke, aubergine, butternut squash, carrots (multi-coloured), celeriac, fennel, Romanesco cauliflower, samphire, sweet potatoes… Yes, Mrs… um—'

'Britton. Audrey Britton.'

'You've had the full "heritage" range, near enough. Very traditional. I'm sorry, but I can't quite see the problem.'

Thinking that she was getting nowhere… rather fast – with this 'Noah', whoever he was – and also sensing that she was somehow being belittled – Audrey decided to leave matters there, for now. 'I'm just asking if you can "mix things up a little" … next time,' she said, forcing a smile – of sorts – into her voice. 'Thank you so much. Goodbye.'

Later, while peeling and slicing two of the mysterious orbs and one of the long roots, Audrey grew resentful of the way the young man on the phone had dealt with her enquiry. Who was *he* to lecture her about 'heritage'? She had been a resident – a *valued* resident – of Titchmore Green for sixteen-and-a-half years. She was practically a native! There was also something posh – not snooty or grand, exactly – but posh… educated… *privileged*… about the way the young man had spoken. Suddenly, she felt very aware of her own accent, never mind that Arthur had told her – more than once – that it was 'slight' and 'barely there'. She called to mind the pretty young woman (who she thought now to be the wife of this *Noah*) who she'd seen queuing at the post office – the girl had worn a long dress of the kind young girls seldom wore these days – all natural fibres, nothing man-made about it – you could tell. Yes, she'd had Wellies on, beneath her dress, but they, also. were of a posh and patterned kind. Through the post office window – not that she'd been looking especially – Audrey had seen her drive off in one of those big, four-wheel drive things that had the look of being new.

'Noah!' she now thought to herself. Whoever would give a child a name like that? Nigel – her nephew's name – now *that* was a nice name. But Noah… well, it was… like something that had gone out with the Ark!

She stopped slicing for a moment and chuckled at her unintended witticism.

When the next box came it was – to Audrey's eye – no different from the first. There was, perhaps, more colour to it, yes. Some of the carrots, as she took them to be, were very dark indeed and others a waxy white. But, as a whole, the box was – *fundamentally* – no different: a preponderance of the same, long, slightly lewd shapes, and everything crusted with earth.

'No!' Audrey decided. She would have no more of it. *This* would be the last. Happy as she was to support the village and all those in it, she would go back to buying her veg at the supermarket. No one could blame her. She would cancel her custom with a polite note and deliver it early the next morning… the earlier the better, before she set off for the hairdresser's – when no one would be up and about. She began to put pen to paper on the kitchen table. 'Keep it short and to the point, Aud. That's the secret. No need to tell them *why* I'm withdrawing my custom. Sweeten it a bit. A few white lies. Soften the blow,' she told herself.

> *The Thrushes*
> *Titchmore Green*

> *Dear Noah (sorry but I don't know your surname),*
> *As a widow on a pension living on my own, I'm finding – like so many of us in this world – that I'm having to keep a watchful eye on my budget these days. Also, my appetite isn't quite what it used to be. Therefore, I'm sorry to say that I shall be cancelling my order. Forthwith. I do hope you'll understand.*

> *Yours sincerely,*
> *Audrey Britton (Mrs)*

Early next morning, as mist shrouded the still and mostly sleeping village, Audrey pushed her envelope through the letterbox.

The house – no humble cottage as Audrey had first presumed – where Noah, his wife and – by the looks of it (from assorted trikes and bikes scattered outside) – their children lived, was the grandest of several in Titchmore Green that went (to the consternation of deliverymen) by the names of The Vicarage or The Old Vicarage or indeed The Old Rectory. The vicar nowadays lived elsewhere – in a new-build on a housing estate in the town, his remoteness being a nuisance as far as Audrey was concerned (although possibly not to him).

She felt a twinge of regret as she heard her missive fall to the floor on the other side of the front door. Still – it had to be done, she told herself. Her action was for the best.

Having driven to the town, she was the first customer of the day through the doors at the supermarket, stocking her trolley with familiar, clean and comforting vegetables, handily bagged, for the most part, in see-through plastic – her eye untroubled by anything that was livid, or puce, or long, or hairy, with a curve to it of a suggestive kind.

Later, as she sat under a dryer at the hairdresser's, she thought how well the morning had gone, and flicked at a magazine.

In the fortnight that followed, all was reasonably well in the world of Audrey Britton. The word *reasonably* is used because, as she went about her business of being active and involved in the affairs of the village, she had the mounting sense that things had grown different in Titchmore Green. By 'things', she meant the people who lived there, their outlook, what they were... *about*.

When she knocked – for example – at Pear Tree Cottage on a flag day for one of the many charities for which she collected, it was no longer Ned Nobbs, the old gamekeeper, who came to the door, but a young man who introduced himself as 'Zeb', who in turn called out to his 'partner' – Persephone – to see if she had any change for a lady – no name, no 'Audrey', let alone 'Mrs Britton' – who was collecting at the front door.

And the story was the same at other addresses at which Audrey called: Marshbank House, Honeysuckle

Cottage, Tiptree Mill, Dingle Terrace, The Nest, The Nook. Their former occupants – Dr Pewsey, Miss Finch, Major and Mrs Clyde, Herbert Frost, deaf Mrs Pike, and more – gone… all gone. The houses all now being lived in by various Tarquins and Jocastas and Calebs and Allegras and Venetias and Felicias, so it seemed. All nice enough, civil enough, smiley enough and all happy to find some change for her tin. But all rather like… *Noah*, of the vegetable box. Posh (in the way that they spoke, never mind, in some cases, their beards and rather 'casual' appearance) and all cut from the same cloth – they each seemed to have the same dresses, the same dungarees – as 'N'… or so she imagined (they'd yet to meet in person).

Making her way home to The Thrushes. Audrey suddenly felt very old. Opening her front door, she realised that, for all of her desire to be busy, she hadn't, in fact, been very busy in the village for quite some time. Indeed, it dawned on her that nowadays, save for her trips to the supermarket and the hairdresser in town, she very rarely left her house at all.

On the day after her charity collection, Audrey made her regular trip to the hair salon and, while in the town, stocked-up with a few supplies from the supermarket that she wheeled in a trolley to her small blue car.

Having returned home, she was taken by surprise by the presence in her front porch of a large cardboard box. Stuck to it was an envelope bearing her name.

Setting down her bags of shopping from the supermarket, she reached with her key and unlocked her front door and then bent over and dragged the heavy box into the house through the hallway and onto the quarry tiles of the kitchen floor.

Having replaced her driving glasses with her reading ones, she opened the envelope and studied the letter inside. The handwritten note – on a single sheet – read:

Dear Audrey,

Thank you for your letter. My wife Willow and I fully appreciate your situation. As neighbours and fellow villagers, we would very much like – in a gesture of community spirit – to supply you with a vegetable box twice a month, free of charge.

Herewith, the first.

We are very happy to do this. It is no problem. Although there is absolutely no need, doubtless you'll do us a small turn of your own one day.

Yours with good wishes,
Noah and Willow
(plus Sark, Herm, Hamlet, Ptolemy and Skye – the kids – our tribe!)

Audrey Britton wasn't normally a woman to be flummoxed. But now she was flummoxed indeed. For a moment, she seemed to lose a little of her footing, the toe of her shoe colliding with one side of the cardboard box.

Her slight stumble caused the flaps of the box to open sufficient for her to catch sight of certain of its contents, her eyes falling for an awful (to her) moment on a bunch of mud-crusted carrots that seemed longer, hairier, and all together more sinister, than ever: a malign rainbow of weird, *un*carroty colours – blood reds, tongue pinks, forest blacks, ghostly whites and thunder cloud mauves – where the flesh of the root vegetables lay hideously exposed.

An earthy, dirty smell assailed Audrey's nose.

She felt the need to sit… to *lie* down. Her legs were like jelly.

Clutching table edges and doorknobs, she made her way to the living room and lay on the settee.

When Audrey awoke, several hours later, it was to a dusky light and an eerie quiet, any birdsong beyond her windows having long ceased for the day. For a strange moment, she seemed to hear Arthur's voice, calling to her: 'Aud! Aud! Look what I've grown!'

Rising from the settee, she entered the kitchen. 'Where are you, Arthur? What is it?' she asked.

She made her way to the kitchen window and looked through the glass. In the half-light, and without her spectacles, she seemed to see something. Forcing her eyes to focus, she saw – or thought that she did – a scarecrow-like figure… that had slumped forward… as if over a garden fork.

Audrey recoiled from the window. As she did so, her heel caught the cardboard box of vegetables that lay on the floor.

And, suddenly, her head was spinning… spinning into a whirl.

She had the strange sense that all of the people in the village – the settlers, the incomers, the *new* people – the Noahs, the Willows, the people on their 'list' – were talking about her and laughing at her, as if they knew and had always known about Arthur's carrot, that *he* was Mr Pennyfeather, of Crewe… that, all along, *everyone* – not just the newcomers but the people who had left: Mrs Pike, Miss Finch, Major and Mrs Clyde – had been sniggering at them – *guffawing* – for years over not merely Arthur's carrot but her accent, her trips to the hairdresser, her notices in the newsletter, her floral arrangements in the parish church, her flag days, the very sight of her: coming up their paths, rattling her tin.

Suddenly, she removed her cardigan and began unbuttoning her blouse. Then she undid her skirt.

Fingers still flying, she unhooked her bra behind her back and pulled down her knickers… till she stood there… naked… in her kitchen.

Plunging her hands into the vegetable box on the floor, she grasped the bunch of carrots she'd seen earlier.

Then she ran out of the house with them and into the lane.

Separating specimens from her cluster as she hurried, she hurled them – as if they were sticks of dynamite – against the windows and doors of her startled neighbours.

'There was nothing wrong with my Arthur's carrot, if that's what you're thinking… if that's what this is all about. He was a stallion! A Casanova! We made love every night! I could have had dozens of children. Scores… if I wanted. He was *that* virile. But things were different back then. He was making his way in life – in the planning department at Mulverhampton. He rose to become assistant deputy chief surveyor. And besides, money was less plentiful then. We made… sacrifices!' she shouted. 'Oh, how my tuppence longs for him now! These carrots and whatever else it is that you taunt me with… let me tell you, they don't even come *NEAR!!*'

For almost an hour, Audrey Britton ran amok in Titchmore Green, as if she were some wild Earth Goddess that a whirlwind had propelled from the darkness.

Eventually, a police car arrived, and she was wrapped in a blanket and taken away.

Audrey Britton no longer lives in the village of Titchmore Green. She is instead a resident of the Sycamore Slumbers rest home in the nearby town, her nephew Nigel having helpfully sold her house to a nice young couple named Silas and Cordelia, who are friends of Noah and Willow, and Tarquin and Jocasta, and Caleb and Allegra, and everyone else who now lives in Titchmore Green (a name, incidentally, that they're thinking of changing).

On Sundays at Sycamore Slumbers, a roast lunch is always served. It is, in the words of the management, a 'traditional' affair for the pleasure of residents. Soggy miniature cubes of what – prior to their dicing and deep-freezing – may once have been root vegetables are dolloped onto Audrey's plate, and those of the other seniors, by a smiley young woman from the kitchens who has a name that Audrey – frail now after her final 'turn' for Titchmore Green – can't quite remember, but who she considers to be… nice.

The Lamb of God

Like many in the coastal reaches of my country, I was faintly familiar with the island. I had never set foot there, of course, and I knew of no one who indisputably had. But from my boyhood onwards I had heard references to it, and the ancient order of monks who were said to live there, cut off from civilisation.

It was difficult for me to be sure from these fragments – most of which had the ring of fishermen's tales – if the island really existed. Once, in what I thought at the time might have been an appropriate area of the sea, I seemed to detect – in the distance – a cloud hanging above what had the look of an islet of the remote and rocky kind. But having had two almost entirely barren days in those waters, I had no reason, or desire, to sail any further near it. And, having drawn-in my empty nets (with more than a degree of frustration), I turned my small vessel, the *Santa Maria*, about and headed for home.

Several times, on that homeward voyage, I glanced back to where the white cloud – and possibly the island – had been. They no longer seemed to be there. On the last occasion that I did so, there was unquestionably nothing but blue sea and the eventual line of the horizon. *If* the island had indeed been there, it had now retreated... beyond the ocean's great curtain, as if reclaimed by mythology and those stories of the kind told by sailors with minds addled by alcohol and long years alone out on the saltwater.

And so, some months later, it was with joy and yet at the same time near-disbelief that – though too feeble to express anything – I found myself alive, on its shores, after being caught with my boat in the most tremendous storm. This latter had unleashed itself with almost no warning: one of those strange, sudden and very violent cyclones that happen when a day overheats to the point of explosion and the place where you stand, sit, or steer – be it on the land or on the sea – becomes a scene of the utmost madness: lightning, gale-force winds (that seem to sweep from nowhere), and the sea – all too abruptly – your mortal enemy. An Act of God, of the cruel and terrible kind.

How long I had drifted in the hull of the *Santa Maria*, I could not say – dazed and bewildered, as I was, for so much of it. A collision with her woodwork had cut open my head and, for a while, rendered me unconscious: the blood drying and flaking from me in the subsequent – skin-blistering – sun, as if in mimicry of the old and peeling paint of my blessed *Maria*.

As I lay, burnt, bruised and dry as tinder, in the cup of her beams… waves rocking the *Maria's* hull at the edge of the pebbled beach where we'd run ashore, I became aware of the eyes and face of a monk, staring into mine, a corona of white sunlight circling his head and his beard.

He lifted me, awkwardly, from my vessel.

Carrying me over his shoulder, he took me – by way of a steepening path through rocks and then bushes – to the high-perched walls of what I realised had to be a monastery. My principal sight through all of this was of his scurrying, leather-sandalled feet, from which I noticed a number of his toes were missing.

Unless I am mistaken, a bell heralded our approach – this possibly being rung by a brother who had seen us; or maybe it was tolling coincidentally, as part of their mass.

Inside the monastery's cloisters, I was – amid various whispers – laid on a bed within the whitewashed walls of a small and simple cell. There, cold water was raised to my lips, which I half drank, half dribbled… down my rough and stubbled jaws. This sweet and lovely liquid, I presumed, had been drawn from a well.

With the driest of croaks, I thanked the priest who gave it to me... the same one, it seemed, who had carried me from my boat.

Touching my arm, he responded: 'We are a poor order. But what we have, we share. Rest now. The Lord has delivered you unto us. And we shall abide by His will.'

In the days and then weeks that seemed to follow, I sensed myself repeatedly passing in and out of consciousness.

My recovery would take time, I knew.

Morsels of food were fed to me, sometimes spooned, sometimes pressed with fingers to my lips. At such times, aromas of herbs – rosemary, sage, thyme... garlic also – filled my small and unadorned room.

On occasion, I heard sounds that – in my weak and confused state – seemed like those of a *lapping*... which were a mystery to me, given that I knew that I had left my boat, the *Santa Maria*, and the sea, some distance behind, at the foot of the island's cliffs.

The length and angle of the light from the small window to the outside world in my cell, and the way that shadows altered and lengthened in my room, told me – thanks to the many years I had spent at sea – that time was passing.

In spite of what seemed to me the long nature of my stay, I felt myself to be growing no stronger. Quite the reverse, in fact.

Although the brothers fed and watered me, in the way that I have described, my legs in particular – shrouded by my bedsheets – became so light they no longer seemed to be there.

One day, during a moment of lucidity, I reached to the priest who had plucked me from the *Maria*. He had come to my room to see me, in the company of a number of the other monks.

I went to take his arm in my hand. But when I closed my fingers, they gripped nothing… save the cloth of his habit.

Puzzled, I let go and fell back on my pillows.

And that was when he lifted, from the sleeve of his robe, what remained of his limb, and wiped at his mouth with the stump of his elbow.

The Feast

The white and wind-flensed tree that was the twisted, cysted skeleton of Enoch ap Owain of that scrag of farm called *Y Pinsiad* (in English 'The Pinch') had, so it seemed, always been dry and cinderous, scraping and splintering inside the thin, shroud-skinned rest of him, like the cold clinker of a fire long extinguished, or the harsh-grinding innards of an ancient cased clock mute of chime.

So when those same chafing, grating bones sounded – of all things – one strange, sunlit morning… *soft* – his ribcage no longer a beamed beast-house but instead a kind of squeezebox (as he had once seen and heard in the hands of a gypsy woman) – he knew that inside himself he was rotting, dying – and that it was time for him to prepare.

And so he set about destroying all that there was of *Y Pinsiad*. For such was the meanness of ap Owain that he was determined that nothing of that pathetic place, be it so much as one single sour seed, or one bent and headless nail, should fall to the clutches of anyone else in Wales.

Not that any heirs awaited, or friends and neighbours, expectant of alms.

Enoch ap Owain's lifelong observance of the ways of the miser had entirely precluded any possibility of marriage and progeny. And those families who *had* once lived near *Y Pinsiad* had long abandoned their homesteads, these being now mere ruins in those unfertile uplands where ap Owain – threadbare and of pallor grey and bloodless – alone lingered, like lichen on a stone.

So it was that he starved to their deaths his flock of sheep – which, in truth, had never been more than ragged and scabied – not taking them, on his old and rusted tractor, so much as a single rough swede, even when the slopes and ridges above *Y Pinsiad* were white with snow and bled, so it strangely felt, with their bleating.

The skin-and-bone horse of the farm he neglected so completely that its hoofs grew cruelly contorted and, in time, could barely stand, the animal resembling in its awful clumsiness nothing so much as one of the pantomime kind seen on stage in a seaside town; the empty-bellied creature collapsing while in giddy pursuit of its tail and, unable to right itself, eventually dying in the farm's very yard, ravens and other scavenging birds of the hills swooping and ripping its sorry carcass clean.

His old cow – 'dry', of course (on account of its ancientness), as one of its brittle, sun-bleached pats – suffered a similar fate… crawled-over by wasps and flies in its grassless field of thistles and thorns.

His pigs, for their part never more than thin, devoured one another, yellow teeth crimsoning in the gloom of the charnel houses that their sties became – the last of them taking its own trotters in its hungrily-grinding jaws.

Meanwhile, ap Owain busied himself with a great bonfire of all of the miserable furniture and fittings of *Y Pinsiad*.

On this he threw, among other things, the cracked forms of two china dogs, a wormed wireless whose stations in England (and Cardiff also) had long stopped 'calling', and a great quantity of catalogues for ploughs (in full colour) over which he had lusted but never bought (their price to him a sin), tossing also to the flames the sheet of manuscript that bore the words *Y Weithred* ('The Deed'), its copperplate page curling to ash.

Also to the pyre, he dragged, never minding his years, a wooden dresser of linen and blankets whose drawers had stuck fast, and the springless armchair in which it was his habit to sit, candle-less of an evening, in the freezing cold kitchen of *Y Pinsiad*.

He even cast to this inferno the Bible that had been at *Y Pinsiad* for as long as any person had been at *Y Pinsiad*: its black binds and mildewed verses smouldering in surly spite as ap Owain stared on.

Throughout all of this killing and firing, one matter exercised ap Owain's miserly mind greatly. Haunted him... *howled* at him, in fact, like the wind that rose and roared on the ridge above *Y Pinsiad* on nights of pit-shaft darkness.

This troubling, *festering* sore of a matter was the business of his funeral, and, more particularly, the cost – the wounding... heinous... *sin*ful cost – of the simple enough business of his despatch.

He would be cheated. Oh, of that, he was convinced: the rapacious rates of some undertaker stealing his hard-won savings, not unlike (ap Owain wincingly recalled) the calf of his former neighbour, the shameless Shenkyn Fferm Goch, that had once invaded his pasture and fatted itself on his grass – *his* grass, mark you – in an outrage still raw.

Yes, the magpie men... in their black coats and white collars. He remembered how they had come to *undertake* the removal of his father and mother. Father first: body found (finally) – skull-split – in a crack of the ridge that ran deep in its rock. (A 'fall', as entered in the record, while looking for lost sheep... though some said different.) Then Mother, thirty years later, when *Y Pinsiad* had leeched the last of her – life draining from her, a jar more each year, to join the blood that had seeped from her husband's split head.

For a moment, alone on the step of the house, their *son* – how strange that word seemed to him in his ancient body's winter – saw again the streaming, wind-tossed tails of a dark, silk top hat: feathers of a magpie (that most *thieving* of birds)... all aflutter.

In his meanness and his madness, Enoch ap Owain killed all and burnt all in that dismal, dying season. Smoke spiralled from the acidic acres of *Y Pinsiad* almost constantly.

'*All*', that is, save one final – and feathered – thing.

The creature that Enoch ap Owain spared... that he had *other* plans for... was a turkey: one that occupied its own stone-walled pen, from where it followed with some interest the farmer's perverse doings, in those days and weeks of death and incineration, through the gaps between the green and rotting struts of its gate.

Like everything at *Y Pinsiad*, the hen bird was a shabby and under-fed thing (lean, in fact, as a favour ap Owain might once have frugally done for a neighbour, entering the deed in a ledger kept for the careful recording – and future use – of such things).

Notwithstanding the bird's unwholesome appearance, ap Owain resolved (smiling to himself, bleakly) that he would make it the subject of his final act – the last supper at *Y Pinsiad*, so to speak – to mark his departure from its poor pastures for good. He would take his leave with... a feast! Yes, a fitting end, Enoch ap Owain nodded to himself (flypaper tongue drawing over thin, dry lips)... with Christmas coming near... that time of good cheer.

As *Y Pinsiad* descended into its final, Hellish ruin, ap Owain came to think of nothing but this hen bird and the meal that there would be.

Yet, in an echo perhaps of those relations that pertain between condemned prisoner and guard, he conducted himself discreetly around his feathered prize: eyeing it from behind the torn curtains of his windows, creeping softly (and slyly) around the walls of its pen.

Sometimes at night, on his bed in the darkness, his empty sunken stomach rumbling like the growl of a storm in distant peaks, ap Owain seemed to sense the hen bird's black eye upon him and to even hear the rustle of its feathers… the click of its claw feet on the cobbles of its pen.

On such nights he thought also of the monstrous hearse that threatened: a more expensive one than had been ordered, of course… all bright-shining chrome and polished sloe-blackness, smooth pine coffin catafalqued on its back (satin-lined and brass-plaqued), its brazen sumptuousness an horrific sin. Like the claw of the turkey, he heard also, or seemed to, and with a shudder, the rattle of the buckled iron grid brimming with nettles that was the gateway to *Y Pinsiad*… signalling the death-chariot's approach.

Forcing his mind back to the turkey, with an effort that fair creased the tight-stretched skin of his face and brow, ap Owain conjured an image that, notwithstanding the bird's true meagreness, was both full, rounded and almost sensual to behold: its breast, its legs, its wings, its tongue… its beak.

'*Y Wledd*,' he whispered to himself in his mothed overcoat on his bare mattress in his bitter-cold room. '*Y Wledd*.' ('The Feast… The Feast.')

In the darkness his cataracted eyes seemed to see the fleshy pink smear of the hen bird's wattle and snood.

A red poppy bedraggled by rain that he had once noticed as a boy in a green meadow below *Y Pinsiad* came back to him now in the blackness: its sagging, bloody rosette.

The appointed hour fell on a morning of hard frost and thin snow that blew about *Y Pinsiad* in an icy, eye-streaming wind, as if in search of somewhere more hospitable to settle. And with it there came at *Y Pinsiad* a frenzy of squawking and ripping and clawing… a riotous scramble of plucking and stuffing… and an orgy of gorging and gorging, and gnawing.

When, come spring, a walker, lost on the hillside, happened to enter *Y Pinsiad*, the hill-farm was quiet as the mossed graveyard of a mountain chapel or church. A 'graveyard', that is, save for one living thing: a hen-bird turkey of unusual plumpness whose eyes rose up from its pen, with a slow and sated look.

New owners are, to this day, still sought for *Y Pinsiad*. Its grim house and land-gone-wild have grown more ghostly – and ghastly – by the year. The agents have not *quite* given up on the possibility of a purchase. 'Going for a song,' they like to say.

It is, of course, one of the most remote of all Welsh hill-farms, its isolation seeming to weigh heavy on the minds of those few potential buyers (city folk mainly, with dreams from magazines) who've drawn near.

The slimed windows, slipped slates and spattered walls of the deserted farmhouse have been sufficient to deter many.

But it is an eerie *sound* – with no evident source – that has really harried visitors to hurry from *Y Pinsiad*, away and over its buckled, brown-rusted grid.

Those who've heard the curious 'call' have spoken of something unsettling and murmurous, sweeping the mean yard and meaner fields, swelling – from nowhere – to a shrill clamour.

Pressed to explain, they speak thus of the blood-curdling cry which at certain, strange hours is said to consume that lonely, old hill-farm:

Gobble… gobble… GOBBLE!

Devilled Kidneys at the House of Mrs Usher

I had been in clerkship to Judge Jawlock for a little over six months when, returning to chambers from lunch one day, I found a typically terse note from him on my desk.

We leave for Bonebury Assizes on Sunday night. Arrange for me to lodge with Mrs Usher.
Jawlock

Not for the first time in my tenure with the judge, I set down his missive with some puzzlement. Never mind my nineteen years in the Law, I had never heard of the Bonebury Assizes. Nor even of Bonebury. And as for how I would contact any Mrs Usher…

My several months of clerking, corresponding and general bag-carrying for the judge, not to mention advising him (in so far as such a thing was possible) of reforms (by which I mean modernisation) of the laws of England, had taught me that it was unwise to query any of his instructions in a direct manner with questions of the yes / no, 'head-on' kind. One of the main reasons for this was his temper. When I use that word, I don't mean to suggest any tendency on his part to fly into a rage. Far from it. I can affirm that I never once saw his tall, lean, grey-faced form ever become flushed. If anything, his manner – already chill as a church crypt – turned several degrees colder (whatever blood that washed thinly about his gaunt frame seemingly draining from him completely, as if his human juices were being sucked into the marrow of his skeleton).

He was, without doubt, one of the strangest figures on Her Majesty's judicial bench. Ancient but of an indeterminate age, he had – apparently – always looked the same: stiff and straight as a ramrod, spare – in terms of flesh – as a permanently-fasting priest, severe as… well, a judge… before whom, as a defendant, you would very much *not* want to appear. Members of London's criminal classes were well known to feign all kinds of sudden affliction – deafness, blindness, madness, not to mention infection with any number of highly transmissible diseases – to obtain some deferment or alteration to their hearing, in order to avoid the attentions of His Honour Judge Jawlock.

How I came to be 'in service' with him is still something of a mystery to me. I was a figure neither committed to liberal interpretations of the law, nor, for that matter, enforcement of the more draconian kind. I suppose it might be said that I had an 'open' mind. Perhaps this was the reason for my selection. Jawlock – though I had never appeared before him (as a *lawyer*, I mean) must – I suppose – always have been watching me. One way or another, I had succeeded in catching the old devil's eye.

And so I judged it best that I should – if at all possible – find quietly, by myself, these Bonebury Assizes, Sessions, or whatever they were, and, with them, the curiously-named Mrs Usher (whoever she might be).

My enquiries at the Bailey and the Lord Chancellor's office, however, drew an utter blank. Likewise, my searches of the internet.

Eventually, with only two days until our departure, there was nothing for it but for me to 'come clean' and face the judge.

I knocked his door with some trepidation.

'Y-e-s,' came the reply.

His manner of speech at such times always had about it something of what I thought of as 'the trap door': a long, low creak, the pitch of which curled upwards – slightly – at the end. Its timbre had to it the suggestion of pre-occupation with some profound question of law, philosophy, religion or science. (I felt sure he must have been a scholar at one of our leading schools before gaining a double first at Oxford or Cambridge. Yet, strangely, *Who's Who* omitted all mention of him. Likewise all of the other heavyweight guidebooks to the great and the good.) The exception to this contemplative – if rather intimidating – tone of his came when he was sentencing. When 'administering justice', he was – in a word – terrifying. Not in any theatrical 'fire and brimstone' way, but through his briskness, his directness, his utter *un*readiness (much to the chagrin of the barristers who appeared before him) to break for something as tedious as lunch. At such times, everything with him was rapid-fire (defendants being 'sent down' before they could blink), his knowledge of the Law encyclopaedic (especially when it came to the older statutes). In his scarlet robes and his full-bottom wig, his majesty was undeniable. At such times he was no mere instrument of the Law. He *was* the Law, without a doubt.

When I entered his room, he raised his eyes from some papers on his desk and looked at me with the sort of silent incredulity he might have given to a turtle or similar unexpected creature that had sallied in from the street.

'About, um, Bonebury, judge,' I began, nervously.

'Yes?' he replied (surprise evident in his voice at the subject of my enquiry).

'I'm having trouble… locating it,' I said. 'It seems to have gone… astray,' I added, in an attempt at a joke (which I regretted – instantly).

'Astray? Lo*cating* it?' he replied (his state of mystification quite clear – as if I had reported that Big Ben, the Tower of London, or the Bailey itself, had gone missing. Not, I should say, 'a show' on his part of horror of the jaw-dropped, throat-clutching kind – Judge Jawlock never remotely stooped to theatrics as obvious as that – but more a response of intellectual bafflement (and perhaps even disappointment), as if I were unaware of some scholarly volume on the British constitution or great work of art painted by one of the masters and kept in the private collection of some elderly aristocrat who was known to him personally.

'I wonder if you might just remind me which circuit it's on.'

His look of utter wonder continued. A clock ticked heavily in the otherwise still and silent room.

'Why, the Inner Circuit,' he began finally (speaking in that way of his that for some reason made me think of the oldest and darkest mahogany). 'You're familiar with it?'

'Oh yes… of course, judge,' I now responded, attempting a frown at my own feigned forgetfulness. 'And Mrs Usher's address?' I continued after a moment. 'It seems to have gone missing.'

'Missing?' he responded, with what seemed genuine concern. 'Mrs Usher? Well, we can't have that.'

He rose from behind his desk in his strange, stiff, cantilevering way and made for his bookcases (where, among other things, he kept his *Halsbury's* – by which I mean to say his own peculiar (at least in my eyes) edition of England's laws, the acts and statutes of which seemed not to extend beyond the mid-part of the 17th century).

I watched as he drew down from a top shelf a small volume bound in a dark-red cloth. BONEBURY – A GAZETTEER its front board proclaimed, in black-inked lettering of a kind that seemed to brook no compromise.

'I think you'll find all you need in there,' said Jawlock.

'Thank you, judge,' I said and turned to leave, knowing him to be a man uninterested in social chat and what are called 'pleasantries'.

As I did so, the tick of his clock – on the mantel over the hearth (where, in the winter months, I'd come to notice Jawlock's relish of what seemed one of his few luxuries in life: a fire of molten coals) – was now interrupted by its chime: a songful peal, which had for some while seemed to me at odds with the judge's outward austerity. It rang now as if in celebration of something… a private matter between it and the judge… some business that had been sealed.

Back in my own office, I turned the dry, tea-brown pages of the gazetteer. The archaic content – including advertisements for ladies' parasols, corsets and sundry 'surgical appliances' – surprised me (even allowing for my knowledge of Judge Jawlock's tendency to things of yesteryear). I wondered if Mrs Usher could truly exist. Although encyclopaedic in his knowledge of legal esoterica, particularly in areas of ancient law that many would presume to have long rationally been reformed, the judge was almost entirely hopeless when it came to mundane details such as people's names. A 'Mrs Usher' – I knew all too well – might easily have derived her name from having a husband who'd worked as an official in one of Jawlock's courts, or who had possibly served in one as an usher herself. Jawlock would, similarly, address a churchman as 'Mr Dean', or a cabbie as 'Mr Driver', and frequently spoke to – or hailed – me as 'Mr Clerk'. On the matter of Mrs Usher, though, he was as good as his word. For there (a few pages into the volume) lay a quarter-page advertisement for 'Mrs Usher's Boarding House… *lodgings for professional gentlemen*… No. 8 Stewleigh Street, Bonebury' (the whole panel heavily-ringed in black ink… presumably by the judge's own hand).

An illustration showed a terraced, three-storey townhouse, with railings to the front and steps up from the street, of the early Victorian kind. There was no sign of any telephone number, let alone an email address. 'Telegrams: Mrs Usher, Stewleigh Street', a line at the foot of the advertisement proclaimed (causing me to wonder if the current Mrs U. was carrying on a profession first begun by a forebear to whom Judge Jawlock's book related in terms of its age). The only thing for it, I decided, was to write to the current Mrs Usher: a letter, making reservations for rooms for the judge and myself, getting it in the post – if I could – first-class. And this, I duly did, having consulted a timetable for trains to Bonebury, at the back of the book. The judge and I could reach its 'shores', it seemed, by way of – to me, at least – a number of little-known connections and routes through various backwaters.

Two days later, having finished our respective business in chambers, Judge Jawlock and I were in our seats on an early evening train from Paddington… the architecture of London slipping from us, likewise the daylight from the sky.

After an uneventful hour in which the judge studied his newspaper (his narrowed eyes searching out, I well knew, court reports) to the sound of intermittent sighs and tuts (in the matter of the sentences that had been passed, I didn't doubt), and in which I looked through the window at the darkening landscape and wondered what might await us at Bonebury, our train suddenly entered a tunnel. A weak light – not much better than that which might have been offered by candles – came on in the carriage, as our train rattled into its long, dark throat.

The judge and I stared at each other in silence, the faint light doing more to shadow than illuminate his features (and, doubtless, mine). And, although I had by that time known him – as I say – for some six or so months (dealing with him almost daily), his appearance now… in that pallid light, in that clattering carriage – lips thin and grey, like old, tarnished knives; eyes dark as mineshafts; cheekbones high as any eagle's eyrie, with –

below them – cliff-faces of flesh, drumskin-tight on his firmly locked jaws… I was – I admit – unsettled.

When – eventually – we emerged from the tunnel's blackness, into a dusky, pewtery light, I had the strangest sense that our carriage had changed.

We no longer seemed to be in a carriage at all – certainly not one of the long, open kind – but in a small compartment of our own. The judge and I sat opposite one another on upholstered, bench-like seats. Above his head – where I felt sure previously there'd been a shelf of metal rods (running to one side), was now the netting of a parcel rack; on it, the trunk for his robes and the box for his wig.

Beyond us, the train itself seemed to have altered. Instead of the hooter or klaxon that had sounded from the engine earlier, I now heard a long whistle – some might even have called it a 'scream'. And, unless I was mistaken (it was difficult for me to be sure in the dying light beyond them), there were – as we exited the tunnel – clouds outside our window of what seemed to me to be smoke. Added to which, rather than our earlier whooshing rush along the rails beneath us, our progress seemed now to have a slower, steadier, percussive rhythm.

The guard drew open the door to our compartment from the corridor. He was the same man who'd checked our tickets earlier, I felt sure. But he also now was *different*. For one thing, his face sported whiskers – mutton chop sideburns, that extended over his jaw – like brambles down a bank. Indeed, these seemed to sprout and writhe into place as I watched.

And that wasn't all: a watchchain sagged in half-moons across his waistcoat. Surely when we'd spoken previously he hadn't worn anything like that?

The man drew out a silver timepiece and held it in his palm.

'We're running to time,' he said, smiling. 'Another five minutes and we'll be at Skulwick Cross. Change there for Gravesditch. And from then on you'll want the nine-ten to Bonebury. But you won't need *me* to tell you that – will you? – your lordship?' the guard said to the judge, in a manner that I worried the judge – given his natural reserve – might find over-familiar.

To my surprise, Jawlock responded with a smile. 'Oh, I think – after all these years – I shall find my way. Thank you, Mr Guard,' he said.

'So very nice to see you again, if I may say so, my Lord,' added the man, to a nod from the judge… after which the guard retreated from our compartment in a dutiful way (as if knowing he'd been dismissed).

Skulwick Cross was a bleak spot indeed to wait for a train – the judge's breath and my own rising in pearl-grey plumes in the vaporous night air of our otherwise empty platform. I was glad when our engine eventually came in. Yet Skulwick had nothing on the subsequent grimness of Gravesditch, where, on the other side of the tracks from where the judge and I stood waiting for our final connection, the headstones of a cemetery loomed. I wondered if its occupants might have been the victims of some Victorian railway disaster. The platform was icily cold. Our train seemed to be running late. I took out my phone in the hope of establishing its whereabouts, only for the screen to yield nothing.

'Pah!' the judge snorted beside me. 'That *thing* of yours will be no good *here*. This is deep country. The Inner Circuit. All of *that* nonsense,' he nodded at my phone, 'has been left behind.'

To my astonishment, our train arrived, utterly without sound: its carriages – wreathed in smoke – suddenly standing there… in front of us.

The engine let out a hiss.

'There she blows!' declared the judge, advancing in his long, dark overcoat in the direction of a carriage door. 'The nine-ten. Ten minutes late, as always. Dead on time!'

I followed him with our luggage.

As I did so, I wondered about the whereabouts of my holdall (the one I'd had with me at Paddington). In my right hand, I now felt and saw the unfamiliar handle of an old-style Gladstone bag. Keen as I was to go back and search behind me, the judge urged me onto the train.

'Quickly!' he called out, one foot already on the step of an opened door. 'We must get aboard! Bonebury is beckoning! *Justice* is beckoning! We spurn her at our peril!'

As we journeyed on to Bonebury, the vista offered by our windows was now one of utter darkness. From what I could see of it, the sky – never mind a moon – held not a single star. Opposite me, the judge fell in and out of sleep: the lids of his eyes shutting, then – as we rattled and jounced on what seemed a very old and rickety line – lifting… his pupils immediately fixing on mine, as if he were distrustful of me – as if, as well as his clerk, I might have been some sort of assassin.

Eventually, he seemed to lose any inclination that he might have had for sleep, and his face acquired a certain contemplative look.

I decided to venture some conversation.

'We must nearly be there, judge,' I said. 'What sort of place is Bonebury?'

He eyed me keenly for a moment. Not, I sensed, because he had any doubt as to the character of the town; more – it seemed – as if he were weighing-up whether I could be trusted with the majesty of his answer.

'It is a Hellish place,' he began, finally. 'A lawless place. A snake-pit. A veritable Sodom and Gomorrah. The den of knaves and brigands. And not only knaves and brigands, sir, but every verminous alley rat, blackmailer, body-snatcher, bootlegger, cadger, cattle-rustler, charlatan, deceiver, drunkard, Fagin, fence, footpad, forger, fornicator, fugitive, hooligan, horse-thief, hussy (of the most brazen kind), importuner, liar, mobster, mountebank, perjurer, pervert, pickpocket, poacher, sheep-stealer, shyster, slacker, swinger of lead, trickster, twister and general blackguard you could *possibly* imagine. And that is why *I* am sent to it, Mr Clerk… Old Jawlock… once a year… to give it some *justice*… and *not* one of those other, namby-pambies who presume to sit on the sovereign's bench. And there shall be some law in it by the time *I* am done, sir. *That*, I can promise you.'

The whistle of our engine let out a long (and, it seemed to me, awful) wail. It was as if the very night through which we were passing was a cause of terror to its steam and its steel... as if our speed, like that of a bolting horse, was prompted not by shovelled, molten coal, but by sheer, deep dread.

'Yes, Mr Clerk… Bonebury nears,' said the judge. 'I can smell it, sir. I can taste it. And *it* – I feel sure – can smell me.'

The taxi driver who greeted us – well, the judge, more than me – at the rank outside the railway station did so in the same familiar fashion as the guard on the train.

'The house of Mrs Usher, if you please, Mr Driver,' said Jawlock, as we got into the cab.

I felt the need to name the street and give the house number, but my intervention was unnecessary.

'Right you are, your honour!' said the driver, speaking over me.

He was a cabbie of the old-school, in a flat-cap and muffler, whose vehicle looked as ancient as him (our luggage being strapped in a doorless stow by his side that was open to the elements).

'And how *are* things in Bonebury, dare I ask?' enquired the judge.

The cabbie shook his head and shuddered. 'All the better for seeing you, your grace.' The man's shaking of his head turned to a nod. 'All the better for seeing you.' A smile joined his nod.

The streets through which we passed seemed to me quiet enough. Given the comments of the judge, and the cabbie, I had expected unsettling sights, at the very least: a burning car; hoodlums on a corner; women of the night in the arc of streetlamps; perhaps a robbery in progress as we passed. But there was none of that. The town – my watch told me it was not quite eleven o'clock – was in near-total darkness and quiet as the grave. I wondered if this was on account of some curfew, perhaps one that Bonebury's citizens – in fear of the lawlessness that the judge had spoken of – imposed on themselves.

We pulled into a street that Jawlock seemed to recognise. A gas lamp, unless I was mistaken, gave out a weak, yellow glow. In the window of a terraced townhouse, a light shone. The cabbie pulled up at the kerb.

Unloading our luggage, the driver refused to accept any fare or tip. 'There is *one* thing you might do for me, judge,' said the man, as he set down my bags and the judge's trunk and wig-box. 'Me and the other lads in the trade have been having more than our share of trouble with "runners" just lately – dodgers making off without paying the fare. I believe a couple of these…' (he hesitated for a second, seemingly to alter his choice of word) '…scoundrels are on your list, your honour. And if you wouldn't mind…'

'Say no more, Mr Driver,' said the judge. 'If it should prove to be in the interests of justice, you can rely on me to lick them into shape.'

With this, a smile seemed to pass over Jawlock's lips – his right eye (unless I was mistaken) even closing for a split-second, in what, to my great surprise, seemed like a wink.

I was puzzled by this reference to what sounded a rather minor crime (except, of course, in the eyes of cabmen and women), given the state of near-insurrection I had expected to find in the black heart of Bonebury. Doubly so, given the suggestion that such a felony was deemed worthy of the attention of a visiting red-robed judge. I imagined it could only be there as a case to be 'taken into consideration', in the language of the courts, alongside matters of far greater moment.

The driver and his cab departed into the otherwise silent night.

I rapped the knocker on the door of 18 Stewleigh Street, the wan beam of the pavement lamp and the light inside the property illuminating, faintly, the handle held by my fingers and thumb. They gripped, I saw, a ring that was suspended from the jaws of a brass, lion's head knocker, of a particularly striking kind: its mouth being open in such a way that – queer as it may sound – I feared, for a moment, my disturbance of it might cause it to bite. From the other side of the door, I heard the sliding of bolts, the jangling of keys and various excited, female tuts and clucks.

The nightgowned – and bonneted – figure of Mrs Usher greeted us keenly – one hand supporting an oil lamp, the other alternately beckoning us and clutching at a shawl draped over her shoulders, all amid many noisy exclamations on her part of 'Bless you!' and 'Come in! Come in!' and 'Such a journey, I expect!'

I took her for a woman of late middle age. Never mind the lateness of the hour and her seeming readiness for bed, I noticed that her face appeared to be rather heavily made-up. Not quite the greasepaint of a clown, but, as the saying goes, 'getting there'. Stepping over her threshold felt like stepping back in time. Scenes of a less than fashionable kind hung from picture rails in the hall. On a table, near the foot of a staircase, I detected – in the gloomy light – the large, dark leaves of an aspidistra.

'Oh! How wonderful it is to see you again, judge!' exclaimed our hostess.

'It's good to be back!' responded Jawlock, with enthusiasm (in a manner that, after six months in his service, I found difficult to credit).

'And how are you, Mrs Usher?!' he went on. 'How *are* you?!'

'Oh, as well as can be… in a place like *this*,' she responded, with a shudder.

'Is Bonebury very bad?' asked Jawlock.

'Wicked as ever, judge! Wicked as ever!' she answered. 'But all shall be well now that *you* are here,' she added, her demeanour quickly brightening.

'Yes, I've been telling Mr Clerk here all about the place,' said Jawlock, prompting the landlady to look at me for a moment, with – I felt – more than a small degree of curiosity being evident on her part.

'*I* see,' she said, elongating her words, as she eyed me.

'And there shall be some justice in this town by the time I'm done with it,' Mrs Usher. 'I promise you that.'

'Yes, you'll get your teeth into it all right,' she said, her joviality deserting her for a moment – a certain coldness flashing over her features in the glow of her lamp. 'But never mind me!' she said. 'Look at you! White as frost and thin as a rake! You've been letting yourself go in London. Working too hard, I don't doubt. What on earth is wrong with the womenfolk there?! Why aren't they looking after you?! Well, never mind them. You're here now. We'll soon get you fed right and some colour back in those cheeks. A proper breakfast in the morning, of course – just as you like it.'

'Thank you, my dear Mrs Usher,' interjected Jawlock. 'You're so very kind. What would I do without you?'

'And tonight, before cocoa and bed, a good platter of meat sandwiches.'

'Oh really, Mrs Usher, you oughtn't to go to any trouble.'

'It's no trouble at all, judge. Not for you. You know that. They're already prepared.'

With that, she led us up the staircase and showed us to our rooms – the judge's and mine being at separate ends of the same first-floor landing, its boards cracking and groaning in the dimness, as we stepped over them to our bedchambers.

Whilst washing my hands and face with water from a jug-and-basin on an old-style stand, I heard a knock at the door to my room. Drying myself, I opened it. On the floor outside, I found a tray covered with a tea towel. Beneath it, my cocoa and sandwiches, as pledged by Mrs Usher. Hungry (having not eaten for hours), I took these inside and – although the cold cuts in the sandwiches were less than to my taste – I cleared the plate.

Later, in bed – on a mattress that I found hard and unyielding – I struggled for sleep (wondering if I'd been given the judge's mattress, by mistake).

Something other than my berth's board-like nature contributed to my restlessness. From along the landing, came the squeaks and creaks of what sounded very much like a bed. And, above these noises, cackles of laughter from a source I strongly suspected to be the rouged lips of our landlady. Drowning these (at times), came a singularly sonorous bass chortle that kettledrummed over our hostess's high squeals.

Daylight, at the edges of the curtains of my room, together with the chirping of birds beyond my window, caused me to wake. I rose stiffly from my bed and drew open the drapes. It was my first real look at Bonebury (its rooftops, spires and towers, at least). Far from a place of unmitigated anarchy, my eyes met a scene of a surprisingly peaceful kind: a small and traditional market town, so it seemed, bordered by green countryside. My room appeared to be at the rear of Mrs Usher's house – my window looking out on a pretty back garden. A blackbird crossed its dew-sparkled lawn. A robin redbreast – since when in London had I seen one of those? – hopped along the brick wall that separated us from the property next door.

For breakfast, Mrs Usher served a dish with which I was unfamiliar.

'Devilled kidneys!' she announced proudly, as she set down plates before the judge and me. 'Your favourite, your judgeship, unless I'm very much mistaken,' she added, beaming.

'Ahhh, Mrs Usher, you spoil me, ma'am,' said Jawlock.

He – I noticed – seemed (never mind the delight with which he greeted her dish) even more grey and drawn than usual; his eyes red-ringed and bloody. Sleep had been in short supply in *his* bedchamber, too, I thought to myself, as I turned my attention to the contents of my plate.

'Well, with all that judging you'll have to do today – the very worst of humanity, I don't doubt – a good, full stomach is what you'll be needing.'

'Quite so, Mrs Usher. Quite so,' purred Jawlock, slicing open what looked to me to be a large – and by no means overcooked – lump of internal organ.

I watched – more than a little apprehensively – as a wave of pink juice sluiced onto Jawlock's plate.

'Rare!' declared Mrs Usher. '*Just* as you like 'em.'

Jawlock sank a forkful into the severe ravine that was his mouth – grimly guarded by jagged ranks of grey and twisted teeth (that seemed to me like ancient standing stones). As he did so, his seldom less than stern features melted into something that appeared very close to… a picture of ecstasy.

'Come on now, Mr Clerk. You, too. Eat up,' Mrs Usher enjoined me. 'Let it not be said that any man left the house of Mrs Usher without enjoying a hearty breakfast.'

The court building was – as a seat of justice – the most strangely ancient I had ever encountered: a higgledy-piggledy structure off Bonebury's main square, and about as far from the majesty of the Bailey as could possibly be imagined. The courtroom itself was a cockpit of overhanging galleries and benches all crammed-in on each other and hewn from wood that had turned black with age. To the touch, the timber was as cold as stone. Such was our proximity that, at my desk, in front of and below the judge, I felt sure I could sense on my face the breath of the defendants in the dock before me – and Jawlock's exhalations (chill and damp) down the back of my neck.

Amid its rustic simplicity, the judge was received with great deference (even reverence), the officials of the court bowing before him with solemnity; every other local, so it seemed, either doffing a cap or tugging a forelock, and generally hailing him – with evident respect – as 'Your Lordship'.

What surprised me – given my memory of Jawlock's description of the town as a veritable Sodom and Gomorrah – was the piffling nature of the prosecutions brought before us: larceny of the pettiest kind. One case centred on the theft of an orange from a market stall in the square. Others involved minor infractions of this and that in the sale of merchandise (alleged abuse of lead weights and – to my genuine mystification as to how such a thing could ever have reached the crown courts – the under-cutting of cheese). Beyond these, were appeals over land ownership and rights of way. As ever, Jawlock, who had an innate dislike for what he considered to be the impudence of appeals, dismissed these instantly, while sentencing – in the other cases – as formidably as ever, to the maximum that the law allowed. That none of the convictions could be considered custodial matters appeared to irritate him greatly. At the Bailey, I had developed a system for reining him in when I thought his zeal for the supreme sanction was getting the better of him. This involved some conspicuous coughing or shuffling of papers on my part in an attempt to halt what I feared might be coming next: some reference to transportation, the stocks or even the scaffold. At this, and with an irritated 'Yes? What is it, Mr Clerk?', a discussion between us would ensue, often at the pitch of stage whispers, as to why 'a damn good flogging' might be 'just', or ever so slightly out of the question, in a case that hinged on evasion of a bus fare. In these disputations of ours, he would invariably cite his edition of Halsbury's – the one that expired circa 1650. Most of the time, I managed to come out on top, causing Jawlock – in our hours of recess – to become even more terse than normal, eyeing me enigmatically on those occasions when I had reason to disturb him in his rooms.

In the matter of the orange that I've mentioned (it had been taken by a youth who was clearly not very bright), Jawlock beckoned me to his bench – 'A word, Mr Clerk, if you please'.

I rose to hear him advance his view that a period of detention – possibly with hard labour – might well be permissible as a sentencing option. 'The sanction is here, quite plainly, in my Halsbury,' he said. He rotated his cracked volume towards me, planting a yellow-nailed finger on a mildew-blighted page: Ye *f*ale of *fy*tresse Fruites Act, 1553.

'I was thinking of six years,' said Jawlock. 'A hardened criminal of his kind won't be missed by society.'

I – eventually – beat him down to one month. 'I feel sure twenty-eight days will make the lad's pips squeak,' I sighed.

The low-key nature of the morning's proceedings led to a morose atmosphere at luncheon in his chambers, the judge and I eating meat pies and sausage rolls that Mrs Usher had prepared and packed for us.

In the afternoon, came the case that the cab driver had told us of on our arrival at Bonebury. Jawlock's mood brightened visibly as the prosecutor announced the case. It was as if he sensed that here – at last – was something that had 'potential': jurisprudence of the kind that would make our long journey from London worthwhile.

'Bring in the defendants!' he said, grandly – adding to me, under his breath: 'Time – Mr Clerk – to teach these fare-dodging hooligans a lesson.'

On sight of those charged, however, his previous low spirits swiftly returned.

Far from facing – as I sensed he'd expected – a gang of tearaways of either the common or garden hooligan or the Hooray Henry kind (who might, above all, have been young) – Jawlock found himself confronted with a group of senior citizens of an age quite possibly approaching his own, who had seemingly forgotten to take enough small change with them to cover the return fare for a trip to – as far as I could make out – the bingo, or similar, in the next small town.

Jawlock sighed and tutted, audibly, behind me, as the evidence and mitigation were given.

While I sensed he had no real 'beef' (to use an expression) with these pensioners, he nevertheless jousted with me, as usual, when it came to the matter of their sentencing. When I pleaded that they were all of previous good character, he spluttered – with incredulity – that they had been caught red-handed, returning from what was clearly a viper's nest of a gambling den 'of the most pernicious kind'. Eventually, he relented and acceded to my suggestion of a community punishment. 'The stocks, you mean?' he interjected, wholly seriously, before my correction that the matter would be best dealt with by the relevant probationary authorities. 'Oh, all right,' he sulked, finally. 'No one's interested in their old bones, anyway.'

That night, Mrs Usher served us rump steaks for dinner.

'Oh, this is wonderful, madame. You have no idea how much I've missed your cuisine,' enthused Jawlock, as he masticated merrily on the meat that had been presented to us – *tartare* – by our landlady. 'I don't know how you manage it, I really don't. But, after all these long months, this is… heavenly, if I may use the word.' Juices dribbled down his chin.

Mrs Usher tittered at the tableside. 'It's just so nice to see you enjoying yourself, your lordship. But it isn't getting any easier. The way things are these days, your honour. The contents of my larder are looking rather lean. How was it in court today your worshipfulness? Much luck?'

'Dismal, Mrs U… utterly dismal. One thief (of oranges) sent down – and he'll be out before we know it. An orange, I ask you. What on earth is the good in that?'

'I don't know *what* the criminal classes of this town are coming to, your grace. I really don't.'

'Things can only get better,' said Jawlock, between chews… wistfully.

'Oh I'm sure they will,' our hostess – seeking to encourage him, so it seemed – responded. 'What's it they say about markets – going up as well as down? You'll know better than me, your majesty.'

'Quite so, Mrs U. Quite so,' replied Jawlock.

'Anyway, you tuck into your rump, sir. We'll soon get some blood back in your cheeks. Don't you worry about that.'

That night, I had the strangest dream. The lion's head knocker on the front door transformed into the head of Jawlock. When I took hold of its ring, Jawlock's mouth took hold of my arm, which sank in his maw, up to my shoulder.

Coming to, I found myself weirdly contorted in my pyjamas: their front unbuttoned and my arm awkwardly angled in a sleeve… as if it were in a sling.

Over the following days a steady flow of cases more serious than those that had been presented at the opening of our session now came before Jawlock. Although none of them could be considered particularly grievous (bicycle thieves, scrumpers of fruit from orchards, and pilferers of women's underwear from washing lines, being the offences that I vaguely remember), the judge – as was his wont – imposed custodial sentences on almost all of the defendants, which improved his mood greatly. Something I noticed was that he was no longer the virtual walking cadaver that, during my previous months of service, I had known him to be. At Mrs Usher's, he seldom dined less than vigorously, consuming great quantities of tongue, brain, liver, heart and tripe, in addition to the more usual chops, cutlets, steaks, mince and faggots that our landlady liked to serve. Soups, stews, pâtés, casseroles and jellies (containing indeterminate items of anatomy that she had either pickled or pulverised) were also laid before us – our entire menu never once, so far as I can recall, being adorned with a vegetable – root or leaf – of any variety.

Jawlock's rake-like physique grew sleek (and even stout), and his grey, gravestone face jowly and ruddy.

In our third week at Bonebury a case came before us of a kind that I thought was no longer brought in England – namely one of witchcraft. On seeing the court list,

I immediately raised the matter with Jawlock, who insisted that the case was within his competence to hear and that it would proceed before him as listed.

Within no more than a few minutes of hearing the prosecution's 'case' and seeing the young woman who'd been arraigned – not much more than a girl, in fact – I was firmly of the mind that the whole matter was a fabrication and that the charges had, quite plainly, been trumped-up.

Turning to the judge on his bench behind me, I gave him my opinion that this prosecution was a scandal that should be ended immediately, with the whole matter being referred to the office of the Lord Chancellor.

'These proceedings must be stopped!' I demanded. 'Letting this go on one minute longer will constitute the most grievous miscarriage of justice. This young woman is the very picture of innocence.'

'Innocence,' echoed Jawlock, eyeing the defendant keenly. 'Pure… sweet,' he added, ostensibly listening to me but in what seemed – and sounded – like his own reverie. 'Tender,' I seemed to hear him say.

Suddenly, he came-to from this seeming muse. 'Yes, you're quite right, Mr Clerk. There is no need for us to continue with this. I shall put an end to this matter forthwith and give my direction to the jury.'

I slumped back into my chair at my desk beneath his podium and sighed with relief.

'Members of the jury,' Jawlock began. 'There is only one verdict that is appropriate in this case. I therefore direct you to find this defendant… GUILTY!'

To my horror, he continued: 'It is well known that there is only one sentence for such a case. Warders, take her down! Prepare the faggots… and the stake!'

It may not surprise you to hear that that night I could not bring myself to eat. When the judge and I convened as was our custom for dinner at the house of Mrs

Usher, our landlady fussed and clucked as never before. Jawlock, whose physical being had by now long entered the realms of the gross, gorged with unprecedented fervour. 'Another leg, your worshipfulness?' enquired our hostess, as she danced at his sawing elbow and shoulder. 'Some more thigh? I've plenty more breast – such lovely meat! – don't you worry about that. I think I can fairly say, your imperialness, that I've always known you as a breast man.'

Jawlock answered her witterings with nothing more than the mashing, opening and closing, of his jaws, his whole being monstrous and whale-like, in Mrs Usher's lace-frilled parlour.

That night, having barely picked at a bone at dinner, I struggled for sleep on an empty stomach. My restlessness was made worse by the whooping and cackling that poured from the judge's room at the far end of the landing. Although I had grown used to its near nightly occurrence, the laughter, shrieks, squeaks and creaks that emanated from his chamber now rose to new heights. Till suddenly, with a great, primeval *bellow* that fair shook the frames of the pictures on my walls… then died (in the manner of the cry of a climber plummeting from some altitudinous peak)… the raucous chorus ceased.

Only one place had been laid for breakfast the next morning, and that was for me. Mrs Usher, significantly subdued, said Jawlock had been 'called away' in the night. Unless I was mistaken, she uttered this explanation with a catch in her voice and – turning from me – a dab with a tissue at her cheeks.

Jawlock, I presumed, had been summoned back to London to explain his conduct in the witchcraft case, news of which had doubtless already reached the ears of the Lord Chancellor and was, I suspected, exercising the minds of politicians and jurists in the capital at the very highest level.

'*You* are to take his place – in the court,' Mrs Usher (to my initial bafflement as to her meaning) now told me. '*You* are his nominated heir.'

As I began to grasp the intent of her words, her more customary manner overcame her. 'I'm sorry that it shall be such a poor breakfast this morning, sir – just some leftovers from last night. Mercy me! I simply haven't had the time, as you'll perhaps appreciate – what with Judge Jawlock going… off, all of a sudden, in the way that he was… taken.'

I looked at my knife and fork on the tablecloth and considered her words.

'I know you were off your supper yesterday evening,' continued Mrs Usher. 'But you'll do it, won't you, sir? You have the appetite for it – the Law, I mean… the great "body" of the Law. That's what Old Jawlock used to call it. You'll have the taste for it, by now?'

I thought for a moment, then answered her. 'Plainly,' I said, 'Justice must be… served.'

'Oh, that's right, your worshipfulness… that's right, your majesty. Music to my ears! Words that might have come from Old Jawlock's very own mouth!' my hostess trilled. 'Good and plain, that's it. None of your *horrid* fruit and vegetables, or any foolishness like that. Just good, strong meat and drink. That's it, sir.'

She fingered a ribbon on her bonnet, then continued: 'I'll pack you a lunch. Something to get your teeth into. And there'll be a proper cooked meal tonight, of course (and anything else that might… take your fancy) after all your trying and sentencing and everything. As luck would have it, I've some nice joints just in. They may need a little longer in the pot, mind – to tender 'em. Either way, it will all be good and hot. But I'll let *you* be the judge of that…'

Active

Richter and Minkov stepped through the snow together. It was their first real opportunity for a private conversation since Minkov's arrival at Richter's estate.

'And your daughters?' asked Richter. 'How are they these days? Aleksandra and…'

'Irina,' said Minkov.

'Irina. That's it, of course.'

'They are well, thank you. Growing up fast.'

'They must be teenagers, at least.'

'Alexandra is fifteen and Irina is two years behind.'

'Really? As old as that? What are they like now? It is so very long since I saw them.'

'Active.'

'Active? In what way?'

'Outdoor types. They like their sport.'

'Ah, like their father.'

'Aleksandra is quite the swimmer. She has been asked to train with the Russian squad.'

'Well, that's marvellous. That's really something. You must be so proud.'

'I am. And Irina is quite the footballer.'

'Football? Do girls play that now?'

'Oh yes. Last season she was the top goal-scorer of her team. Just a moment. I can show you.'

Minkov loosened his right glove with his teeth, removed it and reached inside his thick, quilted coat. He drew out a wallet that showed a photograph of the girls, in a window in the leather.

'Well, fancy!' said Richter. 'They look so *well*. So *healthy*. And to think how small they were when I saw them last.'

'You must come and stay. It's been too long, I've told you.'

'Oh, I don't know. I don't think such things will happen now. But I will never forget them. I can assure you of that.'

The men stopped where they were for a few moments, mainly so that Richter, given his age, could catch his breath. Against the trees that flanked their figures, their exhalations rose, like the smoke of a small fire.

They walked on.

'It must be nice,' Richter said. 'To be a father and see your children growing up.'

'Yes, it is. I am lucky.'

'My father was killed. In his Panzer. At Kursk. 1943. I was two years old – if that. He had the Knight's Cross, with Oak Leaves. A curious thing to mention, really, I suppose: here, walking as we are, beside this forest. He was a favourite of the Führer.'

'I know. You've told me. But things are different now, Thanks be to God, between your country and mine.'

'Things *have* changed,' said Richter. 'There is no doubt about that. And yet—' He cut himself short. 'Oh look!' he said. 'There's one. Your rifle. Quick!'

Minkov aimed, fired… missed the boar.

Spinning to its right, the animal ran away, swerving through the trees.

'Der'mo!' (Shit!') said Minkov.

'Don't worry,' said Richter. 'There will be others. There are plenty these days, believe me.'

'How long can we stay out here?' asked Minkov, putting his rifle back over his shoulder. 'I don't wish to sound impertinent, but is it safe?'

'Oh, don't worry,' said Richter. 'We've a while yet.'

They walked on.

'You know, it really is very beautiful here,' said Minkov.

'It is. It is. And that, of course, is the sadness… the irony. The *maddening* irony.'

'Oh, I think see one,' said Minkov, stopping.

'You do? Where?'

'Eleven o'clock. One hundred metres.'

'Ah, I see him,' said Richter, softly. 'Yes. A male, by the looks. There are no juveniles in attendance.'

'He's big,' whispered Minkov. 'Unless I'm mistaken, a fine pair of tusks. In another age, his head would have looked good on my office wall.'

'Well, get him anyway. Think of it as a service.'

Minkov fired. The boar staggered for a second, went down.

'Good shot. I think you've got him in one.'

'I'll give him another, to make sure,' said Minkov. He fired again. The boar's body twitched, then held still. 'What do we do now?' asked Minkov, lowering his rifle.

'Leave him. One of my men will take care of it. They know what to do. Come,' said Richter, turning. 'I think we'd better go. It's been long enough. Apart from anything, I'm getting cold.'

They were in the helicopter now, looking down, as the aircraft was piloted by one of Richter's men.

'Look at it!' said Richter. 'Kilometre after kilometre… of my poor, beautiful Bavaria. Useless. Ruined.'

'It is sad,' Minkov acknowledged.

'Sad?! It is far more than that. I can't tell you how it breaks my heart. The forests are full of it. They say the caesium has sunk into the ground – in some places by fifty metres. The plants suck it up and then the animals eat the plants and then, well… Argh, that day, that awful day. You blasted Bolsheviks! You're as bad as those idiotic Americans!'

'Bolsheviks no longer,' said Minkov. 'Come now. Life hasn't been all bad. You're a rich man, and so am I. From what I have heard, the land will be clean in twenty or thirty years. That isn't so bad, really, is it? Besides, it's all about oil and gas now. That which lies *below* ground. Not the trees and lakes on the top. Anyway, it was Ukraine. Another country. It won't have escaped your attention that we're at war with them, more or less, these days.'

'*You* may have thirty years.' answered Richter. 'I don't. This was the Fatherland. The land of plenty that my *own* father would have come home to. Had he made it. Old and unmarried as I am, I feel that without the land, the boars, the deer, I have nothing. I have no children, no issue; my life is without point. Where is *my* legacy? You Soviets could never make a damned thing and could never run a damned thing. That was your problem. In Germany we know how to do things. Or we did… once.'

'It will be all right, eventually, so the scientists say.'

'And you *believe* them? A single mushroom, those same scientists state, has the radioactivity of an X-ray in a hospital. And we all know how those people run and hide in their white coats when they X-ray your chest or your leg or whatever. What are they going to do? Go round checking every mushroom and berry with their machines? So much for the "fruits of the forest"! It is too terrible… too *awful*. Really, I can no longer speak of it.'

The old man turned away, morosely.

At his schloss, on its peak, Richter persuaded his guest to stay for several more days. Minkov was unsure why the older man desired his presence: his host hid away for most of the time in a tower, materialising only for meals, when his manner was distant and curt. Yet Minkov remained, out of respect for their business relationship, which had grown to be a long one.

On the morning after their walk, Minkov noticed, through a window, a dead boar – seemingly the one he had shot – hanging on a wall in a courtyard of the schloss. He wondered about the wisdom of this but chose to say nothing, judging that it could only have been done with the authority of Richter, who, as a native and indeed the suzerain of those parts, surely knew what he was doing.

When it came to the agreed final day of his stay, Minkov told Richter that he would give his family Richter's regards.

'I've sent them something,' Richter said.

'Oh, you shouldn't have.'

'I know, but I had to. Forgive me. Your wife, as I remember, was an excellent cook. Is that still the case?'

'Definitely.'

'And two "outdoor" girls, as you describe them,' continued Richter. 'Just as they ought to be. I shouldn't say such a thing, but the Führer – I feel sure – would have approved. It's a shame that you are hurrying back. Really, there is no need. *Active* daughters – yes, I like that.'

With Relish

Of all the shitty snack stands and tea stalls in the world that Marcus Carver – lifestyle commentator, TV 'personality' and feted restaurant reviewer for foodie bible *Gullet Magazine* – could have walked up to… and the man had bowled up to *his*.

Never mind that it was nearly midnight. Never mind the darkness that, beyond the floodlight fixed to its roof, surrounded Darren Bunn's trailer (in a way that made it look faintly like a lunar landing craft) at his not entirely legal pitch on the pay-and-display car park at desolate Scraggby Sands. The figure who'd stepped from the shadows was Carver.

Bunn *knew*.

How could he *not* know? Besides, as if proof were needed, a magazine that looked mightily like the latest issue of *Gullet* – where Carver was the glittering star-writer – was poking its furled and fat, glossy top from a pocket of his patron's cashmere overcoat – right beneath Bunn's nose.

Yes, it was Carver all right: acid-tongued darling of the London smart set, the 'wittiest man since Oscar Wilde', so someone had said, and about to 'dine' *there*… at Seafront Snacks in spectacularly dismal Scraggby, where the sea – *if* it even existed – had only ever been sighted with the aid of binoculars: a coastal 'resort' of last resort, as Bunn often thought of it, a one-horse town whose sole donkey had long been shot and pulped into pet food, a dull and stagnant dump of a place… on the lardy, unwashed arse of a cruel and conniving world.

Rootling around for an onion and other odds and ends, Bunn hadn't – at first – fully caught sight of his customer: an accent – plummily out of keeping with those 'parts' – and a glimpse of a felt fedora (now resting on Bunn's counter), being all that had registered with the stand's proprietor, waiter and caterer-in-chief.

Which meant that – it being Bunn's habit to confect (mainly for his own entertainment) something 'different' at the end of a night – he was now serving Carver possibly his finest ever burger – the 'Scraggby Supreme', as Bunn had christened it during its creation: a deluxe mound of ground beef (sourced from a pedigree herd), lightly seasoned with salt, and served with a garnish of samphire and sun-dried sea kelp (never mind the squirts of mustard and the powdery clouds of pepper with which, to Bunn's dismay, his patron was napalming it)… all attractively presented in a hand-crafted, artisan-baked, organic-flour bun.

Having delivered it – wholly unwittingly – into the hands of the VIP who was standing at his hatch, all that Bunn could think (and very nearly say: biting his tongue at the last), was: *You bastard! You absolute bastard!! If only I had known!!*

'That really wasn't too bad. Not too bad at all,' Carver (Bunn was convinced) announced some minutes later.

The sleekly-built visitor took a serviette from Bunn's counter and wiped his mouth. For some seconds, Carver's face bulged as he worked his tongue inside his jaws, seemingly determined to loosen – and swallow – any morsels that might remain. Having done this, he let out a loud and unpleasant belch into the chill night air.

'I must come here again,' he said, in the wake of the tonsillar thunder-rumble – his tone one of puzzled surprise.

Bunn watched as, beneath the flap of his coat, Carver stuck his hand in a pinstriped trouser pocket and drew out some coins. He dumped them on the counter. 'Keep the change.'

Bunn looked at the money and saw that – never mind any tip – there was barely enough for the burger… but said nothing.

'Couldn't do me a receipt, could you?' Carver asked. 'Stick on an extra tenner, there's a good chap. You know how it is: expenses. A man's gotta make a living in this world.'

Bunn found a Biro and scribbled some figures on a pad. He peeled off the top page and gave it to Carver, who stuffed it in a pocket (unaware that Bunn had rounded the sum *down*, so that it now stood at pence rather than pounds).

For a moment, Carver looked around – in the manner, thought Bunn, of some risen mole: sniffing the air, nonplussed by the environs in which he'd surfaced.

'Well, I'll bid you Goodnight,' said the visitor, placing his fedora back on his head. 'Toodle-oo.'

Bunn watched him go, heard the leather soles of his shoes scuff the surface of the car park. The blackness beyond the stand's floodlight was suddenly noisy with screaming gulls. A car that had the sound of something 'sporty' started up and drove away.

Some short while later, Bunn towed his trailer out of the pay-and-display. After a journey of not much more than a mile, he unhitched it – as he did most every night – next to the static caravan he rented at Scraggby Seasons – a 'home park' on a sloping scrap of land, exposed to the elements and overlooking the infinite, desert-like sands of Scraggby Bay.

After his encounter with Carver, Bunn found it impossible to sleep – his mind churning with the living nightmare that had engulfed him four years before.

Again and again, Bunn's brain came to rest on the same, one thing: the broccoli, herbed cheese and wild salmon soufflé he'd created on that now distant – but haunting – evening at the top-line London restaurant which wasn't merely his place of employment but his *stage*... as the brightest young star in the capital's culinary firmament; what was more, a kid from a council estate who'd made it on his own merits, with no leg-ups or lucky starts.

He'd prepared the soufflé to perfection. Its edifice was a masterpiece – as elevated and noble as the dome of St Paul's. The entire restaurant, it seemed, had fallen silent in awe. Applause wouldn't have been out of place, as the maître d' carried it to the table of one Marcus Carver – Bunn watching from a porthole window in his kitchen's swing door.

Carver had consumed it without a word, his face blank – betraying nothing.

And then, two weeks later, in his review for *Gullet*, he had… demolished it, utterly – swinging a wrecking ball of smart-arse jokes against Bunn's creation: 'The soufflé had *not* risen – or, if it had done, it had surely done so, from the dead.' If the establishment in question expected to retain its star rating, Carver concluded, it would definitely have to raise its game.

Bunn had been sacked the very next day… the first step on his long and painful road to Seafront Snacks at Scraggby Sands.

Come morning, Bunn took his trailer to an outside 'event', its success severely hampered by driving rain and heavy winds. Sausages intended for hotdogs congealed in grease-pool pans… serviettes blew away or became sodden on the counter.

Ahead of what he knew was likely to be a long and slow night on the seafront, Bunn towed his trailer home. As he did so, he became aware of the impatient tooting of a car horn behind him.

Amid a further flurry of toots, a red roadster roared alongside and overtook him before disappearing around a bend. The toots of the roadster were joined by audible hoots of laughter from those inside it. At the wheel, unquestionably, was Marcus Carver; in the passenger seat, a young woman, who, in spite of her headscarf and sunglasses, Bunn felt sure was Shelley Leggley, a waitress-cum-barmaid (and quite a looker, it had to be said), at The Succulent Shrimp (a 'gastro pub' known to Bunn, not that it was a term he much liked) at Nettlethorp Cliffs.

As Bunn drove on, unwelcome mental images of Carver pawing Shelley Leggley's 'assets' in a layby jostled in Bunn's brain with the realisation that Carver clearly had to be *staying* somewhere... doing something... *locally* (in all probability, a write-up on The Succulent Shrimp)... and that therefore Carver might indeed return to Bunn's stand in the car park. He remembered what Carver had said (after that belch of his): 'I must come here again.'

Driving over the humps in the avenue at the home park, Bunn's fingers drummed at his steering wheel... his mind deep in thought.

Given the usual, quiet nature of the afternoon, together with a similar shortage of trade come tea-time, Bunn pulled down the shutter of Seafront Snacks and went out onto the sands.

Returning from their near-empty expanse some two hours later, he didn't bother to open for business but instead set about preparing an extra-special burger for Marcus Carver... in the hope that Carver might indeed come back.

Later, in large part due to his disturbed previous night, Bunn fell asleep in the chair that he kept behind the stand's counter.

Towards 11 p.m., he awoke. Rubbing his eyes, he remembered – none too happily – where he was and what he was doing with his life. He slid-up the shutter, switched on his floodlight... and waited.

Apart from a couple canoodling in a car in one corner, the pay-and-display was empty.

A sea breeze – as it might correctly have been called in the event of Scraggby actually being in sight of saltwater

– rolled a tin can in the melancholy lot and lifted and blew the sheets of an old newspaper.

In the extreme distance, Bunn's eyes made out the tiny white dot that was the lantern of the lighthouse that stood on a spur of the coast.

Bunn noted how the light seemed not to revolve in a consistent way but in a changing pattern of 'dots and dashes' (as he thought of them). It was as if the keeper of the lighthouse – if there were still such men (or women) – was trying to communicate with him… sending a signal that he ought to take down.

Not for the first time, Bunn found himself wondering *why* Carver had done what he had: destroying his soufflé and – with it – him.

With part of his mind on the small, faraway white flashes, Bunn seemed able to make sense – cruel as it was – of the behaviour of the other man – the fact that, for Carver, it had all been… calculation. If he or any reviewer didn't dynamite a restaurant every so often, then what was the point of printing – or reading – his reviews? What would be the point of Carver? No one wanted to read that someone's apple pie was *nice*. Every so often, a restaurant and its chef had to pay. Something had to be sniped-at, mocked, exaggerated… out of all proportion… *knifed*. Fairness didn't come into it. People like Bunn were expendable. It was all about the self-preservation of the Marcus Carvers of this world.

When his watch showed 1 a.m., Bunn judged that Carver wouldn't come: the grasping hands and greedy mouth of the London man were doubtless occupied with something sweeter – Bunn's mind turned again to Shelley Leggley.

He shut-up the stand, hitched it to his clapped-out Vauxhall, then drove home.

As with the previous night, sleep proved impossible.

Lying on his back on his bed in the caravan, Bunn recalled Carver's appearance on a TV quiz. Minor 'celebrities' occupied pods and answered moronic questions, with unfunny (and clearly scripted) answers.

Bunn remembered Carver's clothes: an electric-blue velvet jacket and a crimson-and-white polka-dot cravat; the camp, Scottish host – Kenny McDyre – wore a ridiculous spangled suit.

'So, Marcus Carver,' McDyre had asked, 'have you ever given a restaurant a deliberately *bad* review?'

'*Only* when I've been in a bad mood, which – *un*like the way I like my steaks – take note all you chefs out there…' – at this point McDyre had made eyes (of mock-astonishment) to the studio audience – '… is *very, very* rare.'

This, of course, had been the cue for the audience, and Carver's fellow contestants, to dissolve into laughter, which they duly did.

In a crass follow-up, McDyre had said: 'There you are, ladies-and-gentlemen… Marcus Carver… dished-up straight from the horse's mouth.'

Carver sat sneering in his pod, like the smuggest Cheshire Cat.

Horse's *arse* more like, Bunn now thought to himself, cutting short his hated memory of the programme… appalled by the intimacy of his familiarity with its script.

He heard rain on the caravan's roof.

The following day, Bunn opened for business as usual. Trade at his stand, which bore the legend 'A Taste of Scraggby' (not his idea: he'd acquired the 'business' fourth-hand), proved 'sporadic'.

Come evening, he found himself thinking of what he felt had to be Carver's impending review of The Succulent Shrimp, at Nettlethorp Cliffs… whether this might be sufficient reason for Bunn to buy the next *Gullet*.

As usual, the lighthouse began its distant wink. The car park and seafront assumed their standard, cemetery-like quiet.

Bunn struggled to stay awake.

Suddenly, the silence was broken – by the throaty roar of a vehicle, smartly followed by the squeal of brakes.

In the darkness of the pay-and-display, the engine sound ceased.

A door opened and swung shut.

There were footsteps.

A plume of breath climbed the night air, like a vape cloud, as Marcus Carver stepped into the floodlight at Seafront Snacks.

'Evening!' he said. 'Chilly one, isn't it?!'

Although wearing his fedora and coat, he made a mock shudder, which sent Bunn's mind back to the artifice of the awful TV show.

'Said I'd be back,' continued Carver, not uncheerfully. 'One for the road. Then I've got to get off. Can you do me another of those specials of yours?'

For a moment, Bunn was thrown. He hadn't been expecting Carver. Not now. Clearly, Carver had made a weekend of it, had done his love 'em and leave 'em act (quite probably with Shelley Leggley), and was now driving back to London to get to either his office or flat some time near dawn (the roar in the car park having come from his roadster).

Bunn remembered the burger he'd prepared the previous afternoon. He'd left it – unrefrigerated – on one side in the stand. But that would hardly matter.

'Uh, yes, of course,' Bunn said, locating the burger and putting it on a plate in the microwave.

'Good!' said Carver. 'Need something to keep me going. Time of night. Been a busy weekend, one way or another. Famished, if I'm honest.'

Using tongs, Bunn placed the burger between two thick slices of crusty bread.

'Is it the same as the other night?' asked Carver.

'A bit different,' said Bunn. 'See what you make of it.'

'Quite a bouquet – that's for sure,' said Carver.

'Help yourself to mustard, salt and pepper. There's some relish as well.'

'Looks a good piece of meat,' Carver said, lifting the upper slice of bread. He dolloped it with three spoons of relish, spraying-on a double squirt of mustard in support.

Call himself a gourmet? thought Bunn. He wouldn't taste anything after a creosoting like that.

Carver took hold of it with his hands, opened his mouth.

'Bon appétit,' said Bunn.

He watched as Carver's jaws closed on the bread and the burger inside.

'Uhmm,' Carver murmured, thoughtfully. 'This one *is* different. What's in it?' he asked between chews.

He bit into it anew, without waiting for Bunn's answer.

Lugworms, Bunn thought to himself, picturing the bucket he'd brought back from his excavations on the sands. *Dogshit.*

'Meaty – but I'm also getting something… "crunchy",' said Carver, chomping and chewing.

Ground cuttlefish bone and the mashed skeleton of an unidentifiable seabird found rotting.

'And yet, at the same time, that crunchy-nutty texture is offset with something quite soft and moist.'

A beached jellyfish – quite possibly a Portuguese man o' war, that had to be scooped into the bucket v-e-r-y carefully, in case its sting had survived.

Carver was nearing the last of his late supper now: swallowing the final mouthfuls.

Diced rat's tail (Bunn recalled the spreadeagled shape of the rodent – poisoned and floating on its back – in the fetid effluent of an outfall pipe).

'Well, that's filled a hole,' said Carver, chirpily, the burger and bread entirely devoured. 'How much do I owe you?'

His choice of words unsettled Bunn. *Owe? Owe?!* Bunn thought of the humiliation, the misery, the loneliness he'd endured.

'Have it on me,' he said, eventually.

'Are you sure?' said Carver, looking up – genuine surprise, it seemed, on his face. 'That's awfully kind. Thanks very much.'

'My pleasure,' said Bunn.

'Right then. I need to get off. Thank you, and, um, cheers.'

Carver turned and walked away from the stand. But then he seemed to haver, on the edge of the light. He stepped into the dark but stepped back and turned to Bunn.

'I don't suppose there's a toilet around here by any chance?' he asked. 'Bit of a journey ahead. Don't want to get caught short on the open road.'

He drew a handkerchief from a pocket and, despite the coolness of the night, mopped his brow. 'You know, I suddenly feel rather…' he began. He seemed to stagger, but then he straightened. 'I don't quite know what's come over me. Well, um, cheerio then,' he said, not waiting to hear if Bunn had an answer.

Bunn heard the roadster roar to life. Its headlights swung across the car park as the vehicle headed to the exit and joined the road along the seafront.

Bunn listened as the car's engine changed pitch, as Carver went through the gears, on the front's otherwise empty straight.

Looking out across the sands, Bunn saw the remote lantern of the lighthouse – winking.

When Carver had gone what Bunn felt must have been half a mile, the roadster (still audible) seemed to lose its rhythm, its driver appearing to 'miss' a change. On the night air… for a couple of seconds… there was the sense of the car drifting. After this, came the muffled bang of what Bunn knew could only be a collision.

He drew down the shutter of Seafront Snacks... and turned out the light.

That night proved Bunn's last at his pitch in the pay-and-display. He shut Seafront Snacks for good. Not that there were many who'd noticed his 'business' (on the dark side of the moon that was Scraggby Sands).

Some days later, Bunn bought the new number of *Gullet Magazine*.

Several items in its pages attracted his attention.

The first and most obvious was the prominent and long obituary to Marcus Carver. Bunn skipped the paragraphs of praise, his eyes alighting on the few facts the magazine seemed to possess about its writer's 'sudden death': the critic's crash – in his 'much-loved' and 'signature' roadster – from the seafront at Scraggby Sands; the sweeping away of both Carver and his car by Scraggby's highest tide in living memory; the discovery of Carver, still strapped in his seat – apparently some seventy-two hours later – on the rocks of the lighthouse at Hookem Head; toxicology tests now underway in an attempt to establish the cause of Carver's death.

Bunn looked up from the magazine for a moment. He wondered about the state in which his nemesis had been found. He imagined Carver being recovered from the cold, blue-green seawater: swollen... bloated... a human soufflé.

Returning to the contents of *Gullet*, Bunn's eyes were caught – some pages in – by a small panel of print which stated that an intended review of The Succulent Shrimp at Nettlethorp Cliffs had been 'unavoidably held over'.

Amid the pages of advertisements at the back, Bunn spotted the line ad he'd submitted for his catering trailer – 'free to whoever will collect'.

Of far greater interest, however, was the advertisement he saw under 'Situations Vacant' – a chef required 'with immediate effect' (someone had obviously had to leave in a hurry, thought Bunn – another case of the kitchen copping the blame for something, no doubt; what *could* have gone wrong?) at 'a prestigious foodie pub'... no name, but a phone number whose code Bunn recognised as being that of Nettlethorp Cliffs.

Taking a red pen, he smiled and circled it – with relish.

A Piece of Cake

The birthday cake of Don Alberto Ercolano was a wonderful sight. It was carried through the darkness of the reception room and set down, carefully, on the dinner table before him.

The many candles guttered like a forest of fire-lit trees, then shone, upright, like votive flames of the kind that are left in a cathedral.

Ottavio Giulio Pirovano, who was the new baker in the village, having inherited the business of his deceased uncle, sensed the awe of all those present – their collective holding of breath.

Albeit requiring more than one attempt, Don Alberto – the candlelight playing on his face like the flames of a torch, or a fire, on the walls of a cave – blew out the candles quickly, without speaking.

Having done so, the lights were turned on and there was loud and enthusiastic applause.

The only words Ottavio heard were from a woman to her husband near whose table Ottavio was standing: her observation – made during the zestful clapping – that there had been a great many candles on the Don's cake. '*Mininu cinquanta*,' ('At least fifty') she said.

Her husband did not respond to her comment but instead increased the intensity of his clapping, seeming to want his wife to hush.

Somewhat to Ottavio's surprise, Don Alberto now called for the cake's removal.

The heavy-set men who had laid it there promptly carried it away.

Although disappointed, Ottavio did not dwell on this fact, fully expecting the cake to return at some later stage, a slice perhaps being given to each of those present to take home with them as they departed.

And yet there would be the irony that he, the baker, would not get to sample his handiwork because of his necessary early departure (to go to bed and rise before dawn to begin his baking for the next day).

For a moment the young bachelor found his thoughts returning to the evening of his arrival (from the mainland) on the island: the way the sun had set on the waters of the harbour.

As Ottavio left the party he saw that Don Alberto was dancing – and smiling – with one of the prettiest girls in the village.

For an instant, the eyes of the girl – looking over Don Alberto's shoulder – met Ottavio's, and she smiled.

Ottavio smiled back.

Don Alberto, for his part, was beaming – until he noticed the girl's glance at Ottavio, whereupon his own smile seemed to slip from him, like – so it seemed to Ottavio – a heavy anchor to the bottom of the sea.

Some while later, when it was noticed his bakery had not been opened for several days, and the local people were anxious for bread, the police broke in and searched Ottavio's premises.

His corpse was found in a chair at the open door of one of his ovens: a piece of cake wedged in his mouth.

Don Alberto was thirty-nine years old – and had been for some long while. All the locals – from the barber who dyed his hair to the tailor who made his corsets – knew that.

Vamp

'Martin,' said Fiona Briggs.

'Hmm?' her husband answered.

'There's something in my salad.'

'What?' said Briggs, in an uninterested, not-really-listening voice.

'I *said* "There's something in my salad".'

'Oh, I heard that,' he replied hastily, sensing the need to correct any impression of casualness on his part. 'I meant "What" as in *What's* in your salad?'

'A bug. Some sort of crawly… *sluggy* thing.'

'Are you sure?'

'Perfectly.'

'It's not a herb or something?'

'Of *course* it's not a herb. D'you think I'm stupid?'

'No one's calling anyone stupid, Fiona. Least of all me. I only asked.'

'Well – aren't you going to *do* something?'

'How d'you mean?'

'Look at it? Call for the manager?'

'Me?'

'Well, who else? I can't see anyone else at this table. Or *anywhere* in this dump, for that matter.' She glanced around the dimly lit interior of *Restaurant Sânge*.

'I was merely, um, deferring to the fact that I was under the impression that a woman is quite capable of summoning the manager herself these days, without the intervention of a man,' said Briggs. He chewed – a little uncertainly – on what had been listed on the menu as *ghoulash*, the spelling (and his selection), he sensed, having been a mistake.

'So that's *all* you're going to do, is it? Carry on eating?'

'Calm down, Fi. Let's not have an argument in public.'

'In public?! There's no one else here. The place is deserted. That's the point. Where on earth did you find it?'

'Just a quiet night, I expect.'

'Quiet?! Is *that* what you call it?'

'Fi, please. Keep your voice down. People are watching.'

'Who?'

'Well… the staff, I expect.' Briggs momentarily eyed the bored-seeming waiter who'd served them: a young man in a red waistcoat, with bags under his eyes, who looked in need of several nights' sleep. He leant, half-shadowed, against a pillar twined with plastic ivy.

'Look, are you going to look at this slug… or not? You know, it would be nice if just for *once* in our marriage, you could—'

From somewhere, a voice broke in: 'Excuse me, but I don't think I can take any more of this.'

Fiona Briggs nearly dropped her knife and fork. 'Did you hear that?' she said.

'What?' asked Briggs.

'*That*,' she said. 'It… spoke.'

'I'm sorry but this balalaika music, or whatever it is, they've got playing,' said Briggs. 'It's rather loud. *What* spoke?'

'The slug. The slug in my lettuce. It… talked.'

'Thank goodness for that,' the voice came back.

'Oh my God, Martin… it's off again.'

'What is?'

'The talking slug thing. Can't you hear it? Listen!'

She pushed the plate across the table towards Briggs.

'Whoah! Steady on!!' the voice complained.

And *this* time Briggs seemed to hear it, too. He stopped chewing.

Simultaneously, the couple bent forwards and studied the pile of green leaves on Fiona Briggs's plate.

Adjusting his glasses on his nose, Briggs saw there was indeed something bug-like, on a rather limp-looking lettuce leaf. What was more, it appeared to be looking up at them and... talking.

'Right!' it said. 'Now that I have *at last* got your attention, I'd like to make something quite clear. I am *not* – madam – a 'sluggy thing', but a caterpillar. And *one* day, I shall become a very beautiful butterfly, conceivably a Monarch, Emperor or Red Admiral. The lord and master of all that I shall survey, in an English country garden. Until then, and Heaven only knows why, I was picked to help *you*.'

Briggs suddenly felt nauseous. Unpleasant as it had been, he'd just about managed to force down the strange-tasting pâté maison he'd had for his starter (which now seemed to be coming back up). He couldn't believe his eyes, nor ears. He saw that his wife's eyes had swollen to the size of dinner plates.

'What sort of circus have you brought me to?' he heard her say. 'One with a... talking caterpillar!!'

'It looked all right on the internet,' he heard his own voice answer, rather lamely (not mentioning that it had been the eatery's 'all-in bargain' price that had caught his eye). Anyway, he reminded himself, someone had to keep an eye on the housekeeping. Just lately, with her, it had been spend, spend, spend. New shoes one minute, coat the next...

'Oh, *don't* start all that again,' said the caterpillar, as if it could not only hear his wife's words but read Briggs's mind. 'And keep your voices down – the pair of you – *if* you want to get out here...'

'Oh, we certainly want that. Well, I do anyway,' Fiona interrupted.

'... alive,' continued the caterpillar.

'Alive? What d'you mean?' said Briggs, struggling to believe that he was speaking to a caterpillar. Eyeing its mandibles, he wondered if there hadn't perhaps been some kind of narcotic in his pâté: perhaps a weird mushroom that had been blended-in. And yet – unless he was going mad – the caterpillar's mouth seemed to be... moving... matching the dialogue that Briggs could hear.

'This restaurant is run by vampires,' said the caterpillar.

'Vampires?!' the couple responded (Briggs's tone one of bafflement, his wife's more a shriek).

'I knew it. I bloody knew it,' said Fiona. 'You and your bloody bargains, Martin. Well, you've topped the lot this time: this is the 'dead end of town' all right. I hope you're pleased with yourself. Just what sort of coupons were you planning to cash in tonight? Hey? We didn't see a soul for half a mile, save for that old bloke on his scooter. *Restaurant Sânge...* what sort of a name is that? "Mange" I'd call it – like something on the back of next door's cat.'

'I believe,' said the caterpillar, 'it is a word they use in Transylvania.'

'Transylvania?' said Fiona.

'For blood,' added the caterpillar.

'Oh, that's all we need! So that's the proof, then. Jesus Christ, Martin! What *have* you gone and done? "Let's go out," you said... like the last of the big spenders. "It's our wedding anniversary." I should have known. My mother warned me. You're cheap, Martin Briggs! Cheap!! And you always have been. And look where it's got us. Look where we are: a table for two in... Dracula's diner – with me and you on the menu, according to this... *caterpillar.*'

'Now hang on a minute, Fiona,' said Briggs. 'Let's not get into prejudicial stereotyping on the back of the word of a... um... caterpillar. I've heard some very nice things about Transylvania. It's a land of beautiful forests and castles, apparently.'

'Yes! Like Vlad the Impaler's! Oh, do shut up, Martin! No one's the least bit impressed with the silly courses you've been on at Hareditch bloody council.'

Briggs glanced around him. He couldn't help but feel that his wife might have a point. He'd noticed, on stepping in from the street, how the staff had seemed grey-faced, red-eyed. Unless he was mistaken, their waiter was no longer lounging by the pillar with the fake ivy but had moved closer. For a moment, Briggs's eyes met those of the chef – how large and bloodshot his eyes seemed – peering from beneath his *toque* through the porthole window of the door to the kitchen.

'Enough! Please!!' said the caterpillar, which, never mind its ambitions of becoming some sort of winged dandy, wore – for now, at any rate – an unappealing coat of lime-green and canary-yellow… like a squirt of strangely garish toothpaste, thought Briggs.

'If I'm to get you out of here, the one thing you must do is act normal,' the caterpillar continued.

'Normal?' snorted Fiona. 'Us?!'

'Now, just sit back and carry on and I'll talk you through ev—'

The caterpillar stopped talking. The waiter who'd been lurking at the pillar suddenly appeared at the table.

'Is everything all right? Can I get you anything?' he asked.

What Briggs – who couldn't help but notice the man's 'lived-in' look, the five o'clock shadow on his jaw – wanted to answer was: 'Some stakes… and I don't mean of the meat kind – and plenty of garlic!' But he was speechless, as if struck dumb. Other than the waiter's questions, all he was aware of was his own heart… pounding. It seemed so powerful he wondered if the man could hear it… if the organ might jump out of him and carry on pumping, in a bloody heap, in the middle of the table (to be pounced upon by this fanged man-cum-bat creature who was there, by his side).

For twenty-six years, Briggs had worked for the same department in the same office at Hareditch council. 'Outreach & Interface' it was called now (though he could count on the fingers of one hand the number of times he'd left the building, or 'interfaced', with anyone). Occasionally, he'd written reports of a minor, inconclusive nature. From time to time, he called his own desk phone, having obtained an outside line on another in the building, hoping his would be answered by a colleague who'd take a message, Briggs pretending to be people with whom he was liaising on non-existent projects: Lionel Lear, Sean O'Connor, Krish Patel, Marjorie Kinsey. Mostly, he just stared at his computer. People thought he was working but, aided by the corner position of his desk, unaltered in three decades, he passed days, and indeed weeks, reading trivia on the internet, including comments 'below the line' left by people he supposed were just like him. He'd risen effortlessly – on the back of nothing more than his longevity – to a comfortably-pensioned, middle-management rank.

Then, one day, someone new – someone *not* from Hareditch – had entered his world, *breezed* in, and asked him to make a presentation. The 'stress' had sent him to pieces. There'd been time off work, visits to his GP, prescriptions, pills. At home, he'd moved into one of the spare bedrooms. Fiona had seemed to change. He had the sense that she might even be 'seeing' someone. There'd been endless bickering. He went no further than the end of the road (with their chihuahua), usually wearing his dressing gown and slippers. Eventually, with the aid of some medication prescribed for his nerves, he'd gone back to the council, but things had never been the same.

The waiter seemed unsettled by the way Briggs was just staring up at him, open-mouthed. The man repeated his enquiry about whether everything was all right.

Suddenly, Briggs felt a painful kick in his right shin under the table, and sensed Fiona: scowling.

'Uh yes, fine. We're fine,' said Briggs. 'Thank you very much.'

The waiter walked away.

In a somewhat hushed voice, the caterpillar resumed talking: 'Phew. That was close. Look, we need to act fast. I don't doubt it's already well past sundown. Leave it much longer and every bloodsucker in town will be flying in through the door.'

Briggs noticed how, even as the caterpillar spoke, a pallid-looking couple were being shown to a table.

The caterpillar continued: 'Here's what we're going to do. When he comes to take away your plates, ask for a finger bowl.'

'A finger bowl?' queried Martin.

'Yes,' said the caterpillar. 'With some luck, looking at the configuration of your cutlery and crockery, he'll place it directly over your escape route.'

'Escape route? How d'you mean?'

'For some time, a division of beetles has been boring a safe passage through the table leg, to your right. It's your 'lift-shaft', if you like, to liberty (except we'll be going *down* not up). Once we hit the carpet, we'll rendezvous with a party of cockroaches. *Don't* be alarmed, they aren't bad lads, never mind their media.'

'Finger bowl... table leg... beetles... cockroaches,' said Martin, in a bewildered voice. 'I'm sorry, but I'm having trouble taking all of this in.'

'Oh Martin, just *listen*, for heaven's sake!' said Fiona. 'This caterpillar's trying to help us.'

'Thank you, madam,' said the caterpillar. 'All you've got to do is dive into the finger bowl. As you've probably noticed, ninety-nine per cent of the china in this dump is either chipped or cracked. The vortex caused by your entry into the bowl will take you through its base to the tablecloth. Although you may not be able to see in this light, its cotton is distinctly on the threadbare side. Some friendly moths have been finishing the job, clearing a portal to the table leg.'

'I'm sorry,' said Briggs. 'But I still don't understand. How are *we* going to fit in a finger bowl?'

'Oh Martin! *Really*,' said his wife. 'You and your bloody questions! I've never known a man have such… negativity.'

'It's a fair question,' said the caterpillar. 'And one to which I don't fully have the answer. All I know is that you'll undergo a process of miniaturization. I'm not an expert in particle physics. I'm just a talking caterpillar – isn't that enough?'

'He's right, Martin,' said Fiona. 'For once in your bloody life, be satisfied. This caterpillar's trying to help us.'

'Yes, but why?' said Briggs. 'I don't—'

'What about *you*, Mr Caterpillar?' Fiona asked. 'What will *you* do?'

'When the waiter comes to take your plates, I'll jump – or try to – from this lettuce leaf into the finger bowl. Just make sure, the bowl's in place *before* he takes away this plate… or it could be a case of one crushed caterpillar – and "chips" for me, on the tabletop.'

'Will you make it?' asked Fiona.

'It's going to be a leap of faith. But I *have* been practising. Thanks for your concern.'

'I just can't believe this,' said Briggs. 'It *can't* be happening.'

'Well, it *is*,' said Fiona. 'Get a grip. Just like that presentation you were supposed to make. *You* can bottle it again, if you want to, Martin Briggs. But I'm not. *I'm* getting out!'

Briggs looked around the room. The place was filling up. Unless he was mistaken, the faces of the customers all seemed a shade of grey. At the table of one couple, the waiter uncorked a bottle and poured a red liquid into their glasses. Was it wine, Briggs wondered, or… something else?

Suddenly, the waiter was beside him. 'May I take your plates?' the man – if that's what he was – asked.

Briggs felt the toe of Fiona's shoe in his left shin.

'I wonder if we might have a finger bowl?' he said.

There was another – painful – stab in his shin.

'I mean *first*,' he added.

'Yes, of course,' said the waiter, with a somewhat puzzled air. 'If sir would like one.'

The waiter retreated.

'Can't trust you to get any bloody thing right, can I?' said Fiona. 'Even if our lives depended on it.'

The waiter returned with the finger bowl. He placed it at what seemed the spot wished-for by the caterpillar. Perhaps not 'bang on', thought Martin, but – maybe – near enough.

Briggs watched as – with one hand – the waiter picked up Fiona's plate.

Suddenly, in the dim light, Briggs saw the small form of the caterpillar leap from its edge.

As it did so, everything in the restaurant seemed to Briggs to enter a strange and silent slow motion. From the corners of his eyes, the lifting of forks to their mouths, and the levering of ruby-filled glasses to the lead-grey lips of the other patrons, seemed to take an eternity.

The caterpillar flew through the air above the table in a manner that caused Briggs to bring to mind the feats of Olympian ski jumpers – and landed, with (unless his ears were mistaken) the tiniest *plosh* in the pool of the finger bowl, before climbing onto the half-slice of lemon that floated within it, as if it were a raft.

Briggs looked around the restaurant. All of the other tables were now full. What's more, the tables seemed to have come nearer: their edges and cloths within touching distance, the would-be diners almost in his face.

He heard Fiona's voice: 'I'm leaving, Martin. Even if you're not.'

Turning, he saw – for an instant – his wife's scarlet-painted nails over the edge of the finger bowl, before they slipped inside.

Since when had she been painting her nails? he wondered. New shoes, coat and now… nails. He thought – again – of her visits to the hairdresser: she'd been going once a fortnight (he'd followed her).

What *had* got into Fiona?

Mystified, Briggs jumped into the finger bowl.

To Martin Briggs's amazement, the caterpillar had been right. Although the experience had been like going through the spin cycle of a washing machine, he and Fiona had indeed passed through first the base of the finger bowl, then the tablecloth and its wooden top, before plummeting down the shaft of the leg to the floorboards below. There, to his continuing disbelief, a party of cockroaches – in the manner of *partisan* commandos – had greeted and directed them to a tunnel they were guarding beneath the carpet, where – now – the caterpillar led them on.

'These are the hard yards,' the caterpillar said. 'I'm afraid we're going to have to expect some turbulence.'

'Turbulence?' queried Martin.

'Carpet bombing,' said the caterpillar.

Above them, the heels and soles of boots and shoes pressed down on the carpet. Chair legs dragged over and dug into the fabric. It was like burrowing along the London Underground in wartime, thought Martin: Hitler's doodlebugs raining down from a raid up above.

The dirt and fluff were almost unbearable, never mind the obstacles posed by the salt and sugar that had been ground into and through the (obviously ancient) carpet. Sharp grains of rice lurked in the blackness, like ice floes. Worst of all were the ends of fallen cocktail sticks. These speared from the gloom like horrific boobytraps set to protect the tombs of pharaohs.

Somehow, they managed to reach a cliff-face. Its sheer – and surely unclimbable – wall loomed above them.

Martin worked out that it was one of the steps up from the dining area – the first of several.

In their miniaturized form, the step was like the face of the Eiger. How on earth would he and Fiona ever climb that?

'Get on board!' said the caterpillar.

'What?' said Briggs.

'My back. Two legs good, sixteen legs better.'

Martin helped Fiona onto the creature.

'Hold on tight,' said the caterpillar over its shoulder. 'We're about to make some caterpillar tracks!'

They sat astride as the creature headed upwards, the carpet pressing down on them like the roof of a collapsed marquee.

The caterpillar climbed one step... and headed up another.

On the third cliff-face, however, it began to cough.

To his alarm, Briggs sensed that the caterpillar's strength was fading, that its legs were losing traction – giving way.

Suddenly, its tail end swung loose from the face of the step.

'Oh my God!' screamed Fiona as, turning her head, she saw the near-bottomless drop that beckoned below them.

Briggs sensed that the caterpillar's front end was 'going' as well... its whole body buckling on the sheer cliff-face of the step.

'Please caterpillar! You can do it! We *believe* in you! I didn't at first,' said Briggs, 'but I do now!'

The caterpillar spat out a dustball, and looked back over its shoulder.

'You... do?' it spluttered.

'Yes! And that's a tier-three deputy-assistant officer in outreach and interface at Hareditch unitary authority (with twenty-six years' experience) speaking. Believe me, one day you're going to be a beautiful butterfly... in a garden with birds and bees and honeysuckle and—'

'Okay,' the caterpillar, short of breath, gasped. 'I've got the picture. Let's not gild the lily.' It cleared its throat. 'Right, Mr Briggs. Now that you seem to be fully "on board", let's get out of here!'

It took a deep breath – one that seemed to inflate its whole body. Then, one leg followed by the other fifteen, it hauled the three of them up the face of the step – as if conquering some great tower-block in the clouds: the Empire State, the Shard, or even Hareditch council's concrete multi-storey car park.

They were up and over... on the flatlands of the foyer, mere feet from the front door.

Even though their subterranean world was now more filthy than ever (thanks to the 'traffic' tramping in from the street), the trio could smell freedom. The Hareditch night – with its gasworks, abattoir and railway sidings – beckoned, like Switzerland's snow-capped peaks.

However, no sooner had they scented its sweetness than a fresh terror struck.

Above them, whether by accident or design, someone was vacuuming the carpet – with a nozzle whose power seemed set at 'full blast'.

The carpet lifted, as if in the grip of a typhoon. Martin and Fiona held on to the caterpillar. Its back rose, taking on – in the super-charged suction – the humped-and-hollowed shape of a tiny rollercoaster.

'I'm... going, Martin – I can feel it!' screamed Fiona, her hair standing on end.

'Don't!' answered Martin. 'Hold on! I *love* you, Fi! I've *always* loved you!!'

At which point, the suction died – the Hoover above them seemingly having been switched off.

'It's a bit bloody late for that,' she said of Briggs's declaration, her hair collapsing from its vertical state. 'Come on. I want to get out of here. My hairdo's been *bloody* ruined. What a night!'

They emerged through a small hole, inches from the door.

It swung open, to admit what seemed a huge pair of highly Gothic-looking boots. Suddenly, seeing its chance, the caterpillar broke into a gallop and then, in the manner of a racehorse clearing a hurdle at a classic of the turf, it leapt over the threshold and into the street.

Out of the blue, Martin and Fiona were themselves again – 'normal', life-sized.

Briggs shuddered for a second as he looked at himself in the window of *Restaurant Sânge*, with its fairy lights, plastic ivy and faded menu. Tomorrow, at work, he nodded to himself, he'd give the place one Hell of a bad review on the internet. No sane person in Hareditch would set foot there (no matter how many vouchers they had).

'Well, I guess that just about wraps—' began – and ended – the caterpillar, on the pavement, somewhere near Briggs's feet.

The old man they'd seen earlier, on his scooter, pulled past them, steering whilst emitting a cloud of smoke from a vape pipe, not wholly unlike a steam locomotive appearing from a tunnel.

'Oh my God!' said Martin. 'The caterpillar!! And we never even knew its name!'

In almost the same second, the metal cellar doors in the pavement on which he was standing opened and swallowed him, before slamming shut to their previous state.

Fiona Briggs, who'd winked at the elderly rider of the scooter, made away – heels clacking, into the chill damp of the Hareditch night.

A Good Egg

'An egg?' queried Gertrude Gore. 'What kind of an egg?'

Although surprised by the ringing of her telephone, and instinctively cautious – these days, on those rare occasions when it rang, the caller always seemed a snake oil merchant wanting to sell her something – this voice sounded… genuine. The accent was 'continental', sophisticated. It sounded rather like that of a *maître d'* she half-remembered: a rather suave type, with brilliantined hair, at a restaurant she couldn't quite place.

'Oh, Miss Gore. I couldn't tell you that. It would spoil the surprise. But we would be honoured, truly honoured…'

It had been years since she had received such a request. Standing there, holding her phone, it was as if something strange had happened to her hearing aid: some sort of surge in its power, or a fortuitous fusing of wires, that had reconnected her with her past.

It was not for nothing that she had once been celebrated as 'England's greatest trencherwoman'. Unlike the old lady of nursery rhyme (who died… of course), Gertrude Gore *had* swallowed a horse… and lived – eating her way through the equine in a single sitting: soups, pâtés, jellies, stews, meatballs, roasted joints and pan-fried steaks – till not a morsel remained. Her feat had entered the pages of gastronomic legend.

In her career as England's most celebrated eater, there was, so observers said, no known species of animal, bird of aquatic life that her tongue hadn't tasted and her stomach hadn't held: no swan or swallow she hadn't swallowed, no pike or sturgeon she hadn't stuffed, no squirrel – red or grey – whose small skeleton she hadn't sucked clean. There was, it was generally agreed, no eel, badger, goat, pigeon, frog, newt or owl that Gertrude Gore hadn't gorged.

In her heyday, the tweeded spinster (who – though certainly 'stout' – was no giantess, nor possessed of the girth or manners of a glutton) had been a celebrity in the pages of England's popular press, the editors of newspapers portraying her as a sort of cross between Miss Marple and Boadicea: a 'national treasure', gallantly wolfing her way, for the good of Old Blighty, through whatever it was that had been placed before her. Owners of new restaurants in London and on seafronts in coastal towns would pay her to dine at their tables, photographs of the flashbulb kind capturing her cracking open the claws of king-sized crabs and carving her way through enormous T-bone steaks.

In interviews, she attributed her 'healthy appetite', and her insistence on leaving her plate 'clean', to her Christian upbringing as the daughter of the rector of a clutch of country parishes in the English shires…

'May I take that as a "yes", Miss Gore?' the voice on the other end of the phone enquired.

Looking around her, Gertrude was suddenly struck by the dullness of her living room, also how very long it had been since she had set foot beyond her apartment's front door.

She became aware of a faint watering in her mouth.

'Very well,' said Gertrude.

Rain squalled at the windows of the taxi as the driver headed to what her caller on the telephone had proudly proclaimed as 'The Jurassic Coast'. Gertrude had hired the cab from a stand near her apartment block. 'No need to inconvenience yourself with a train all the way from London, Miss Gore,' the man with the accent had told her. 'We'll pay for your cab.' Ensconced, rather regally, in the rear of the taxi, Gertrude had the sense of 'old times': the feeling – at this rather advanced stage of her life – of being 'back in the game'.

Some hours later, the taxi driver was threading his way (not without difficulty), along narrow and winding Devonshire lanes.

The headlights of the cab flared against banks and hedgerows where the road twisted in serpentine bends.

Amid the growing lateness, the worsening weather and deepening dark, Gertrude began to have doubts. Might it not be best to abandon all of this and head back home to London, she wondered. Was there perhaps not something rather *odd* about this invitation?

But then she also thought of the taxi fare, which had surely to be a fortune by now.

Her eyes – no longer as sharp as they'd been – struggled to find the cabbie's meter.

When she finally located it (above the driver's head), the machine's digits moved in a scarlet smear, as if the rain had somehow streamed inside the vehicle, the cold water from the outside world running down its walls.

In the cab's dark womb, Gertrude fingered her pearls.

The driver drew up with a suddenness that caused Gertrude to slide on her seat.

'I think *this* must be the place,' he announced.

He let the vehicle idle at what – between the swinging of its wipers – seemed to Gertrude a rather forbidding set of gates. Either side of their ironwork, stood a high, stone wall.

'I say, driver, couldn't we just—' Gertrude began.

The cabbie cut her off: 'Hang on. Look! There's life out there! Thank God for that!'

Through a rain-sluiced side window, Gertrude saw a scurrying figure: a man with a lantern and some sort of cape that he was holding over his head, like a tarpaulin.

He hurried from a gatehouse and drew open the gates.

Ahead, Gertrude noticed the dark outline of what looked to be a large property, at the top of a long drive.

Suddenly, a flash of lightning illuminated a great and ancient mansion of the grey-stoned, creeper-clad kind.

The retainer who'd opened the gates swung his lantern in a gesture to the cabbie to drive on… up to the house.

There'd be no turning back now, Gertrude knew.

'Good evening, Miss Gore.' A butler, clutching a candelabra in one hand and the handle of an umbrella in the other, greeted Gertrude.

He stood at the cab door, which the driver had managed – via his window – to swing open without leaving his seat. The manservant, attired in dark tails, waited at the foot of a set of steps that rose behind him, wide and magisterially, in Parthenon fashion, to the house that loomed above.

'Would Madam be kind enough to follow me?'

In her heart, which seemed to be beating rather fast, and her head, which was perplexed (not least with the probably unpayable price of the taxi ride back to London), Gertrude was strongly inclined *not* to step into the butler's dark night.

Yet, somehow, her voice seemed to be lost. And there was something else. As well as feeling foolish in her bewildered state in the back of the cab, Gertrude felt… obliged.

'They're waiting for you, Gertrude,' a voice seemed to say above the rattle of the taxi engine and the rain falling on its roof. 'They're waiting.'

Climbing the steps to the house, her voluminous handbag looped in the cruck of her elbow, Gertrude wondered how it was that the flames of the candles carried by the butler managed to burn so very perfectly, given the stormy nature of the night.

Rain beat on the black fabric of the umbrella that her saturnine escort held above her.

'We are without *earthly* power tonight,' he said, stepping carefully in time with her, 'as I expect you have noticed. But I dare say the master will manage. Everything has been prepared.'

Behind her, Gertrude heard the engine of the cab diminishing, as if it were disappearing down the drive. Amid the rain, which was splattering the stonework of the steps, and the wind, which was still blasting in bad-tempered gusts, Gertrude seemed to hear the clatter of the iron gates in the perimeter wall… the sound of them being shut.

The butler seated Gertrude at a table in a great, baronial hall. Banners emblazoned with dragons, bears and unicorns that seemed to Gertrude to be of considerable antiquity hung from staffs that protruded from wood-panelled walls. Before her, on a table whose length appeared infinite, candles cast a golden glow over crystal glassware, gilded china and silver cutlery. A log fire waved in a huge stone hearth.

'Good evening, Miss Gore!' a voice announced, in a rich bass-baritone. 'Truly, I have waited such a long time for this night.'

Looking about her, Gertrude divined no one amid the gloom that seemed to encircle the enormously long table. Perhaps – thought Gertrude – it came from above her: a gallery, or maybe from an ante-room or an alcove of some kind?

She recognised the voice as that of the caller (from those days earlier) on the telephone.

The speaker continued: 'The consumer of two hundred and twenty-three kippers… in one weekend… at the Tarmouth Smoked Fish Festival.'

'Two hundred and twenty-eight, actually,' corrected Gertrude, somewhat nervously, 'though I'm surprised anyone remembers that. It was such a long time ago.'

'Thirty-nine marrows,' the disembodied voice boomed on, 'at the internationally famous Marrowby Marrow Marathon…'

'And nineteen courgettes,' added Gertrude, in a timid semi-whisper.

'A feat unbeaten to this day.'

'Well, the rules were a little different back then. They were allowed to serve them stuffed. Mincemeat, you know. That sort of thing.'

'And, Miss Gore, your coup de grâce, your entry into legend, the feat that will for ever secure you a place at the table of the greatest gourmands this world has ever known. I refer – of course – to the horse.'

'Well, horse is putting it a *little* strongly,' said Gertrude. 'More a pony, actually. At the Nogborough Horse Fair, true enough. But, a Shetland, and, on the whole, a little one. The poor old thing had passed away. And they were looking for some publicity or something. You know how it is. And good meat was so very hard to get hold of at the time – worse than rationing. So, you know… "When your country calls" and all that. All in the line of duty.'

While rather enjoying the flattery of these reminders of her past glories, Gertrude was aware that she was gabbling. She couldn't help but feel that even allowing for some of the strange things she'd done in her life, *this* engagement was by far the strangest.

'Well,' she began, all set to remove her handbag from the table and rise from her seat, 'it really is such an awful night: the weather, the power cut. Not your fault, or course. But I think, really, I ought to go home. So, if you'd just be kind enough to telephone for a taxi. Clearly, no one can be expected to cook on a night such as this. I expect you haven't been able to do a thing.'

'Oh, Miss Gore. We cannot let you go just like that. Not after all this time. Goodness, it was so very difficult: tracking you down, to your little flat. And after your long journey here. You must stay, I insist. I can think of no one more suited to this task than you,' said the voice.

Task? thought Gertrude.

'Besides, in this weather, all of our telephone lines are down.'

'Really?' she said, in a small voice.

Suddenly, there was a great rumble of thunder over the house. Wind roared down the chimney, flattening the flames of the fire… before they drew up again, resurgent, amid a shower of sparks and a chorus of hisses.

'Where… *are* you?' asked Gertrude?

'Anyway,' her host – ignoring her question – continued, 'the… *dish* that I have for you is a simple one. Unique, yes, but simple. We have no need of fancy grills or anything like that.'

'The egg?' said Gertrude, remembering what he had said to her on the telephone: the peculiar-sounding single dish that her mind had somehow lost sight of in the excitement of her preparations, the thrill of being *needed*, at *her* age (in what nowadays seemed very much a young person's world). She cursed herself inwardly: vain, foolish, silly *old* woman.

'And so, to dinner, Miss Gore – if you please.'

From the gloom, the butler who'd greeted Gertrude, approached the candlelit dining table with a large, silver cloche. He set it down in front of her, and, with a white-gloved hand, removed its great dome. He then retreated into the dark.

A large egg – a *very* large egg – sat on the platter before Gertrude. Its shell – if it had had one – had been removed. The ovoid was white, solid-looking and with a faint sheen, as if made of marble.

What could it be? wondered Gertrude. From an eagle? An osprey? A duck-billed platypus? No, surely too big.

It reposed on the platter: enormous, enigmatic, like something extra-terrestrial.

Sitting, in that great hall, with the giant egg, she suddenly felt terribly tiny. Although she knew herself *not* to be small and, never mind that she was no longer quite the same size as 'in her prime' (the kind of woman who tended to be referred to as 'imposing' and perhaps 'formidable'), Gertrude *felt* small and child-like... as if she were sitting in an infant's highchair.

Before she knew it – the butler was back: smoothing a bib over her front, tying its strings at her neck.

The disembodied voice returned. 'And now, if you please Miss Gore, I require you to consume the egg.'

More than a little flustered, Gertrude sought to compose herself.

Eyeing the enormous egg, she brought to mind the conquests of her heyday – the oysters, cucumbers, pigs' trotters, lampreys, sheep's eyes, oxtails, tripe puddings, squids and sweetbreads, among other things – that she'd consumed, up and down the land.

Well, she said to herself, this egg *was* on the large side, but she probably had the beating of it. What could be the harm?

Gertrude looked down at the table for her cutlery – and saw there was none.

'I'm terribly sorry,' she said, lifting her head and calling into the darkness, 'but I don't seem to have a knife and fork.'

'Oh there's no need for those, Gertrude – may I call you Gertrude?' asked the voice. 'The very *last* thing I want you to do is to carve this egg.'

Gertrude sat in silent puzzlement for a moment. Looking at the egg on its platter and then into the darkness of the hall, she asked: 'But how shall I eat it?'

'Whole!' the voice boomed back at her. 'You must swallow it, Gertrude! You must swallow it whole!'

Gertrude's body stiffened with shock. Not only at the nature of this challenge, but at the way in which it had been issued: an order... a command.

She looked again at the egg. It was surely the size of a rugby football, if not bigger. How on earth would she—

'I don't think I can,' said Gertrude.

'You must!' the voice thundered, drowning any sound from the storm outside.

Suddenly, Gertrude sensed herself not in that dining hall, but in the rectory – the house where she grew up. She saw – quite clearly – her father wringing his hands – and her mother, the real force in the family (constantly furious at the puny nature of her husband's stipend as a country parson), telling her she could *not* 'get down' from the table, and she would *never* get down from the table until she had cleared her plate of 'Every last scrap!' – the whole unwholesome lot of it: the scrag end of meat from the butcher's bin, the flyblown vegetables from the bitter earth of their garden, the wormed fruit from their horrible so-called orchard. God's bounty… for which (ridiculously)… the good Christian Gores even said grace.

'What sort of an egg is it? Why is it so large?' Gertrude asked in a timid voice, her eyes refocusing on the ovoid before her.

'It's a dinosaur egg, Miss Gore,' the voice responded.

'A dinosaur!?' she repeated, with incredulity. She looked around her, shifted in her seat, tried to catch sight of whoever it was that was speaking to her. 'How on earth… why on earth?' she spluttered.

'Appropriate, is it not?' the voice came back at her. 'You see,' the voice went on, 'I would very much like to turn back the clock.'

'With an egg? How do you mean?' Gertrude, still astonished, interrupted.

'Consider your position, if you will, Miss Gore… Gertrude,' said the voice. 'Not so many years ago, you were a heroine… a "national treasure", no less. Rarely a week would pass without your photograph appearing in the newspapers: an epic episode consuming Cumberland sausages in the North Country; an extraordinary feast of eels, some days later, in the East Anglian fens; a world record – which I believe still stands – for whelks devoured in a single sitting at a seaside resort on the South Coast…'

'And your point is?' asked Gertrude.

'Look at you, now, in your autumn years. And – who knows? – maybe even your last winter… too timid to go out. Childless. Grand-childless. I have no wish to be cruel, but I am right, Miss Gore, am I not? I have seen you twitching your curtains, looking down on the scenes in the street, turning away with dismay, putting a record on your gramophone player, pouring yourself a small glass of sherry, pouring yourself another one…'

Gertrude felt herself blush. 'The world *has* changed, rather,' she said. His comments about her status as an 'old maid' had wounded her but she decided to let them pass. 'You know,' she said, 'there's a place across the road that calls itself a "takeaway". It sells – what do they call it? – "fast food"… yes, that's it. It really is the most awful—'

'Some might think it nice to go back to the time of Adam and Eve,' the voice broke in, above her. 'But I say: why stop there? We can go back further – much further – than that. And so here we are… on the Jurassic Coast – what better place could there be? – with our egg, and our Mother Hen, as I have come to think of you.'

'I'm sorry but I'm having trouble taking all of this in,' said Gertrude.

'Oh, but you will,' said the voice, 'all of it… *and* the egg.'

For a moment, neither spoke: the only sound being the rain, squalling against the hall's high windows, and the continuing crack and lick of the log fire.

'Please, Miss Gore,' the voice returned now. 'It is time to begin. Feel free to use your fingers,' the voice went on. 'No one is watching.'

'*Whole*, you said?' asked Gertude, a small part of her wondering if her host might have had some change of heart.

'Down in one,' the voice came back.

Gertrude leaned forward. She took a sniff. Well, at least it didn't *smell* rotten, she consoled herself (never mind its alleged ancient nature).

She cupped her hands beneath either end and took hold of it, as if she were receiving something sacramental, or even a new-born child.

It was heavy, smooth and slightly greasy on her palms. She felt the weight in her wrists and her forearms.

'You know, I'm really not sure if I *can*,' she began.

'You must!' the voice came back at her, imperiously.

And again, she thought of those wretched lunches and dinners in the drab dining room of the rectory... the angry face of her mother – so full of hate for her lot in life: 'No, Gertrude, you may *not* get down.'

Gertrude thought about the odd things – the *really* odd things – she'd eaten in her life. Among them an octopus. She'd eaten all of it – head, tentacles, every last sucker – at the gala opening of a seafood restaurant, somewhere miles from the sea. There'd been a jazz band and a red carpet (rolled out especially for her).

Well, if she could manage something like that and, of course, the horse (albeit that it was really a pony)...

Straightening her back, she upended the egg, sliding her hands so they gripped it at its girth, with its pointed extremity poised above her, like an outsize artillery shell or a curiously coloured weight from an antique longcase clock.

Beneath it, Gertrude opened her jaws – as wide as she could – and lowered the egg to her mouth.

Her tongue touched its waxy whiteness, the edge of the egg contacting the tips of her upper teeth, which – unlike many people of her age – she'd been careful to keep.

As the egg now began to enter the silo of her open mouth, Gertrude flared her nostrils in bovine fashion, foreseeing that, in the moments to come, she would be dependent on her nasal passages for any breath she might draw.

'G-o-o-d,' came the disembodied voice, in something like a purr. 'G-o-o-d.'

Gertrude sensed the egg moving slowly, steadily into her – somehow, unless she was mistaken, elongating its shape slightly, in her hands and in her mouth, as its great weight slipped into her, in the manner of some gigantic ship, inching its way through the waters of one of the world's great canals.

Fraction by fraction, she felt the egg enter her.

'That's it, Gertrude,' came the voice, with encouragement. 'That's it.'

And the egg continued its slow descent, like a nuclear missile into the bunker of its launch site, after some apocalyptic drill.

Suddenly, with the tip of the egg somewhere near her tonsils, Gertrude sensed its progress stop.

She moved her hands from that large part of it which remained exposed, till they were each at its rounded base, furthest from her, and, with one hand by the side of the other, she pushed.

The egg, however, would not move.

She returned her hands to the sides of the ovoid and attempted to first swivel, then wriggle, it free.

But the egg would not shift.

It was stuck there, like some cannonball that had become lodged in the masonry of a castle wall.

Gertrude attempted to swallow. Oh, *how* she attempted to swallow.

But the egg would not budge.

Pressing her palms on its sides – its rubbery mass prohibited any penetration by her fingers and nails –

Gertrude now attempted to squeeze it away from her: to 'uncork' herself, if she could.

Yet the egg *still* would not shift, let alone come out.

It was – without question – jammed.

Gertrude sat there, with her head uplifted and her throat utterly blocked, as if she were some goose or duck being force-fed with grain for *foie gras*.

Terror took hold of her extraordinarily stretched features.

'Arghh… urghh… garhh,' she let out in cries strangulated by the egg, stopping-up her throat.

She slapped the tabletop with her hand, a glass and side-plate crashing to the floor.

In her mounting panic, she found it increasingly hard to breathe. Her nostrils seemed incapable of inhaling or exhaling, so close as they were to the exposed egg, which seemed to press down on her, like a boulder.

'Gaargh… urghh,' uttered Gertrude, her eyes watering now and her neck and face turning first pink, then red, through the suffocating weight of the egg.

'You must!' the awful voice from the dark came at her. 'Swallow it, Gertrude! Swallow it! *Every* last scrap!!'

Suddenly, with these words, she was once again not there, in that strange baronial hall, but at the dinner table in the rectory, where she knew she had somehow been not just in her childhood but for *all* of her life.

She heard her mother's martinet voice, as clear and sour as the meal-time gong of some side-street hotel of the small and penny-pinching kind: 'No, you may *not* leave the table!'

Oh, how she longed to spit out the egg… *if* she only could.

Gertrude sensed her whole body locking and stiffening now, an inability to utter any sound, and not just a shortness of breath, but its absence. She was – she knew – choking.

Was *this* what her whole life had been for, she wondered. Her death... pre-destined at this dining table? Sucking an egg?

Her consciousness began to leave her: not gradually but as it if had been running and had leapt from the edge of a cliff, from which she was now falling... plummeting.

Suddenly, she caught sight of her girlhood self: she was running through a field at the back of the rectory. And she remembered – she remembered how she *had* got down from the table that day – never mind what her mother had said... how she had run out, through the back door, and across the garden – straight through her father's barren little vegetable patch – and over the fence and into the field beyond, her mother all the while calling after her... demanding: 'Come back here, Gertrude! Come back!!' And Gertrude *had* – that evening – gone back (with blackberry-stained fingers and lips) and been smacked and sent to bed. But that rebellion had also been her beginning.

And she remembered now how the newspapers had made her their darling. Yes, she knew that some of the laughter was 'at her'. But most of it – far and away the greater part – was 'with her', and always had been.

Now... without, it seemed, any mental instruction... her body made one last, instinctive attempt to swallow the egg.

Gertrude's whole being seemed to undergo a peculiar convulsion, like a twitch from some kind of electric shock.

Suddenly, in the manner of a keystone slipping from an arch, the egg began to loosen and to sink into her.

Down it went, past her tonsils. Down it continued, into her throat. Further and further, its vast mass fell – easing its way down the tube of her esophagus until, finally, it came to rest in the great cavern of her stomach.

Wearily... groggily... Gertrude came to her senses in her seat.

Staring before her, she saw the empty platter where the egg had been.

She removed her 'bib', rose – a little unsteadily – to her feet, and surveyed once more her strange surroundings: the long, candlelit table; the log fire (now low) in the great stone hearth; the hanging banners with their dragons and unicorns and sundry mythical beasts.

All was quiet in the hall. The storm had long passed.

Suddenly, with one hand clutching the back of her chair and the other on her belly, Gertrude – with an astonished look on her face – called out to the darkness and whoever (or whatever) had been there: 'I can… feel it. I can feel… *her*. I can feel her kicking!'

We Want Candy

They came at him at the end of the pier, in their great marauding army.

The small of his back was against its rail, his legs against its ironwork.

Behind and below him: the churning sea.

Wind pulled at his purple hair, slapped his grease-painted face.

And still they advanced... over the salted, sun-bleached boards; crowds more of them forming on the sand.

The front ranks now went for him.

Biting.

Or doing their best.

The gums of their toothless jaws closing on his arms and his chest.

He beat them back with his candy canes, his sticks of rock and his toffee apples – flung, as if they were grenades.

In time, they retreated – as they always did.

And he returned to his booth... where he spun pink candy floss, and waited, as the sea sucked at the stanchions, from which oily weed waved, like shrouds, in the gloom.

Near the Knuckle

When the clam shut its shell with a *snap* at her table in the Mayfair restaurant *Fruits de Mer*, Claudia Sharp, although startled by its audacity, resolved, for the moment, to do nothing.

She was determined, above all, *not* to be seen to make a fuss, even though the clam was fixed – and not without inflicting some pain – to (what was nominally) her ring finger.

Her reasons for her feigned insouciance were twofold and interconnected.

For one thing, she was not – as a high-powered executive – in the habit of permitting herself to be troubled by an inconvenience of the kind that might be offered by a mere mollusc, crustacean, or whatever it was that the clam might like to be known as.

Also, she felt foolish, because, despite several discreet initial attempts to shake it off, the clam would not let go. And Claudia Sharp did not like to be made to feel or look foolish – especially in public.

She was a regular at the *Fruits de Mer*, invariably dining solo at the table the staff knew she preferred: prominent and set slightly apart in the restaurant's red velvet cavern, a position that made her seem aloof and superior – like a heron, on a private islet… yet always with an eye out for any acceptable male who might happen to be supping singly. (Not that there were many who in her eyes ever passed muster.)

So it was that, when the waiter approached to enquire if all was well with her meal, Ms Sharp moved quickly – with a napkin – to conceal the clam.

And later, when the same waiter returned to her table with her bill, she hid the hand in question in her understated yet very definitely high-end bag, while producing with the free fingers of her other a platinum card from a private bank.

Content with the smoothness of her public performance, she rose – at a juncture when the room's other diners appeared to her to be occupied – and moved to the exit (doing so, with seemingly languid – yet innately steely – heron-like strides).

Snatching her coat from the cloakroom attendant and using it as cover for the creature with which she had become conjoined, she then hastened into the street and hailed a cab (initially doing so with her clam-caught hand… before downing it quickly and hoisting her other).

At her flat in a 'good' part of London given over to mansion blocks and white-painted townhouses fronting safe, quiet pavements leafy with trees, Claudia attempted to beat off the clam. This she tried by means of a series of downward blows to a marble counter-top in her minimalist 'designer kitchen'.

Failing to free herself of its embrace, she then tried swinging the seizing shell against the white enamel of her roll-top slipper bath.

Again getting nowhere, she then remembered the hammer she kept under her queen-size bed (in case she ever found herself on top of it with 'the wrong kind' of man).

But the hammer also proved ineffective: the shell deflecting her blows as if it were titanium.

If anything, rather than coming loose, the clam seemed to tighten its grip.

Back in her kitchen, her eyes fell on a familiar magnet on her fridge door.

The magnet – in the shape of a laundry basket brimming with a jumble of clothes – advertised the services of the local launderette where, on Sunday mornings, having groomed herself for the task, she was in the habit of washing – as publicly as possible – a choice selection of unused and – so she hoped – eye-catching underwear. Pick-ups at the Lewcock Grove Launderland ('Six-Star Service with Stelios') had in fact been few and far between, despite much dangling and stretching of her knickers and bras; such small attention as there was, principally coming from the proprietor: a middle-aged grandfather and would-be lothario with a permanent five o'clock shadow, whose neck, ears, fingers – and possibly *other* body parts – were seldom less than heavily burdened with jewellery of the kind generally known as bling. 'Here. Let me take those. I can see to those for you. How are you off for detergent?' he would purr, gold fillings flashing, as he closed-in on the open door of Claudia Sharp's part-loaded drum.

The fridge magnet – 'Stay Super Clean With Stelios: Lewcock Grove's No 1' – had long advertised a portfolio of sister 'services' that (not that she had time – as a high-powered executive – to waste studying the affairs of a mere humble launderette) – had long seemed strangely... *diverse*: 'Pest Control... Driving Instruction... English Lessens... Wils & Funerals... Landscape Gardenings... Bureau De Change... Computer Repares... Totally Quolified & Insurred'. A shield of some kind, with dubious-looking acronyms and a Post Office box number, completed the picture.

She had, on one occasion, taken advantage of one of his sidelines ('White Goods – Free Delivery'), having correctly interpreted this 'service' on the eve of a dinner party for which supplies of powder of the Colombian kind were looking worryingly low. To be fair, his little nosebags had gone down well with her guests, albeit that its delivery sparked a distinct ratcheting-up of his familiarity in her subsequent visits with her Sunday smalls.

Now, however, she noticed a 'service' that appeared not previously to have been there. What was more, it was one that – in her circumstances – seemed (almost) tailor-made for her needs.

OYSTER CATCHERS

the magnet in small but clear print – between 'Pet Care' and 'Barbecue Supplies' – now proclaimed.

She dialled the mobile number that the magnet displayed.

'Super Clean Launderette and Inter-Global Enterprise. Lewcock Grove's finest,' came a familiar-sounding voice. 'How may we help you?'

'Stelios?' she began. 'Is that you?'

'Hey Claudia!' he responded. 'How are you?'

'It's Ms Sharp speaking,' she continued, keen to put some distance between them, in spite of her predicament.

'Ah, yes, of course, Miss Sharp, I recognise your voice. My favourite customer. How could I not? How may I help you?'

'Are you at the launderette?'

'Why? Do you have some washing you would like me to handle?'

'No, but I may need your services.'

'Anything for you, Miss Sharp. Anything. You only need to ask the word.'

'Where are you?'

'Today, on this lovely day, I am involved in one of my external services.'

'What does that mean?'

'I am in my ice cream van.'

'Ice cream van?'

'Yeah, it's a new line, Miss Sharp. "Stop me and try one".'

'I think you mean "Stop me and buy one".'

'That's it, Miss Sharp. You got it. You're a clever lady, Miss Sharp. Like I've always said. Expansion, Miss

Sharp; it's got to be done. The only way to build the Great British business. Take Leyland cars, Miss Sharp…'

'Look. Stelios. Never mind all that. I need your help.'

'Of course, Miss Sharp. Of course. Twenty-four hours I am at your service. How may Stelios assist you?'

'Your fridge magnet—'

'Yes? You like it? A clever piece of marketing, no? All of the big firms have them now. Coca-Cola, Mercedes-Benz, Stelios Super Clean.'

'What I want to know—'

'Just one second, Miss Sharp – I have a customer.'

She heard the muffled sounds of a transaction: 'That's four ninety-nine… There you go, my Sonny Jim.'

He came back on the phone. 'Okay Miss Sharp. Sorry about that. Go ahead.'

'Four ninety-nine? For an ice cream? That's a bit steep, isn't it?'

'Man's gotta make a living, Miss Sharp. Besides, this is a good area. It's small beers to these kids. He gave me a five-pound note. Told me to keep the change, cheeky thing.'

'I hope that's *all* you're selling them.'

'Hey, Miss Sharp! Come on! You know me better than that. I'm a family man. I have kids of my own. I would do anything for any of them. They all know that. And so does my wife. You should get to know me better, Miss Sharp. I keep telling you that.'

'Look. Your magnet. On my fridge. It says "Oyster Catchers", among all of the other stuff.'

'It does?'

'Yes.'

'Okay.'

'Well, are you?'

'What?'

'An oyster catcher? Personally, I always thought an oyster catcher was some sort of bird. But let's not get into that now.'

'An oyster catcher? But, of course, Miss Sharp. All my life I have been catching the oysters. Honest to God. Ever since I was a small boy. Always, Miss Sharp.'

'Good. Where are you now?'

He told her the street.

'That's just around the corner from me.'

'A good area, Miss Sharp, like I said.'

'Can you come round to my apartment?'

She gave him the address.

'Of course, Miss Sharp. Two minutes and I'll be there. Fast as Jack Frost.'

She ended the call.

On her finger, the shell had grown heavy. Although she tried to dismiss the idea, she had the strange sense that the shellfish – she hadn't managed to eat the contents at *Fruis de Mer* – was somehow trying to drag her in. More to the point, her finger had – between the joint and her knuckle (the metacarpal… was that the word?) – turned a kind of sea green.

'Bloody thing,' she said to herself… and she wondered if the 'thing' could hear her.

Claudia heard chimes in the street. Through a gap in her blinds, she caught sight of Stelios in his van. Above the windscreen of his jangling chariot, an outsize cornet, stuffed with a 'dripping' dollop of vanilla, lofted itself at the world – like a giant, spuming phallus.

Her buzzer went.

'Stelios speaking.'

She pressed the button to open the building's front door.

Moments afterwards, he was on her landing.

'Miss Sharp? I am here,' she heard him call.

She opened her door, expecting his ebullient worst (while wondering why he hadn't knocked or used the bell).

He stood there in a bright blue T-shirt blazoned with the logo of some – to her – plebeian fitness label, its garish, gut-bulging front laden with several gold-seeming chains that over-hung the squishy twin mounds of his man-boobs. His belly sagged above the elasticated waistband of black nylon tracksuit bottoms whose flares concertinaed scruffily to a pair of moon-white running shoes she knew had not for one second been put to the purpose for which they had allegedly been devised.

Stelios's face wore a large, cheesy grin.

His hands were behind his back… until he brought out two ice cream cones – melting – in his curly-haired and sausage-fingered paws.

'Not say it with flowers, but say it with ice cream. Strawberry Surprise – my personal favourite – *or* Marvellous Mint Chocolate Chip… which fancies your tickle?'

She ignored him.

'You hear my music from my van, Miss Sharp? I played it specially for you. Romantic, no?'

'What? *Jack and Jill*?'

She stepped aside. He sauntered in.

'Wow, Miss Sharp! *Nice* place! Classy! Very classy! And only to be expected of a very classy lady, if I may so to you. Tell me, how many bedrooms? Do I get the tour?'

She came straight to it: 'Oyster catching – is that *really* one of your lines?'

'What's that Miss Sharp?' he said, craning his neck to peer into, first, her kitchen on one side of her entrance hall and then her computer-stacked study on the other.

'Oyster catching. Do you do it?'

'Absolutely, Miss Sharp. Absolutely.'

'Well,' she continued, bringing her left hand out from behind her back, '… take a look at this!'

His eyes switched to the clam that she now wielded in front of him. A scattershot of pink ice cream flew from his mouth.

'Holy Mary, Miss Sharp!' he spluttered. 'That's one big one you got there.'

The clam hung from her like some weird contortion of a baseball glove.

'What is it?' he asked.

'I thought *you* were supposed to be the expert?' she replied.

'It's not an oyster. I can tell you that. Too big. A clam, I think. Maybe even a giant one.'

'Clam? Oyster? What difference does it make? They're all shellfish, aren't they?'

'All shellfish? Yes of course, Miss Sharp. You are quite correct. But, you see, I am oysters and—'

'And what?'

'And my cousin, Spiros, *he* is clams. And I cannot go taking his business, Miss Sharp, Not even for you. My other cousin, Lefteris, he is lobsters. My other cousin, Kostas, he is calamari. It is a family thing. A matter of honour, Miss Sharp. I cannot go interfering with their business. Not even for you.'

'All right! All right! I get the picture,' she said. 'This Spiros of yours – when can he do it?'

'Who?'

'Spiros, the one who you just said was your cousin… the one who does the clams. When can *he* do it? When can he take this *thing* off? It's starting to hurt.'

'Oh soon, Miss Sharp, soon. Maybe next week some time.'

'Next week?! He'll have to do better than that! What does he expect me to do? Walk around London with a shellfish on my finger?'

'Oh no, Miss Sharp. Not a fine lady like you. I will use my influence. We will fast lane you. Twenty-four hours… forty-eight at the most… and we will have that monster off. You leave it to me, and Spiros.'

'Right. We'll say thirty-six hours at the max. This cousin of yours can get hold of me here. And I'm relying on the discretion of the pair of you.'

'Absolutely. No one will get to know, Miss Sharp. As well as being a very… attractive lady, if I may say so, Miss Sharp, you are a very important lady. A thing like this can be embarrassing for a high-powered lady like you. But don't you worry, Miss Sharp. You leave those newspaper bastards to me. They won't hear a word. Spiros shall see to it.'

He tramped from her apartment, rivulets of melted ice cream streaking his tracksuit bottoms, a trail of pink blotches on the parquet floor of her hall.

She noted now that – beyond the clamp of the clam – the blue-green of that part of her finger which was visible was deepening in colour – like seawater far from the shore… where the ocean-floor falls away to an abyss.

And there was another thing. Unless she was mistaken – with Stelios and what she suspected had been his large and hastily-applied dose of aftershave now gone – there existed in her hallway and indeed in the rest of her apartment a persistent and unpleasant odour.

The clam – and, with it, her finger – had started to smell.

That night, cocooning herself in her bedclothes, Claudia dreamt that she had dreamt the whole affair.

The weird nature of her nightmare caused her to wake.

She sat up and, pressing her hand down on her pillow, saw – to her horror – that the clam was indeed there – still very much attached. She went from her bedroom to the bathroom. In its tiled, surgical whiteness, she struggled once more to open the shell. She tried to force a nail file between the locked lids and – when that failed – the blades of a scissors. The shell was shut tight as anything she could imagine: the hatch of a nuclear submarine, the door of the safe that housed the Crown Jewels. Even worse, her efforts to free herself seemed only to induce the clam to clamp hold of her more firmly. A small slick of blood showed itself on the sharp edges where the shell seized her. Two crimson droplets crawled in fine streams to the plughole of the washbasin into which she now flung the file and the scissors. She put out the light, deciding she would cope better with the clam if she could not see it. She reasoned that if it were kept in the dark, she might also keep herself in the dark. She returned to her bed and lay there, without sleeping, till dawn.

Shortly before the time of her usual arrival at her office, Claudia telephoned her secretary to tell him she would not be in that day and that she would be working from home.

Later, she wrote a couple of brief emails one-handed and participated in a few Skype conversations and Zoom conferences while keeping her 'clam hand' very firmly *off*-camera.

For the most part, her attention was on her smartphone and the street outside… for either a caller or a figure who might be Stelios' cousin, Spiros – the family member who was said to be the clam-handler of their clan.

In the afternoon, she saw an elderly-looking mini-cab (a tatty sign on its roof appeared to be lacking the *i* of TAXI) pull up at the kerb outside her building. A figure – the driver, it seemed – got out. One of the street's trees, together with a corner of the railings that stood either side of the steps that rose from the pavement, blocked her view, but, within a moment, she heard the buzz of her intercom.

'Yes?' she answered.

'Spiros speaking. C.A.I., Clams Away International.'

'Thank God,' she said, pressing the button that unlocked the building's front door. 'Come up.'

When she drew open her apartment door, her eyes fell on a middle-aged man who bore a close resemblance to his cousin Stelios, save that his nylon tracksuit bottoms were royal blue. His uncanny likeness to his relative in almost all other respects, she dismissed (after a moment's thought) as not completely unnatural in what was, by the sound of it, a close-knit family. More to the point, he came armed with an impressive array of equipment – pliers, leads and screwdrivers – some of which projected from the pockets of his sagging tracksuit bottoms, other of which was strung around his shoulders and neck.

Claudia showed him the clam.

'Sheesh! That's one big one you've got there, lady!' he said.

'Can you do anything with it? You *must* be able to. It's driving me mad.'

He stared at it (jaw dropped). 'I've seen some clams in my time, but this is one *super*-sized son-of-a-bitch – excuse my language.' He paused, then continued: 'But for you, lady, I will give it my best shot. Please, take a seat.'

As she steadied her hand on the smoked-glass top of her dining table, he set about the clam with a variety of instruments. Most of these – there were pliers with bright-red plastic handles and screwdrivers with yellow and green transparent tops – looked as if they'd come from a car-repairs toolkit; there were even spanners. But she decided to say nothing – as long as the clam came off.

At first, he approached the clam with an air of nervousness, as if fearful it might open and shut its shell on him. He stabbed at it while keeping his distance – in the manner of a sword-fencer, lunging with a foil. At the same time, he cursed the clam, under his breath. While doing this, he questioned Claudia. 'How did you come by this monster? Such a devil must have been lurking somewhere very nasty and deep.'

In time, as his patience ebbed and his valour (or carelessness) grew, he began to gouge and smash at the shell… which held fast, even so, throughout.

Eventually, he said, 'Don't you worry, lady – I've got something that will fix this… believe me', and he retreated for a moment to the corridor.

From there, he wheeled-in a box-like device on the base of a small sack truck. To this – removing it from his neck, where it hung like the coiled rope of a lasso – he attached a red lead while clamping the crocodile jaws of its other end onto the shell of the clam.

Shooting a glance at the sack truck, Claudia saw that the bright-orange box bore the wording, HIGH VOLTAGE – HAZARDOUS.

'Are you sure this is safe?' she asked, as he pulled at a lever. 'After all, a clam is a water-dwelling creature, isn't it? And I'm not sure that electricity and water really—'

'Don't worry,' he replied, donning a mask that she noticed wasn't of the kind that a welder might have worn but one that was rubbery and glassy and of the scuba-diving sort. 'All you will feel is…' his words now had a nasal, *snorkelly* tone, 'a small… shock.'

When Claudia came to her senses amid the smoke that surrounded her, her hair was still standing on its ends. Her eyes stung and her mouth seemed to have slipped to one side, like a listing ship – her lips, teeth and gums taking several moments to right themselves.

Somewhere – in the background – she heard coughing.

'Well?' she asked eventually. 'Is it—'

'Yes, it's still there… son-*and*-daughter-of-a-bitch,' Spiros spluttered.

'This is ridiculous! How can it be? A mere clam!'

'This is no ordinary clam, Miss Sharp. This is the Rock of Gibraltar, the Big Foot, the Great White, the Titanic… of clams.'

'What the hell does that mean? This is preposterous! It's just a bloody clam – surely? Can't *someone* free me?'

'This is a job for only one man.'

'Who, for God's Sake?'

'My cousin, Lefteris.'

'But I thought he was lobsters.'

'He is, Miss Sharp. But Lefteris can crack anything, believe me. I have seen him squeeze open the claws of the toughest, ugliest old lobsters you could possibly imagine. He is a genius. To blow open the safe of the Bank of England would be nothing for him.'

'When can he get here?'

'Soon.'

'How soon?'

'Sometime next month.'

'Next *month*?!'

'Lobsters are a popular thing these days, Miss Sharp. He has more cases than he can handle. Famous people – actors, actresses. Distinguished people – archbishops, archdukes… Arch Marbles. Lobsters hanging on to all parts of their anatomies – noses, ears – and elsewhere – believe me. Lefteris is a man in-demand. Everybody wants a piece of his action.'

'Well maybe he should take on more staff.'

'Oh no, no, Miss Sharp. You cannot have 'staff' for such a special skill as his. You need to have the hands – the God-given, *healing* hands of Lefteris.'

'Well get his hands here, and by the end of this week. Tell him I'll pay twice what he's getting from anyone else. This nonsense has *got* to stop!'

That night, in the bright light of the bathroom, Claudia studied that part of her finger which was visible beyond the grip of the clam.

She saw that it was no longer blue-green, but black.

Worse still, she had the awful feeling that, within the locked and merciless shell, something was… nibbling.

Two days later, an orange motor-van with a shutter on one side and the word 'Snacks' pulled into her street.

The buzzer sounded for the building's front door.

'Lefteris speaking.'

Claudia pressed her button to let him into the block.

Some moments later, the smell of fried food made itself felt at her door.

She opened it to find a figure uncannily similar to both Stelios and Spiros, except that this time the caller was wearing orange tracksuit bottoms.

'I'm told you're the one that I want,' she said.

'I couldn't have put it better myself, Miss Sharp,' he replied.

'Sit back and relax,' he said, dumping his gear. 'You have nothing to fear. Lefteris is here.'

As he set to work with a large spatula, Claudia wondered when his famous 'healing hands' would figure in his approach (which seemed as agricultural as that of Spiros who'd gone before).

When his labours with the spatula came to nothing, he looked in a holdall and drew out a stick of dynamite.

'I want you to sit *under* the table with your hand on the top,' he said.

'Tell me you're not serious,' said Claudia.

'It is only a small charge and perfectly safe, Miss Sharp, believe me – a traditional secret of all fishermen going back in time.'

'Look, I'm really not sure that—'

'Three… two… one.'

A shower of ceiling plaster fell to the floor through a mushroom cloud of dust and smoke.

A fire alarm started to sound.

'Well?' she gasped.

Lefteris rubbed his eyes. 'I don't believe it!' he spluttered. 'The bloody thing is still there.'

'How can it be?' she screamed. 'I mean, you used dynamite. What kind of hellish shellfish is this? I don't think I can take any more. What have I done to deserve this? So I've eaten a few scallops in my time. Munched the odd mussel. Cooked the odd cockle. Who hasn't?

Is it a crime? Next people will be telling me the damn things have feelings… hearts… minds. This is like some sort of awful, low-budget schlock movie – *The Seafood Strikes Back* – full of bimbos with beehives.'

'Beehives?'

'Who will rid me of this horrible clam?'

Tears streaked her dusty cheeks. She began to sob.

'Hey now, Miss Sharp,' said Lefteris, softly. 'Please… don't cry. I know who you *really* need.'

'Not another of your cousins. I don't think I could bear it.'

'Trust me, Miss Sharp. I know the one you really need. His ways are different.'

'And I thought *you* were the one who was supposed to have the healing hands.'

'He never fails, Miss Sharp.'

'When will he come? Next week? Next month? My finger has turned black. Look at it!' She shook the clam. 'This *thing* is eating me alive!!'

'I know, Miss Sharp. I know. I did not like to say, but I fear you have the gang green. But try not to worry. He will be here tomorrow. I give you my word.'

'And how shall I know him? This *special* one… in his shining armour. What will *he* be driving? A milk float? A Post Office van?'

'You will know him when he is here, Miss Sharp. There is no one else like him. He will separate you – once and for all. Believe me.'

It was dusk the following day, and a quietness had fallen over her street, when the buzzer sounded on Claudia Sharp's intercom. She had looked out on the road and pavement from her lounge window all afternoon, fearful that, if in her bedroom or kitchen, she might miss the sound or sight of the caller. The noise from the buzzer – she had long complained to the leasing company about its awful 'grate' – surprised her. For though she was sure that her eyes had been fixed firmly on the street she had seen no evidence of any vehicle or figure. All she noticed now was the momentary swirl, near the steps to her block, of a scattering of fallen leaves.

When she said 'Yes?' into the intercom, her question went unanswered. Even so, she pressed the button to unlock the building's front door, and let the caller in.

Similarly, no one announced themselves at her apartment door. Claudia simply sensed 'a presence'. And she opened it.

Her caller's looks, age and dress weren't matters that her mind took in (the events of the previous days by now very possibly taking their toll on her powers of rationality).

All that she really knew was that the visitor was calm, business-like and to the point (reminiscent, in fact, of a private doctor she had once consulted).

'I don't mind losing it,' she said now, of her finger. 'Do what's required.'

It's some while since that quiet evening when those fallen leaves of the plane trees danced in the dusk beyond the window of Claudia Sharp's flat. She remains a patron of both the Lewcock Grove Launderland and the *Fruits de Mer* restaurant in Mayfair's Longkettle Lane. Her ritual Sunday attendance at the washeteria – unworn underwear in hand – is, however, conducted nowadays in a manner that is much less assured. The other customers, busy with their loads, seem to see her – in a way that she is conscious of – as a spinster, or widow, of the elderly type: attending her church devotedly for the reason of having nowhere else to go. Stelios, the proprietor, has little time for her now – as if *she* were soiled goods – even though, on occasion, she wouldn't mind a hand. At times, she seems to detect on his face a satisfied disdain – the sneer of one for whom a score has been settled.

Her money – for now – is still good at the *Fruits de Mer*, where she continues to be shown to 'her' table in the restaurant's red velvet cavern.

(Perhaps surprisingly) she continues to order shellfish but is never now served anything that requires presentation in its shell – a rule that extends even to the most innocent eggs of the smallest of fowl.

The manager and maître d' are always all smiles when they seat her, ensuring that she is waited on by one of their most senior staff.

They are, however, nervous of some of her habits – especially when it comes to the likes of oyster soup, or clam chowder – for which, perhaps in a spirit of defiance, she has acquired a particular taste.

At such times, their eyes dart around the dining room and their ears strain anxiously for the whispers of other customers, as – before consuming a spoonful – Claudia Sharp investigates the broth that has been placed before her.

It is her manner to paddle through it (as a tribesman or woman might in a pirogue on a crocodiled reach of the Amazon), before drying in a napkin and screwing – audibly – back into its socket, her slightly warm – and seafood-scented – left hand.

One Lump or Two?

Never mind the history of military hostilities between the two countries, not to mention controversy on the football field, Helmut Gessler had always been a committed Anglophile and a staunch admirer of all things English. His attitude had been formed during a short stay in London in his youth while a student. He had fallen in love with the city, its sights, its parks, its buses, even the pigeons in Trafalgar Square. His subsequent 'absence' – a long career as a dentist in a small provincial town in Saxony – had only made his heart grow fonder towards England. On hearing the country's anthem, he would feel the need to rise respectfully to his feet; if ever England's sovereign happened to figure in a conversation to which Gessler was party, he would speak, reverentially, of 'Her Majesty' (in a somewhat intimate tone, as if he had met her); such conflicts as there had been between England and Germany, he would characterise as the occasional inevitable fallings-out that were prone to happen in any family, pointing out that Kaiser Wilhelm had been *Her Majesty* Queen Victoria's grandson and that England was, in large part, of course, the land of the Saxon.

As Gessler's retirement from attending to the teeth of his townspeople neared, he promised his wife Inge – who had long been tolerant of (if not perhaps a little amused by) her husband's patriotism towards England, which included lusty singing of 'Rule Britannia' during broadcasts via satellite of 'The Last Night of the Proms' – that he would take her for a *proper* holiday to the country that had for so long, at a distance, entranced him.

Towards the end of their stay, which Gessler pronounced in postcards home to his friends and neighbours had been a pleasant and successful one (pointing out, with a small arrow of ink, that Great Britain was the only country in the world which did not feel the need to name itself on its postage stamps: the presence of the head of Her Majesty was more than enough), Gessler told his wife that there was one last, and very English, rite that remained to them: the cream tea.

So it was that Inge Gessler found herself standing on the pavement of the High Street in the small market town of Frampton Fenwick as her husband peered through the window of Ye Olde Tea Shoppe and pushed open the door. *'Ja, das its der ort,'* ('Yes, this is the place') he said to her over his shoulder after studying the interior. And he stood aside in order that she might step in.

Inge Gessler, it might be fairly said, wasn't quite as convinced as her husband about the tearoom, noting the absence of any other customers. But, on this matter of the cream tea, to which she knew he attached a high level of seriousness, she was content to humour him and defer to his choice.

Gessler was evidently more than satisfied. *'Ja, ja, ja,'* ('Yes, yes, yes') he said to himself quietly as he noted the tick – from one corner of the room – of a longcase clock, the old black beams in the low, curved ceiling, the creak of the veneered boards beneath their feet, and the laced edging of the white, cotton tablecloths.

He drew out a chair for his wife and then, smiling, seated himself at their table for two.

Although his mind was in no doubt as to what would be their choice, Gessler lifted a menu book from its place beside salt and pepper cellars of an old style that had the look of silver plate. He began to read through it, pleasurably. Poached Egg on Toast, Cheese on Toast, Shepherd's Pie, Cottage Pie, Steak and Kidney Pudding, Toad-in-the-Hole, Jam Roly-Poly and Rice Pudding... Yes, all of the English classics were there. Gessler closed the book and put it back, happily.

Presently, a waitress – summoned, the Gesslers presumed, by the short jangle of the bell above the door and the sound of them seating themselves – emerged from a hallway in a wood-panelled wall, at an angle from their table.

Her evident age – she was a lady of clearly very senior years – took the couple somewhat by surprise, and it seemed to take her several minutes to reach them, her progress being marked by the ticking of the longcase clock (which somehow grew louder for the duration). Every so often, the old lady – who wore a waitress's uniform of the traditional kind: in black and white, with a lacy headpiece – seemed to pause, look up at them, and smile, as she advanced. Far from being perturbed, the Gesslers were endeared, especially Helmut, who took the woman's age and somewhat stout physique, as confirmation of the correctness of his choice.

'Lovely day for it,' the woman announced, upon her final arrival at their table.

'It is indeed a lovely day,' Helmut Gessler replied keenly (somewhat to the bafflement of his wife, who could not help but bring to mind a morning of mostly rain showers and who noticed, even now, a darkening of the sky outside the tea shop's window).

'What can I get you?' asked the woman, taking out a small pad and pen.

'Ah, now on that our minds are already made up,' declared Gessler. 'We will have two of your famous English cream teas.'

'Very good, sir,' said the woman, writing on her pad. 'So that will be two rounds of cucumber sandwiches and some fancies from the stand. Right, well that won't take us long. I shall be back with you shortly.' And, with that, the woman began her long retreat to the mouth of the hallway.

Gessler was unsettled that she might not have the couple's order quite right. He felt like calling after her…

'Ah, Miss! One moment, if you please!'… but he decided against it, taking the view that he had ordered quite clearly and that the waitress's response had probably been nothing more than confirmation of what he had said, albeit through use of another description or name.

He smiled at his wife and put his palm over her hand on the white cloth of the table.

Before long, the couple – still alone in the tearoom – became aware of the waitress, returning. The old woman's progress from the hallway was heralded by a squeaking sound that was both intermittent and precise. When the Gesslers turned from their table, they saw her heading in their direction behind a small trolley, which she was pushing towards them, with her hands on a bar, in something of the manner (thought Helmut Gessler) of a traditional English nanny with a pram – the squeak clearly coming from one of its wheels. This particular noise was soon joined by the high-pitched and near enough constant sound caused by the vibration of the trolley's chinaware and cutlery arising from its passage over the uneven old boards of the floor. Inge Gessler bit her lip to stop herself from laughing. Her husband saw this and was uneasy. While he could appreciate the comedic quality of the scene, he had also set great store by the 'event' of the cream tea; it would not be going too far to say that, in his eyes, the meal was to be one of the highlights of his visit to England, possibly *the* highlight.

Eventually, the old woman reached the Gesslers.

Smiling, she transferred a teapot from her trolley to their table.

To Helmut Gessler's surprise, she then took from the trolley and placed between the couple a plate containing what looked like several rounds of cucumber sandwiches. Having done so, she said to them, 'There you are, sir… madam. The fancies of the cake stand are yours to choose from. Do help yourselves. And now I shall leave you to enjoy your tea.'

The waitress began her slow creep away.

Helmut Gessler was confused. This was not what he had ordered. Where were the scones? Where was the butter? Where was the jam? And where was the cream? He wondered what to do. Should he call her back? He turned in his seat to see that – in her plodding way – she was already halfway across the room. Perhaps *he* was wrong? Maybe these sandwiches and the cake stand represented merely the first course? After all, he had given his order quite clearly. There had been no queries on the part of the waitress.

His wife could see that he was perplexed. He recognised this by the slight anxiety that showed on her face. She smiled, in an attempt to put him at his ease. But he caught sight of her worry lines, and this only served to increase his concern.

To Gessler, the ticking of the longcase clock suddenly seemed loud, intrusive, irritating.

Not unlike a novice dental practitioner anxious about the staying power of a newly-fitted bridge or crown, he had the sense that his project of the cream tea was failing... falling apart. He wanted to stop the clock from ticking, to rise from his seat and re-set its hands... and begin everything all over again. His wife knew this, he knew. She touched his hand on the tablecloth.

'*Soll ich gießen?*' ('Shall I pour?') she asked.

'*Ja, bitte,*' ('Yes, please,') he answered her, consoling himself with the thought that maybe the cream tea would yet come.

Gessler found the cucumber sandwiches unsatisfactory. Although cut neatly into triangles, the bread – he judged – was stale: its texture dry and the corners of the sandwiches 'curling'. He felt foolish, embarrassed that he had made such a big thing of this tea, guilty about what he was subjecting his wife to. His behaviour had been ridiculous, like that of a schoolboy. Looking around, he saw that, outside the tea shop, the sky – not unlike his mood – had blackened (as if there would soon be a storm).

'Kuchen?' ('Cake?') Gessler asked his wife, as he leant forward and lifted the stand of 'fancies' from the trolley towards her.

She took a small fruit tartlet of some kind. *'Danke'* ('Thanks').

Unimpressed with what was on display on the stand's tiers – several of the 'fancies' appearing to be shop-bought and mass-manufactured – he found himself taking a slice of Battenberg, which, although not a German cake in substance, had (as he well knew from his Anglophilia) been first baked to celebrate the marriage of Prince Louis of Battenberg to Princess Victoria, Her Majesty Queen Victoria's granddaughter. In Gessler's eyes, therefore, it was not a million miles from being the tea-time equivalent of being served bratwurst at breakfast rather than a British Cumberland banger.

How cruelly ironic, Gessler thought to himself, suppressing a shudder.

Noticing (to his shame) that his wife was barely picking at her tartlet, he bit, miserably, into the Battenberg, whose bright pink and yellow colours only added to his sense of mockery.

To Gessler, this was one of the most ghastly things he had ever experienced. Biting into the Battenberg was like – were he ever to attempt such an insane thing – biting into the pumice stone he and Inge kept in their bathroom for purging their feet of dead skin.

Never had he tried to ingest anything quite as terrible.

And there was worse, because, as he attempted to remove his jaws from the awful (stony yet also somehow adhesive) slice, he felt one of his teeth – his right central incisor – crack and give way.

'Mein Gott!' ('My God!') he called out, removing the Battenberg from his mouth and putting it down on his plate. *'Mein zahn!'* ('My tooth!').

He ran his right forefinger across his front teeth and felt the severed edge of the depleted incisor. Looking down at the Battenberg, he saw his tooth's missing portion – embedded in its lurid marzipan coating.

Gessler stared for several minutes at his sheared tooth, sunk in the bright yellow rind of the Battenberg. His wife was equally agog (if not more so) given her husband's lifelong profession and the store she knew he set by his teeth, which he had always described to her as a living advertisement for his practice.

Save for the ticking of the longcase clock, the tearoom had the silence of an examination hall at a university.

Eventually, Gessler called out to the waitress. 'Waitress! Madam! Come quicky! If you please!'

The elderly woman came forth at her same previous, tortoise-like pace. Angry now, Gessler had no patience for the slowness caused by her senior years.

'There has been a serious incident at our table,' he said, when she eventually arrived. 'I know it is the English way not to cause a "scene", but I feel compelled to ask. How fresh is this cake?' He pointed at the Battenberg.

'Well, I really don't know,' said the waitress. 'But if you'll wait – just for one moment – I'll go to the kitchen and ask.' And off she went, at her crawl speed, back to the hallway.

After several minutes – in which irritation mounted, layer upon layer, in Gessler's normally calm and unemotional mind – an elderly woman in an apron advanced towards the Gesslers, from the hallway in the wood-panelled wall.

So close was her resemblance to the waitress in looks that Gessler felt the woman might indeed be the latter in a change of clothes. This notion was only scotched when the waitress, at her usual glacial rate, came into sight on the other's shoulder.

'May I help you?' the woman from the kitchen asked.

'This… *cake*,' said Gessler, with disgust. 'When was it baked?' (Having posed the question, he felt – for a queer and queasy moment – that the woman might hazard as an answer a year from the Edwardian era… only for him to have to correct her with the date 1884, thereby displaying his superior knowledge of British history, as if he were anchoring some grotesque television quiz of the downmarket kind that he had occasionally stumbled upon when tuning-in his set at home.)

'Well now. Um… ah… yes. Isn't *that* a question. D'you know, I don't think I can…' the woman responded.

'I'm afraid that that is not good enough,' said Gessler. 'Damage has been done here. Severe damage, as you can see.' He gestured at his tooth, lodged in the Battenberg. 'I want to see the manager.'

The two old women – surprise writ large on their wrinkled faces – withdrew in a shuffle.

In their absence, Gessler suddenly found himself struck by the shabby, tawdry nature of the place. He seemed to notice things he had not previously seen (or had overlooked): the grime on the necks of the sauce bottles on their table; the grains of sugar – he and his wife were not consumers – that hadn't been swept from the cloth; the tuppenny-ha'penny 'horse brasses' tacked to various posts that had in reality probably been no such thing; the cheap pictures on the walls – clichéd reproductions of Constable's *Hay Wain* and Gainsborough's *Blue Boy*… in frames that looked to be plastic or fibreglass; the amateurish, typewritten nature of the menu, badly doctored with Biro, all under a plastic cover that had turned yellow-green. An odour of cooking fat that had previously evaded Gessler's nostrils hung heavy in the air. Gessler was appalled.

A third woman, in a tweed suit and pearls but otherwise the spitting image of the others, now journeyed to the Gesslers' table, with the cook and the waitress in tow.

'Madam,' Gessler began, without waiting for her to speak, 'you are looking at a profoundly *un*satisfied customer.'

The woman raised her eyebrows (which served only to madden Gessler the more).

'We have entered your premises in good faith in the expectation of a pleasing English cream tea. Instead of which, my wife and I have suffered one calamity after another.'

'Calamity?' queried the tweed-clad woman.

'We did not even receive our correct order. I specifically ordered two cream teas and instead we have received... *this*' – Gessler flung out an arm – '... culminating in serious personal injury.'

'Injury?' the woman asked.

With wordless fury, Gessler pointed first to his mouth while raising his upper lip and then to his tooth, half-buried in the Battenberg.

'But if you didn't order it, *why* did you eat it?' asked the woman.

'Because—' Gessler began.

Sheer exasperation prohibited him from completing his sentence.

The waitress withdrew her pad. 'I'm sorry, sir' she started.

Oh, thank goodness, thought Gessler, *a sliver of sanity at last*.

'... but I have your order here, written down, quite clearly. Cucumber sandwiches and fancies from the stand.'

'That is *not* what I ordered!' Gessler – reddening, wondering how his dream cream tea could have been become a nightmare like this – shouted in response.

'I'm sorry, sir,' but I shall have to ask you to lower your voice,' said the woman in the tweeds.

'That is *not* what I ordered,' Gessler, in a quieter – but firm – voice repeated. 'Ladies,' he continued after a moment, 'you are letting the home country down. This cannot be condoned and it cannot go unremarked.'

'Unremarked, sir? What do you mean?' asked the manageress.

'What I say. I have lost a tooth in a perfectly hideous cake in a totally monstrous tea. The appropriate authorities will have to be informed.'

'Informed, sir?' said the manageress.

'Come Inge,' said Gessler. 'We are leaving.'

'Oh, but no one's ever had a bad word for our fancies!' said the waitress – with visible alarm.

'No, never!' echoed the cook.

'Well, there is a first time for everything,' said Gessler, wrapping the Battenberg in a serviette and placing it in the breast pocket of his jacket. 'For the good name of England, this cannot be allowed to go on.'

He rose from his seat. Yet, as he did so, he suddenly felt a strange unsteadiness, a wooziness, a weakness in his limbs. It was like that feeling of 'going under' that he remembered from when he'd been subjected to gas in a procedure to remove his wisdom teeth as a very young man.

He sat back down. His vision was blurred. The table in front of him seemed to lift and drift. His eyes fell on the teapot, which – in the mysterious, swirling murk – seemed to throb, as if – like some Aladdin's lamp – it held the answer to all secrets.

What on earth had been in the tea that his wife had poured? he wondered. He remembered its unusually bitter taste. Looking across the table, he saw that – unless he was mistaken – Inge was asleep: her chin on her chest.

Puzzlingly, to Gessler, the three sisters – if that was what they were – seemed to have multiplied. There were eight or nine of them now – all circling the table, in a weird sort of wheel.

What was more, in their hands, they all appeared to have an implement from the kitchen: a knife, a rolling pin, a meat mallet, a cleaver, skewers.

'No, we've never had a bad word said against us,' came the voice of the manageress.

Gessler seemed to see that, outside the tea shop, the street and sky were black.

The sign in the glass panel of the front door was being turned from 'Open' to 'Closed'. A blind was being drawn down.

'*Never… never… never,*' the elderly women said as they rotated around the table.

The last words he heard were: 'One lump or two?'

Mr Yang and the Giant Beansprout

Although members of the community in the district of the city that for generations had been called Chinatown were known for the good manners they showed one another, the success of Zĭháo Yang's restaurant – *The Golden Caterpillar* – created friction.

One day these feelings boiled over: Zĭháo Yang's neighbours, led by certain ringleaders, laid siege to his door.

The ringleaders wanted to know why and how his restaurant could be so successful when Zĭháo Yang never seemed to buy any produce.

The situation made no sense, they said. When the lorries of wholesalers came to the district, his order was always so small that it was barely worth the delivery. And yet he and his cook had a menu of three hundred dishes, which was there for all to see – with numbers and colour photographs – in *The Golden Caterpillar's* front window.

What was more, said these neighbours, they had counted the people patronising his restaurant – both as sit-down diners and as takeaway customers – and Zĭháo Yang had more than any other establishment in Chinatown.

'Your house has a dark secret,' said the ringleaders. 'You must tell us what it is, Zĭháo Yang.'

But Zĭháo Yang hotly denied their claims and accusations, and, after a fierce shouting match on his step, the ringleaders and those neighbours who had stood behind them moved away.

That night, the giant beansprout that Zĭháo Yang grew in the attic of *The Golden Caterpillar* snaked its way through the roof spaces of his neighbours and strangled the ringleaders as they slept in their beds.

After this, there were no more protests about what did or did not go on at the restaurant of Zǐháo Yang.

The Gong

Colin Crisp kept to his side of their bed.

'Ridiculous!' That's what she'd called him, when he'd had it out with her earlier, in the lounge, after the end of that night's episode of *Inspector Sage*. 'You're being ridiculous!'

No explanation… no justification. Only that: her claim, her *dismissal*, made in a sort of snort-cum-splutter.

Well, *he* didn't think that he was. The evidence surely was stacking up.

First, the cigarettes. How long had it been since he'd packed-in smoking? Fifteen… sixteen years? Soon as she hears him getting off to the chemist – wanting some lozenges for his throat, feeling rather 'chesty' – what's he find waiting on his armchair when he gets back? Sixty fags! And not low tar either. Bought, she reckoned, from some scally who'd been flogging duty-frees door-to-door.

As if!

And then there'd been the ale. 'Mr Crisp, you're going to *have* to cut back on your units. I'm serious,' the doc had said, during the check-up for his chest. And what's he find on returning home to Dingleside Drive? A garage bloody full of the stuff! Cider, rum, vodka, gin… rocket fuel of all sorts – booze that, as a draught bitter man, he'd never in his life touched.

There'd been 'a deal on' at the supermarket – that's what she'd claimed when he'd quizzed her.

And now the cheese… 'Exhibit C', thought Crisp – their fridge ruddy well groaning with it – just at the time that he'd been told to lay off almost everything… the lemon-sucking nurse at the surgery serving him with a highly grim-looking 'diet plan'.

Well, if it existed in the 'world of cheese', it was *there*, now, in the fridge, in slices, rinds, tubs and tubes… waiting, with cold, *murderous* intent.

'Death by cheese. That's what we're dealing with here, sergeant,' Crisp imagined D.I. Doug Sage telling his sidekick, D.S. Kareena Singh. 'The question is: by fair means… or foul?'

Crisp pictured scenes-of-crime tape going up around 9 Dingleside. Could *anything* be more obvious?

And yet – he thought – didn't that seem a *bit* of a stretch, just a little over-the-top, faintly 'ridiculous', it might be said… even for *Inspector Sage*?

He finally fell asleep, the word 'ham-and-cheese-icide' spinning to a stop in his head.

'Colin! Your breakfast's ready!!'

Her voice came up the stairs and in from the landing… to the tangle of bedsheets where Crisp lay.

'I said, "I've *cooked* your breakfast"!' she called again.

'Cooked'? Crisp thought, coming to his senses. Since when had she ever *cooked* anything at that hour? Normally she'd still be snoring, hogging the duvet, drowning-out the dawn chorus (such as it was in Dingleside Drive).

Besides, what *he* needed was fruit, vegetables, wholegrains (whatever *they* were), fibre – that's what the nurse had ordered. Not death-on-a-platter in the form of smoky bacon, battery eggs and black pudding, all doing the backstroke in some bubbling-hot lake of lard.

Crisp put on his dressing gown… tied the towelling belt, warily.

As he made his way downstairs, his nose detected no aromas of fat, his ears no whirring of the extractor fan, no hissing or spitting from the stove.

Maybe he was wrong, after all? Maybe he was in for a surprise? Maybe what he was about to receive was something healthy for which he would be thankful:

grapefruit; porridge oats; a plain piece of fish; brown bread, toasted, unbuttered and with the crusts cut off.

In the kitchen, he didn't know for sure what hit him. But when the lights went out for Colin Crisp the sound that he seemed to hear was the gong of a very heavy frying pan.

The Ongleby Arms

Rufus consulted his O.S. map. Cassandra admired the view. It was beautiful, up there, on the hillside above the tarn. But after a morning's hard walking they were hungry and in need of a place to rest.

Wind ruffled and tugged at the map. Rufus managed to keep it still long enough to locate the two black letters he was looking for: **PH**.

'If I'm right,' he said, 'it should be over this brow and around the corner, more or less.' He looked at Cassie and smiled, finding her rather fetching in her bobble-hat, wind lifting the ends of her hair that hung loose below it.

'Come on,' said Rufus, and they continued through the bracken to the brow.

The squat shape of the Ongleby Arms came into sight. It was at the side of an upland lane on which there was a sheep grid. Rufus found its 'look' – the way that it 'fitted-in' with the landscape – pleasing.

Outside its front porch, he and Cassie stamped their feet to free their boots of any sheep droppings.

Pressing down on two old, iron thumb latches, he opened the porch door and then the one to the pub proper.

To say that he was horrified by the scene that greeted him might perhaps be going *too* far. He was, however, distinctly disappointed, unsettled, even disturbed.

He'd been expecting – in a location as out of the way as this and, moreover, in an English national park – a gloomy saloon, occupied by taciturn hill-farmers; a place with a general atmosphere of fustiness; motes of dust, perhaps, caught in shafts of sunlight through the panes of small windows; the smell of woodsmoke from an open log fire; such scraps of conversation as there might have been ending entirely at that moment of his entrance with Cassie.

To his great surprise, he found himself in a brightly-lit lounge which, although empty of customers, somehow contrived a sense of activity thanks to the likes of a fruit machine glowing against a wall, an open fire that – from the constant pattern of its flames – Rufus quickly deduced to be gas, together with piped music of the 'easy listening' orchestral variety (whose strains competed with the bleeps and burbles of the fruit machine), and an array of furnishings and fittings that included highly-polished horse brasses, coach lamps and a very new-looking copper bed warmer, mounted in pride of place above the bar.

From behind it, a large, overweight, middle-aged man, with close-cropped hair, thrust a tattooed arm from the noisily checked short-sleeved shirt which was straining to contain him.

'Ken Smith,' he said, shaking – with a meaty paw – first Cassie's then Rufus's hand, '… ex-twenty-five years Queen's Own Southerners, Warrant Officer Class One for ten of them; these days landlord of the Ongleby Arms. Welcome. What can I get you?'

'We were hoping for some food,' said Rufus.

'Well,' said Smith, 'you can do more than "hope" because we're here to serve – that's my motto. Always has been, always will be. Anyone will tell you that about Ken Smith. You've come to the right place.'

He took hold of, from beside a wooden post in the bar, two menu books, which were large with black covers and had cords with tassels.

'We were just after something simple, really,' said Cassie.

'Oh, you'll find it all in there. Don't you worry about that. The wife – she's in charge of the kitchen. That's her domain, of course. Me? I'm front of house, so to speak. Her English may not be so sharp, but she's a fantastic cook. Best thing we ever did was partner up.'

Somewhat to Rufus and Cassie's surprise the menu seemed entirely given over to Thai cuisine. At home, in North London, they were enthusiastic supporters of restaurants of all kinds. But they hadn't been expecting such fare 1,500ft above sea level at a pub in an English national park.

'Bet you weren't planning on *that*, were you?' said their host. 'Well, this is a local pub and the locals love it. What they say goes, in my book. They can't get enough of the missus's chicken satay and green curry. We're packed out here, five nights a week. But – I grant – Thai's not everyone's cup of tea. You know how conservative some folk can be. So, if you turn to the back, you'll see we do the full range of English classics. Like I said, we're here to serve.'

Rufus and Cassie, who, heading up from the tarn, had been hoping for a simple home-made hotpot, or possibly a ploughman's, turned to the backs of their menus.

Again, the dishes listed were not quite what they were looking for. A slanted, curlicued font proclaimed: 'Deep-fried scampi, garden peas and chips... plaice in breadcrumbs served with a salad garnish and chips... cottage pie, diced vegetables and chips... chicken breast with cheese-drizzled bacon and chips...'

'Do you have soup?' asked Cassie.

'Of course,' said Smith.

'And what is the soup today, please?'

'Tomato,' he answered instantly, as if there were ever any other.

After a moment, she said: 'I'll have the soup, please.'

Rufus followed her: 'Yes, I think I'll have the soup, too.'

'Right then,' said Smith, making a note on a pad. 'So that's two soups for starters. And... for your mains?'

'Oh, I think I'll just have the soup... if that's all right.'

Although he said nothing, Cassie noticed what seemed to be puzzlement, perhaps even offence, on Smith's face: a kind of unvoiced sigh.

He turned to Rufus.

'And for sir?'

'Oh, I'll just stick with the soup, too, I think,' said Rufus.

Smith turned, without comment, and took their order to the kitchen.

In his absence, the couple saw that mounted behind the bar was a collection of shields, trophies and the like, mainly of a martial nature. Positioned prominently was a rifle that appeared to Rufus to be some sort of musket. Unlike everything else in the pub, it had a patina and character that suggested it was not a reproduction but was in fact the real thing: a genuine antique.

Rufus wondered if it was entirely legal to display something like that but decided that it must have been decommissioned.

'That's quite a weapon you have there,' he said, when Smith returned.

'Oh yes,' said Smith, 'you can say that again.'

The landlord was still civil but seemed to Rufus somewhat cooler in manner than he had been.

'Right then, what'll you be having to drink?'

Rather like the menu, the line-up of beers wasn't what Rufus had been expecting. There was nothing that even vaguely approximated a 'real ale'; all the beers – to Rufus's eye – being brash, branded, gas-assisted brews. Better could be had at the street-corner local back home where he and Cassie were prone to pop in for a pint and a plate of paella.

Rufus sensed that Smith could read his thoughts. The landlord's eyes now seemed to wear a suspicious, even hostile, look.

'I'll have a bottle of your dry cider, I think. That looks good to me,' he said, attempting to sound enthusiastic about a middle-of-the-road beverage that seemed the best bet.

'And for the lady?' asked Smith.

'Oh, I'll have the same, thank you,' said Cassie.

'Right you are, madam.'

Smith opened the bottles and poured some of the cider into two glasses. 'Well, if you'd like to take a seat, I'll bring your soup over when it's ready.'

Not that its flames – which danced in only one, monotonous direction – seemed to give out any heat, Rufus and Cassie sat down at a table near the fireplace – in large part because they felt that this was expected of them.

They sipped their cider and said nothing, the pub's interior – beyond the musket – lacking any object or feature that might conceivably have stimulated conversation. The presence of Smith, who was polishing glasses (in a way that seemed to Rufus to be faintly belligerent), and who was easily within earshot, was also a deterrent.

Within a few minutes Smith brought out their soups, which he deposited with some ceremony on their table. 'Careful, mind: it's hot,' he said. Along with the soup – which was obviously tinned – were two soft white rolls of the six-in-a-pack supermarket kind and two small, paper-wrapped rectangles of butter, so rigid they could have passed for stone.

'I'll leave you to tuck in, then. Bon appétit,' said Smith, retreating to his billet behind the bar. On Smith's feet, Cassie noticed, were white slip-ons, which she couldn't help but feel were out of place for an inn that would once have been the haunt of shepherds and drovers – and, if Smith was to be believed, still was (… their present-day equivalents, at least).

She amd Rufus consumed their soup quietly, to the strains of Vivaldi, the bleeping of the fruit machine (which seemed to have a mind and life of its own) and the watchful eye of Smith.

When it was obvious they'd finished, he appeared at the table and began to gather up their things. Cassie sensed him register that she hadn't eaten her roll or her rectangle of butter, which was the same frozen mini-brick that it had been when Smith had brought their order out.

'Come up here for the tarn, have you?' asked Smith, while putting their things on his tray.

'That's right,' said Rufus.

'It's beautiful,' added Cassie.

'It is that,' said Smith. 'But, under-used… in my opinion.'

'How do you mean?' asked Rufus.

'Well, you only have to look at it,' said Smith. 'I mean, there's nothing going on there, is there? No water sports, nothing. No wonder this country's lagging behind. Where's the imagination? If you think about it, they could make a beautiful resort down there. Chairlifts, the lot. They could do all sorts of things. Maybe put a new road in. Carparking. I mean, not that this pub needs it because we're packed out… seven nights a week… but it would bring a few extra coppers my way, 'n' all.'

'But surely that's what makes it beautiful,' said Cassie, 'the fact that it's deserted.'

'Take this place,' said Smith. 'It was a right dump when *we* took over. We had to strip out God knows what. Job took us six months. They won't let us touch so much as a stone on the outside, though. Listed building, national park, conservation area and all that nonsense. Had I known, I might never have taken the place on. The rigmaroles we have to go through. You wouldn't believe it. I mean, as if bureaucrats ever got anything done for anybody. Still, that's the Army in me speaking. What do I know? Only done six tours of active service. Seen ten of me mates die in combat.'

Smith stopped speaking. There was an awkward silence. It was as if he sensed he'd gone too far. He stayed there though, not taking away the tray, just holding it.

'Well, I disagree,' said Cassie. 'I hope the tarn stays as it is – always.'

No sooner had she said this than Rufus sensed Smith's mood darken. Not only *Smith's* mood, but – if such a thing could be said – that of the pub itself. Unless Rufus was mistaken, the Vivaldi disc on the hi-fi had jumped from *Autumn* to *Winter*. And, never mind the plethora of bulbs (the coach lamps, the various garish neon tubes on and behind the bar-top, and the glowing, burbling 'bandit'), the light – the natural light anyway – seemed to dim. It was as if – outside – the sun had become hidden by cloud.

'What d'you mean?' Smith said, setting his tray back down on their table.

'What I say,' said Cassie. 'I just don't want to see it spoiled. That's all.'

'Oh, *I* see,' said Smith. 'You just don't want the ordinary folk – the Smiths of this world – coming up here. Is *that* it?'

'No,' said Cassie. 'I didn't say that.'

'People who might appreciate the availability of a Thai curry or scampi with a lemon slice, tartar sauce on the side, instead of turning up their noses and ordering soup and not even having the decency to eat their roll and butter.'

'I think you'd better leave it there,' Rufus said to Smith.

'No one's asking your opinion, pal,' Smith responded. 'I was talking to the lassie, here. Putting her right. You'll keep out of it if you know what's good for you.'

'I *beg* your pardon?' said Rufus, sitting up in his seat.

'I said keep out of it,' said Smith, his face flushing, the irises of his eyes reddening.

'You can't speak to us like that! We're customers here!' said Rufus.

'And I'm the fucking landlord! One more word out of you' – he pointed a pudgy finger with a ring on it at Rufus – 'and I'll be asking you to step outside.'

'I can't *believe* this,' said Rufus. 'Are you seriously challenging me to a fight?'

'I suggest you just shut it, chum,' said Smith. 'I've had quite enough of the pair of you. Coming in here. Wasting my time with your tomato soups and your little bottles of cider. I'm surprised you didn't ask to bring in your flask and sandwiches. What sort of fucking planet are you people on?!'

'Oh, I'm not having that! You can't talk to us like that!'

'Oh, can't I? Well, who the *fuck's* going to do anything about it, all the way up here? There's no cavalry coming round this mountain, mate. And in case you haven't looked, I'll tell you – there'll be *fuck* all signal on your phone!'

'Let's go,' said Cassie, quietly.

'Aye, you do that,' said Smith. 'You both go and *fuck* off to wherever it is you've come from.'

'I'm not having this,' said Rufus. He was on his feet now, opposite Smith – separated by the small round table with the tray on it and their glasses and bottles.

'Please, Rufus,' said Cassie, placing a hand on his arm. 'Let's just leave.'

Suddenly, Smith's jowly face switched from anger to a sardonic sneer. 'Rufus?!' he snorted. 'What sort of poncy fucking name is that?'

And then Rufus swung. With his right. His fist connecting with Smith's fleshy jaw... an audible *smack*.

Smith wobbled, looked stunned, but stayed on his feet. 'You little fucker,' he said. He grabbed one of the bottles from the table and – hand round its neck – smashed it in two on the table's edge.

Rufus kicked the table so that it drove into Smith. Cassie rolled aside.

Recovering from the shove, Smith came again with the bottle. He swung, laughed. 'You and me, son. Man to man.' He carved the air with his jagged stump of glass, as if in grotesque imitation of a conductor leading the players of the auto-looped Vivaldi on the hi-fi.

He advanced on Rufus, who wondered what he might grab (... maybe the copper bed warmer from over the bar, *if* he could get there). And yet, there seemed no way past Smith, who surely only had to lunge.

'Drop it, Smith!' came a voice, suddenly.

All three of them – Smith, Rufus, Cassie – looked towards the bar.

A small, Thai woman was standing in front of it, holding, as if ready to fire, the musket that had been mounted on the wall. The gun was surely as long as she was tall, if not longer.

The woman spoke while looking down the length of it, its end clearly trained on Smith. Her left eye was closed, as if she were taking aim.

'The bottle, Smith. Drop it… you bastard!' she repeated.

For a moment, silence fell over the scene. A spray of rain fell against a window.

Then suddenly, he charged her, with a scream.

And she fired: an orange flash and a loud crack that overwhelmed everything.

It was followed by the sound of a stumble, as smoke and a gunpowder reek filled the bar.

After several seconds, the woman stepped from the cloud and lowered the musket so that the weapon was upright, at her side, with its butt on the carpet.

Smith lay on his back: a hole in his chest. Around it, a large crimson bloom, that was spreading wetly through the tight, checked cloth of his shirt.

'He no-good liar,' said the woman. 'I only marry for better life. But he chain me in kitchen. Make me his slave. He no soldier. No such regiment as Queen's Own Southerners. I look on internet. Check.'

There was no doubt that the Ongleby's landlord was dead. His great and bloody bulk lay there… like something bovine… felled… a water buffalo.

'What—' began Cassie.

'Don't worry,' said the woman. 'I deal with him. Maybe in lake. You go now. Go.'

They walked away, through the bracken.

Stone Cold

By his ninety-eighth year Seymour Thrayle's skin was the colour of parchment, and it sagged from his long frame not unlike the dewlap or wattle that hangs from a wild turkey's throat. There were other things about Thrayle, not least his attitude and a surprising turn of speed (when needed) on his walker, that were evocative of an old and canny cock bird that had, by dint of its instinct for survival and knowledge of the backwoods, for decades outwitted the Reaper's scythe and the most devoted hunter's gun.

Thrayle, who stood at well over six feet, had always been a spare, lean man, and, in the pale linen suits and white cotton shirts that he favoured, his neck and limbs extruded as if his clothes were mere stows for a motley collection of prods, pitchforks and pipe-cleaners.

Their owner was, however, far from a frail or physically weak man, his large, liver-spotted hands gripping the aluminium walker on which he manoeuvred, like the lock-tight claws of a crawfish.

A concession to vanity were the polka-dot bowties he liked to sport (and, sometimes, in their place, silk cravats that arrived at his house in mail packets from suppliers in London, England).

His head had no hair left to speak of, save a few snow-white strands. And his eyes were blue and watery. Yet – for a man so close to his century – his stare was far from vacant… or tired.

The Southern Peaches Go-Go Club was a bar and 'entertainment' venue in a town of no particular note a forty-minute drive from his country estate – his family or ancestral seat, English commentators might call it – in an American Southern state of which you're sure to have heard.

And Thrayle, unmarried and childless, was the Go-Go's most regular (albeit perhaps not best) customer, driving the dusty roads to its pulsing pink sign (which glowed with two neon peaches), behind the wheel of an old black Buick, or an even older Hudson (of a matching hue) on most nights of the week. Occasionally, when a night was warm and fragrant, and his mood was optimistic, he made the journey in a cream-coloured1959 Lincoln Continental convertible, riding with its hood down.

In the club, which was mainly the hangout of farmhands, good ol' boys, drifters, small-time salesmen and, sometimes, college brats and loud young men on bachelor parties from out-of-town, Thrayle – who was a significantly wealthy man – had his own table, which was situated as close to the stage as the management could put it.

Although he followed with an attentive eye the actions of the women who performed sundry acts of exotica above him, Thrayle was known to almost never become animated. Having paid his entrance fee, he would sit at his table and watch the dancers while sipping complimentary soft drinks. Later, he would drive home.

Most of all, he was known – in spite of his millions – for never giving a tip.

One artiste at the Southern Peaches whose dignity was particularly offended by Thrayle's frugality was Miss Candice Canyons – a relative newcomer to the venue, whose personal curriculum vitae in the cause of adult entertainment included magazine and web appearances (well-received, as she was prepared – if perhaps not proud – to point out, by essayists, readers and viewers in the genre), not to mention roles in a number of straight-to-video R-rated films.

Thrayle had never tucked so much as a dollar bill in her stocking top or suspender belt. Once, the old coot had even had the cheek to yawn through her performance.

'Not a *cent* out of that old skinflint!' she complained one night in the club's dressing room to Sindy McSinn, a fellow dancer at the Peaches.

'Join the club, sister,' said the latter, who was something of a veteran at the venue. 'He's been here years and he ain't given a girl a dime yet.'

'Why?' demanded Candice. 'They say he's a billionaire – near as.'

'Word is the only tip he'll give a lady is after he puts a ring on her finger.'

'What?! You mean *marry?*'

'Uh-huh.'

'An old skeleton like him?'

'I hear he's got a big place out in the country, all very fine and fancy, with horses an' all, running in a field,' said Sindy McSinn. 'He ain't never been wed, folks say. A traditional Southern gentleman. That's how some speak of him – never mind his trips here. A few of the girls have tried it on with him over the years, but they ain't never gotten nowhere – not a nickel for their pains.'

'Anyhow, he *drools*,' said Candice. 'Have you seen him?!'

'I know, honey – his age, I think. Ain't that he's getting excited or anything.'

'Yuurgh!' said Candice. '*Who* the heck would want to be with an old bastard like that?'

Sindy McSinn had heard all this before and felt the need for a change of subject. 'Saw your colour spread with Elroy LeBone,' she remarked. 'Tastefully done, doll.'

'Why thank you, sugar,' said Candice, her mind still partly on what her colleague had said about Thrayle (… the fine old house, the horses that ran in his fields).

Prior to her nightly performances, it was Candice's habit to microwave a meal for herself in the kitchen of the rented trailer on whichever park she was staying during her tours of establishments like the Southern Peaches, afterwards driving to the venue in question and entering via a back door.

One evening, having had difficulty sleeping during the heat of the day, she found herself running seriously late.

Throwing on some clothes, she grabbed some peaches from a bowl in her lounge and rushed in her car to the club.

Bustled on stage by the floor manager, having had no more than a minute to change into her outfit (not that there was much to put on), she grabbed and took with her an aerosol of whipped cream from the refrigerator in which the club's dancers kept a combination of eatables and props for their acts.

The announcer introduced her: 'And *now* ladies-and-gentlemen, brought to you exclusively by Southern Peaches Go-Go in conjunction *with* those good people at Blue Rooster R-Rated Video En-ter-tainment (for *all* your home-viewing needs), please give a big hand and the very warmest Southern welcome to the *charis*matic, the *enig*matic, the sexy *super*matic Miss Can-dice C-a-n-y-o-n-s!!'

The Go-Go's stage lights strobed the platform: a web of silver and blue shafts that reared and clashed and crossed, like giant lightsabres. The drum-and-bass blasted.

Candice saw that Thrayle was at his table: stony-faced, staring… his large and ancient head caught by the glow from the platform – like the topmost part of a totem pole.

She ignored him.

Working her way through her routine, she began to eat first one and then the other of the peaches that she'd brought on with her, squirting some whipped cream on each. This she did more for her sustenance than any other reason, albeit a number of the patrons of the

Southern Peaches seemed to see things differently (not that she cared overmuch).

When her act was done, she saw that Thrayle had risen from his table and was clumping through the audience, on his walker, with his back to her.

Backstage, in the corridor to the dressing room (to which customers were never normally permitted), Candice was surprised to find a caller waiting at the dressing room door.

'May I intrude for a moment, Miss Canyons?' Thrayle asked her. Threads of drool hung from him, sticking to the upper tubes of his walking frame. 'It will only take a moment. I'd like… a word.'

'Well, I suppose I can spare you that,' said Candice. '"The wicked borrow and do not repay, but the righteous give generously." The Good Book, Mr Thrayle. Do you know it? Psalms, Chapter Thirty-Seven, Verse Twenty-One – unless I'm mistaken.'

'I dare say you're right, Miss Canyons. I dare say you're right. I promise I won't detain you for a moment longer than necessary. What I have to say won't take a minute, really.'

She tightened the belt of her robe. The dressing room would be empty at that time: the other dancers either being on stage, rest breaks, or up at the bar.

She pushed the door open. Thrayle clumped in.

Candice made for a mirror, sat in the seat before it and began to remove her make-up. In its glass, she saw Thrayle at her shoulder. The sight of him at least proved he wasn't a vampire.

'Miss Canyons,' he began, 'will you do me the honour of marrying me?'

Some thirty or so seconds later – the words that Thrayle – in his rather hoarse and somewhat slurred voice – had uttered, seemed to register.

'What?' said Candice. She uttered the word not in a tone of denunciation or repudiation but with a quietness that encouraged explanation, clarification, from Thrayle.

'After seeing you tonight,' he continued, 'I think… I believe… I'm *convinced* you're the lady I've been looking for.'

'To… marry?' she said, looking at Thrayle in the mirror.

'That's right.'

Never mind the old man's drool, never mind his rudeness, never mind his *meanness*, Candice found herself thinking about those things that – had Thrayle not been there, making this bizarre offer – she would be doing next: driving back to the trailer park, maybe stopping at a gas station or drugstore and doing some shopping on the way, returning to the club the next night, going 'home' again in much the same fashion, perhaps receiving a call from her agent with the offer of some work that – for a cut – he was willing to put her way (for Blue Rooster or some similar outlet).

She turned to look at Thrayle, not in the mirror now but in the flesh – what little there was on his bones.

How long would he last? she wondered. *Not* in a sexual way – she doubted anything would… could… come to that. But in a… *general* way. How long could a man like that live? He was almost a hundred already, so people said. A man of that age… surely he could be 'gone'… within a week? His heart had to be as old as the rest of him, didn't it?

'Yes, okay,' said Candice, looking Thrayle in the eye.

'You do?' asked Thrayle, disbelievingly.

'I do.'

She and Thrayle were married two days later in a trashy chapel of the kind where anyone who wanted to do so could get hitched. Several dancers from the club attended as witnesses. They tittered at the ordinariness of their real names when asked to supply them for the purpose of the record – Sandra, Darlene, Carol-Ann, Jennifer….

Candice dressed modestly.

Thrayle, who wore a white rose in his buttonhole, had a visible tremor in his hands.

Assisted – amid some awkwardness – by the 'minister', he slid a gold band on his bride's finger.

The ring – for which no measurements had been taken – almost immediately fell off… Candice catching and restoring it at the last moment.

Thrayle had brought the Continental out for the day, and, after the wedding, he allowed his wife to drive the car home.

He directed from the passenger seat.

Never mind his inanimation at the club, his mind seemed now to have only one track.

'I like my peaches. I *l-o-v-e* my peaches!' he jabbered and drooled next to her. 'I can't wait to get my teeth into your peaches. I have hungered and *hungered* – and *now* the hour is nigh!'

Twenty or so miles outside the town, he had her turn off the highway and continue on a dirt road that threw up a trail of dust behind the cream Continental.

Before long she caught sight, through some trees, of a large and gracious-looking house that seemed situated on its own, with no other properties near.

'Is that it?' Candice asked.

'That's the place,' said Thrayle, in a preoccupied fashion. 'Hook a right.'

They drove towards it through groves of trees that seemed to have no end. The groves were of less interest to Candice than the white-painted house, which – having several levels (as its lines of windows made clear) – overlooked the trees and the rest of the grounds in a highly imposing way. As she neared, she could see that part of the front of the property was colonnaded.

The thought entered her head that she would now be the lady here: that any second there would be 'staff' waiting to greet the newly-weds. She was pleased that she had attired herself soberly. If the retainers were old and wrinkled, as she expected them to be, and if Thrayle (or 'Seymour', as she now realised she had better start calling him) had said nothing particular to them, then they might not know anything about her. It was surely unlikely that anyone in a house such as that – Thrayle himself excepted, of course – subscribed to the likes of Blue Rooster Video. They might have their suspicions and even treat her in a way that was haughty. But – if she acted the part – they might never discover. With luck, and the right clothes (which she would be able to buy with the money that was now hers – Thrayle, never mind his meanness in other directions was at least partial to fine tailoring) she would be able to pass herself off as a proper Southern lady.

Suddenly, this line of thought deserted her. For she was distracted by something else: something more pressing… something more *jarring*.

As they drew nearer in the Lincoln, the house (she heard Thrayle call it something but the name passed her by) changed… degraded *physically*. Before her eyes. it became noticeably less white: its colour – with every turn of the Lincoln's wheels – fading to a time-worn grey: the pallor of somewhere that hadn't been painted in years. Not visible from afar, possibly on account of its leafless state, a creeper that looked to be of the old and calloused kind, gripped a large swathe of the frontage. Gaps left by fallen boards showed in the fascia. Several windows on the uppermost floor appeared to have planks of wood in place of their glass. Gutters and drainpipes hung loose as if left semi-detached by scrap-stealers who'd been caught and scared off with a blast of buckshot.

Candice remembered what had been said by Sindy McSinn: about horses – of which there were... none – running in a field at the front of the 'fine and fancy' house.

'Pull up here,' said Thrayle, abruptly.

She stopped the car on a plot that looked to have once been gravel, now overtaken by pigweed, dandelions and crabgrass.

Thrayle, whose mind seemed set on something (and Candice suspected that she knew what), hauled himself out of the Lincoln and clumped with his walker towards the house.

'Mr Thray – *Seymour*,' she corrected herself. 'What about my bags? Is there someone who can—'

'Bring 'em!' he interrupted.

He continued clumping. 'And hurry it along now! There's things, Missy, that you've gotta do!'

Still at the wheel of the Lincoln, Candice – unsettled by the state of the house and puzzled by the absence of any retainers – wondered if she oughtn't to roar off, right there and then.

However, she consoled herself that she was a woman who'd been around, who could handle herself, and that few things in life were quite what they appeared (one recent example being the alleged legendary manhood of Elroy LeBone) and that with some spending here and there Thrayle's undoubtedly dilapidated mansion could quite easily be restored to its likely past glory. Anyhow, their so-called marriage (she looked at Thrayle, who was pausing for breath on some steps) could all be over in a night... their wedding night; the ink on the certificate from that rinky-dink chapel being barely dry – but *legal*.

She took some of her bags from the Lincoln's back seat and entered the house behind him.

Never mind its musty, mousy smell and its accumulations of dry, unswept leaves, the mansion's vestibule was not ungracious, with portraits on its walls of figures Candice took to be Thrayle's ancestors. A large chandelier hung from the centre of the ceiling, cobwebs suspended from it as if in imitation of the drool that dangled from its master's jaws. A large, wide staircase rose to the upper floors (to which Candice suspected Thrayle would soon be escorting – or even chasing – her, though she wondered how he might manage the climb. With some luck, he might not.).

'You can dump your things here,' Thrayle said at last, and she set down her bags, imagining that an ancient retainer might now appear. 'I've got something I want you to put on. Follow me.'

Thinking that what Thrayle had in mind was an outfit of the kind that might energise him for the consummation part of their nuptials – something in lace, chiffon, perhaps an old-style Southern ballgown or even the skimpy costume of a 'French maid' – Candice followed him down a gloomy corridor and through a doorway.

To her surprise, she found they were now standing in a kitchen whose windows… those that were free of the creeper and its vines, looked out over the groves of trees in its grounds.

Thrayle turned so that he was behind her and already in the act of retreating.

'Here!' he said, reaching up behind the door. 'This is for you!'

He tossed something that fell against her chest and chin.

Taking it from herself and holding it up, she saw what Thrayle had flung: an old and faded blue-check apron.

'Get it on, Missy! Get it on!' said Thrayle, who by now was stepping beyond the door and closing it after him.

'… and make me my peach tart! I've been a good boy! I've waited all these years! And all I want now is my tart *full* of my own Southern peaches. My trees are groanin' with them. Groanin! So just get to your cookin' and your bakin'. And don't go makin' a mess of that apron, neither. That was my momma's – the greatest baker of peach tart this side of Atlanta. So, you've plenty to live up to, Missy, believe you me. You'll find all that you need in that kitchen, includin' a basket of peaches I picked personally this mornin'. And now I'll let you get on with it. Let me know when you're done.'

By now, Thrayle had closed the door. When Candice reached for and tried the handle, it held fast – as if, on the other side, it was in the clamp of one of Thrayle's crawfish claw-hands. Unless Candice was mistaken, she heard something turn. She knelt and, peering in the keyhole, saw the end of a key – one of the old, jailhouse kind – turn in the lock and withdraw – and, after that, the cloth of Thrayle's suit and the frame of his walker, clumping away.

She stood up and tried the handle – the door was locked: there was no doubt. 'Thrayle!' she called out. 'Mr Thrayle, sir! Seymour!! You can't do this! Come back here, please. Come back here, right this minute! It's not lawful. It's not how a man should treat his… *wife*! This is far from the behaviour of a Southern gentleman.'

'Whoever said I was a gentleman?' she heard him chortle, from somewhere beyond the door.

'This is kidnap, Thrayle!' Candice shouted, pulling at the door handle.

'You can holler all you like, Missy. Ain't no one here but thee and me, except for the mice.'

Candice stood still for a moment and looked around her at the floor.

'And what if I *don't* bake you a tart? What if I can't?'

'You'll get on with it, if you know what's good for you. Love, honour *and*… obey. That's what the pastor said at our ceremony. *I* was listenin'… every word – even if you weren't. Apparently, it's in that Good Book that you pro-fess to know all about and are so fond of quotin'.'

She knelt back down to the keyhole. 'But I….' She didn't finish her sentence. There was no sign of Thrayle. Any sound from the clump of his frame had gone.

She stood up and looked around the kitchen.

The peaches were in a wicker basket, on an old oakwood dresser.

For the next twenty minutes, Candice considered her situation. Furious with Thrayle, she hammered the kitchen door, yelling: 'And just how do you expect a lady to go to the bathroom in here?'

Some moments later, she heard various clunking and trundling sounds. From somewhere in the kitchen came the muffled sound of Thrayle's voice. 'Open the hatch!' he called.

She saw that set in a wall was a sliding panel, which she now pushed upwards. Inside, on the shelf of a dumbwaiter, was a chamber pot.

'You won't get away with this, Seymour Thrayle!' she shouted up the shaft.

From somewhere above, he yelled down: 'Just make me my tart!'

'Crazy old bastard!' she yelled, and snatched out the pot.

She pulled down the hatch.

She considered her options. She could cook a little but in recent years had mainly relied on take-outs and ready-meals microwaved in the kitchen of her trailer (wherever she'd been shacked up). Besides, she couldn't remember ever baking a tart.

She began to try the catches of the various windows in the kitchen. One after another, they failed to open – the wood being warped and stiff to the point of being stuck tight in the jambs. Either that, or the vines of the creeper – that seemed to grow not only outside but *inside* the house – shrouded the glazing with ugly, impenetrable thickets.

Finally, she found one window that was both loose in its frame and clear of the creeper, through which she figured she might feasibly climb (with some effort).

She still had the keys to the Lincoln.

What to do?

On the one hand, she could simply pile out of there, make a dash for it in the car and never come back. But if she did, she could surely say goodbye to any slice of Seymour Thrayle's fortune. What smalltown judge would believe her tale of imprisonment, against the word of a so-called Southern gentleman like Thrayle? And running out on him after fewer than twenty-four hours of matrimony? No court would award her a cent. She'd simply be portrayed as a gold-digger – one who (for whatever reason) had got the jitters… a tramp who shook her ass in the faces of featherless old buzzards like Thrayle and sought to pick their pockets. Hell, if she wasn't careful, she could end up in jail.

After a moment, her eyes fell again on the peaches in the basket on the dresser.

And she had an idea.

What if *she* didn't make the tart, but somebody else *did?* Hell, this was Peach Country. Stores, bakeries, you name it… they had to be full of all kinds of peachified stuff – if only she went and looked.

She checked her purse: $400.

Heck that was surely enough to buy a peach tart fit for a president.

With a little luck, she could drive the thing back with Thrayle none the wiser – she'd heard nothing of him for a while: perhaps he was asleep – it had been an eventful day for a guy of ninety-eight – and serve the tart up as if it were her own.

Yes, she could get it from someplace high-end – better than any home-baker could make.

She could turn the tables on the old coot, and, before too long – who knew how much living his mean and nasty heart had left in it: a day, a week, a month, a year at most? – his house and money would be… hers.

Come sundown, Candice squeezed out through the window. Outside, she stood close to the creeper for a moment and listened for any sound of Thrayle. Beyond the chorus of the crickets, she heard nothing. She stepped to the trunk of a pine-tree, from where she scanned the mansion. No lights shone and nothing moved. She crept to the Lincoln, praying it would start up without a fuss, her heart beating harder than she'd ever known.

To her relief, the old car fired first time. She eased it down the long drive to the dirt roads and then onto the highway.

As she drove, she was struck by the peach-coloured glow of the sky.

It was as if the firmament consisted of one giant, peach-filled fruit box, suspended above the land.

On reaching the town, the lateness of the hour suddenly dawned on her. Stores, particularly of the small, independent kind, were shut and shuttered. That included the bakery and grocery outlets at which she'd hoped to buy 'her' tart. The only premises open were drugstores, gas stations and big, brightly-lit all-night chains of the stack-'em-high, sell-'em-swift kind. She parked and entered one of these, reluctantly.

A refrigerator unit in an aisle bleached with intense white light boasted twenty-five brands of peach tart. She settled on one that had an illustration of a kindly-looking old woman who reminded her of Dorothy's Aunt Em in the *Wizard of Oz*.

At the checkout, a leery guy took her money and looked her over in a way that suggested he was either a patron of the Southern Peaches, a subscriber to Blue Rooster, or that he just figured he knew the 'kind of woman' that Candice was. 'Pleasure's been *all* mine,' he said, as he gave her her change.

'Betcha it has,' said Candice. 'Can't see any woman wantin' to share it.'

Sitting in the Lincoln on the lot, she looked at the tart.

It had been the best on the rack, but she had her doubts about whether it would satisfy Seymour Thrayle.

That wasn't the only thing about which she wondered. She mulled over the wisdom of even setting foot in that house of his again. And what if he *didn't* die soon? The man was old, yeah – but he was strong… and surprisingly speedy on that walker of his, when he wanted to be. What if he went on for another ten years? Or even twenty? This was the South. Waspy old aristocrats like Seymour Thrayle didn't die young. They lived *long*.

Candice thought also of the life she'd led… and how – if she wanted – could return to it. The Southern Peaches Go-Go was but a few blocks away. She could drive there right now and ask if they'd take her back. But what if Thrayle then showed up – demanding to see his lawfully wedded wife… using his influence… causing a scene? And did she really want to go back to that, anyhow? The videos with Blue Rooster… the 'cameos' with Elroy LeBone? And then there were the 'tours' she made of all the other crummy towns… the two weeks here, the three weeks there… her tenancies on the endless and shabby trailer parks, with no real home of her own, no kitchen or oven that was properly hers in which to… bake a peach tart.

She fired-up the Lincoln, stuck it in 'Drive', swung out of the lot and headed to Thrayle's.

The night sky was starry. The house stood pale and still and temple-like amid the dense groves of dark trees that surrounded it, as if in worship.

As she approached in the Lincoln, she worried that Thrayle might be waiting… watching from a window.

But there was no sign of him – just the house and the trees and the moon and the stars, as she halted the convertible outside the property.

She climbed back in through the kitchen window.

Having done so, she unpacked the tart and concealed the packaging in a cupboard, along with the unused peaches from the wicker basket.

Then she sat in a rocker in one corner and slept.

Come dawn, strong shafts of sunlight – never mind the presence of the creeper and its vines – broke through and warmed the kitchen. Candice woke and, although initially disbelieving the setting, remembered where she was and what she had done.

She saw the tart where she had left it – on the kitchen table.

Having washed her face with some cold water, she resolved to call Thrayle.

Peach tart was surely not a normal thing to have for breakfast, but it occurred to her that the irregularity of eating it at that hour might work to her advantage: Thrayle's senses perhaps not being fully engaged at such a time of a day.

She slid up the hatch on the dumbwaiter.

'Mr Thrayle?! Seymour?!' she called up into the interior of the house.

'Yes? What is it?' his answer – sharp and unhesitating – came back.

Candice tried to sweeten her voice, with a singsong note. 'I have some peaches for you! In a ta-art!'

'Peach tart, you say?' Thrayle's voice came down the shaft. 'It's ready?'

'Yes, it *i-i-z.*'

'Good. It's about time!' he said, gruffly. 'I've been wonderin' what's been keepin' you. I must have dropped off. Get it ready. I'm comin' down.'

Candice pulled open some drawers and found some cutlery and a plate. She laid a place at the table.

She heard Thrayle's walker clumping on the boards outside the door, some muttering (about how long he'd been kept waiting) and then his key – turning in the lock.

'Good mornin', husband,' said Candice, as he entered the kitchen. 'I'm sorry to have kept you but gettin' everythin' ready has taken a while.'

'Never mind your "good mornins". Where is it?' said Thrayle. 'The tart? I've been waitin' sixty years for this – at least!'

She indicated the presence of the tart, on the table.

He eyed it – suspiciously.

'Won't you take your seat?' she said, hoping his fixation would keep his mind from the unease she sensed was audible in her voice.

He slung himself from the walker into the chair she pulled up for him.

'Now, can I get you a napkin?' she asked.

'Never mind that,' Thrayle responded. 'Just pass me my pie.'

She drew it towards him.

He touched it with the knuckles of one of his great crawfish-claw hands.

'It's cold,' he said, grumpily.

His eyebrows scrunched themselves in a way that, had they been observed by another who was equally passionate in the matter of peaches, might have brought to mind the activities of *Synanthedon exitiosa*, the bug better known as the peach-tree borer.

'Well, that's because I baked it last night, when you were sleepin',' said Candice. 'It's been… settlin'… overnight.

And it does say,' she quickly corrected herself (for fear that it sounded as if she was reading the label), '… it's a known fact that a peach tart can be served cold as well as hot.'

'Settlin'? So that's your story?' Thrayle harrumphed, snatching up a spoon.

He plunged it into the tart.

His wife – the realisation of their wedded status dawning on her more than ever in that moment – offered up a silent prayer.

Thrayle lifted the spoon and put it in his mouth.

'Please God,' she whispered.

And then – in almost the next second – the spoon came back out. Not 'came' though – that would be the wrong word entirely. For it *flew* – out of his mouth and out of his hand and across the kitchen and onto the floor. And with, and after, it – in separate but similarly powerful ejaculations – came the portions of the tart which the spoon and his long and bony arm had cantilevered to his maw.

It fell in splats – one on the table, one on the floor.

Within an instant, Thrayle was on his feet, sweeping her aside, clumping with his frame to the old, iron stove. He set one hand on its top, as if about to swear a court oath, and, with the other, drew open its door.

'Cold!' he pronounced, staring at her, his eyes not blue now but blacker than she had ever seen them, his face red with rage.

'I got you the best I could,' she said to him.

'Store bought! Store bought!!' he stormed. 'In *my* house. Of all houses. In this *oasis* of peaches… where my family has been growin' them since before the time of Robert E. Lee?! You have the *temerity*… the *audacity*… to disrespect me… like *that*?!'

He began to clump towards her, spitting… flailing, like some furious combine through a field of corn.

Small as she was compared with him, she stood her ground.

'Now hold it right there, Thrayle!' she said. 'While we're on the subject of disrespect, *your* behaviour hasn't exactly been husbandly.'

Seemingly taken aback, he halted his advance.

'Lockin' me in here. Sendin' me down a chamber pot. That ain't the behaviour of a man, let alone a Southern *Gentle*man. That's the conduct of a… monster.'

He seemed uncertain of her: in his eyes, there was a wariness of her pluck.

'What would your mother say?' Candice went on.

With that, however, she quickly sensed she'd gone too far – for the old man's fury rose again in his face, ten times harsher than before.

'Get out of my way!' he yelled, almost trampling her. 'How *dare* you bring my mother into this! I know exactly what *you* are – hussy! You, lady, are store-bought! Just like your tart!' Drool flew from his mouth. 'Now listen to me. You have three hours to make me a proper one or you'll be out on your ass.'

'You can't do that, Thrayle. This is my home too now. I have rights.'

'Oh can't I? You'll be surprised what I can do – an old man like me. Case you hadn't noticed there's plenty of land round here. And it all belongs to me. Room to dig, Missy… ya dig?'

He snatched the door behind him and turned the key.

She thumped its wood. 'You're crazy, Thrayle! You old bastard! You hear me?!'

Soon she was aware of him clumping outside – in view of the kitchen windows.

His claw hands reached through the vines and pulled at the panes, as if checking for any that might be loose.

When he came to the one through which she'd escaped, he drew some tacks from his mouth and hammered them into the frame.

Thrayle shouted through the glass: 'Clock's tickin', Missy. I warn you. You've got all you need in there.

Fresh peaches, plus anythin' else you might require, in the pantry and the refrigerator. If you've any sense, you'll get to it. I want to eat!'

He let go of a vine that beat down on a window, and disappeared.

Candice sat back in the rocker and did something she hadn't done for a long time. She sobbed.

When she stopped sobbing, she had a hunger to do something else she hadn't done for a time, which was to get stoned… in the way that she had for her early film 'performances': not a line of work she'd taken to easily in a life that had been screwed-up pretty much from the start. She had no hankering for him but remembered, for a moment, Ricky – the photographer and boyfriend (after a fashion) who'd first persuaded her to take off her clothes for the camera: he'd never been short of a smoke, or a snort, or a pill to pop.

Getting stoned, however, was out of the question. There were none of the 'ingredients' in *that* kitchen.

Besides, a much better idea planted itself in her head – which was this: to get Seymour Thrayle 'stoned' instead.

Not with pot, but with peaches.

Thrayle was obsessed with this matter of the tart. Not only was this a danger to others, it might – Candice realised – prove a hazard to him.

All that was needed was for Thrayle to choke while eating. And, for that to happen. what she needed to do was bake a tart not with the stones taken *out*, but with the stones left *in*. Hell, hadn't Dubya Bush – the president himself – had a brush with some kind of snack? Surely no coroner's office or district attorney in the land would press a case of peach-choking as a homicide.

She had him. She *had* Seymour Thrayle.

She just *knew* how he'd guzzle his way through that tart if she cooked it for him. He'd go at it as if there were no tomorrow (which there wouldn't be for *him*, by the time she was done).

It was all… peach perfect.

She jumped from the rocker and moved quickly around the kitchen.

She found the pantry Thrayle had told her of. She saw that – never mind the beat-up state of the rest of the house – it was well-stocked and in good order, likewise the large refrigerator which looked as if it had come from a Fifties movie. It was as if Thrayle had dedicated himself to the maintenance of these – and the dream of his tart – while letting just about everything else go to rack and ruin.

Everything she required was there – peaches, sugar, flour, butter, honey, cream.

Now all she needed was a recipe.

Her mind sharpening to her mission, Candice went through the kitchen – opening cupboards, pulling out drawers. Surely in an old Southern house like this there'd be a book of recipes? Dishes that for generations had been passed down?

She came upon all sorts: old newspapers (one with a report and a photograph – prominent on its front page – that showed a juvenile Seymour Thrayle, receiving a cup for his peach crop, at some kind of county fair); ancient certificates for insurance, shares, land and oil; letters (both typed and handwritten); dark little droppings that looked like the work of mice (from which she recoiled).

Finally, deep at the back of a drawer in the kitchen table, hidden by faded catalogues from a farm machinery company, seed packets and twine, she found it: *The Personal Book of Isabella Thrayle* – Seymour Thrayle's mother. It was a collection of ink-written jottings, poems, pencil sketches and watercolour art, small articles cut from newspapers and magazines, with brittle, pressed flowers and pieces of fine, hand-worked lace.

Candice thought how it was not entirely unlike an album she had herself once kept – about her cheerleading at high school, her prizes at beauty pageants, 'promotional' work at car washes, diners and gun stores (usually wearing something showy and tight) – before her career had taken the fork that it had.

Turning the pages, she came to what she'd been looking for: 'Peach Tart – My Own Recipe – by Isabella Thrayle.'

Candice's heart skipped a beat.

She set to work straight away: turning on the kitchen's old (but electrified) oven. She then put on – and tied behind her – the apron from the hook on the door. She followed Isabella's instructions to the letter. From the first ('Get your cooker good and hot') through all of her little tips (about turning the edges of the puff pastry in order to create a crust and sousing the peaches with honey) to the last: 'And bake in your oven for a half hour or until your tart has begun to brown.' All of Isabella's instructions, that is, save *one*: about being sure to remove all of the stones from the peaches (which Candice noted – and ignored).

For the baking, she selected from the kitchen's crockery and ovenware a dish that was several inches deep – she didn't want any of those stones showing too close to the surface.

When her tart looked the part, she took it from the oven and, with a pair of burnt old gloves, set it down on the kitchen table. On a shelf in the pantry, she found a glass shaker of powdered sugar, and, in the refrigerator, a tub of whipped cream. She set these – with a spoon – on the table at a place set for Thrayle. Having done so, she drew herself a glass of water and drank it.

Composing herself, she stepped to the dumbwaiter, pushed open its hatch and called up the shaft.

'Thrayle! Your tart's ready! You hear me?! It's done! Come and get it!'

She drew down the hatch and said to herself quietly, 'Come and get your desserts, you bastard.'

'Yes, I heard you, madam,' said Thrayle, who, unknown to her, had entered the kitchen silently and was standing, with his walker, inside the door.

She felt herself jump.

Turning, she tried not to show her fear.

His nose was raised, like that of some old, porch-front hound which had noted the odour of something interesting in the afternoon air.

'Your tart—' she began.

'I know,' he said, cutting her off. 'I smelt it… through the house.'

'Would you like to try some?' she asked.

He locked the door behind him and placed the key in a side pocket of his white linen jacket. 'I think I would,' he said, speaking in a much more measured way than his earlier ravings about peaches. His tone and the angle of his head – lifted in a way that suggested he was attempting to get the better of cataracts or some other impairment of his sight – told her he was not unsuspicious of what she might be at.

He clumped and sniffed his way to the table, drool drooping from his jaw (which, for once, she was glad of the sight of – taking it as a sign that his senses had been aroused).

He advanced, eyes all the while on the tart, where it rested, on the long, old table, his ancient, grey tongue switching from left to right in his gulch of a mouth, its movement – amid the evident swelling of his saliva – moistening his thin and cracked blue-pink lips (never mind what seemed an effort on his part to contain himself and give her as little cause as possible for optimism… let alone celebration).

Thrayle swung himself into the chair she had drawn up for him, afterwards shoving his frame aside.

'There's sugar powder and cream,' she said.

'I can see,' he said, gruffly. 'I may be old – in the eyes of some, Missy – but I'm not yet dumb or blind.'

'Now, it's been coolin',' she continued (more than a little nervously). 'But all the same it ain't long outta the oven. Would you like to try—'

'Bring it!' said Thrayle, over the top of her.

She moved the tart so that it was next to the dessert plate and spoon she had laid for him on the tabletop.

'As you can see, I made it nice and deep. *Full* of your own favourite peaches. "Why skimp on a good thing," I said to myself. "When we're surrounded with such bounty." Shall I serve you some?'

He grunted affirmatively.

She spooned a portion onto his plate. She sensed his eyes on her – as if he distrusted her every action and breath.

And yet he was drawn to the tart... *hungered* for it – she knew.

Another surge of drool spilled from his mouth and coated his chin.

She doled him a goodly portion. Even so, she couldn't be sure that the helping she'd given him contained a stone, and she feared that, somehow, they might all have slipped back... deeper... to the far end of the dish.

'Like I said,' she began again, '... there's sugar powder and cream.'

'I heard you the first time, woman!' Thrayle said, angrily. 'Quit prattlin'! Now step back from the table! And leave a man be!'

At first, Thrayle ate doubtfully... cautiously... shooting sceptical glances to where she stood – watching him – by the stove.

He shook onto the tart some of the powdered sugar. Having done so, he lowered his head towards it and sniffed, as if with the sudden thought that the scattering he'd given it might be arsenic or some other poison. He stuck his forefinger in the whipped cream and sucked it. Having satisfied himself that this – like the powdered sugar – had not been contaminated, he dumped a spoonful on his plate.

And now – as she watched – he ate: keenly, hungrily, one spoon after another, shovelling portions from the baking dish on to his plate. In time, he set aside his spoon and took to grabbing at the tart with his fists, throwing it into his mouth, like some infant or a man who'd been starved, scarcely stopping for breath. Within what seemed mere moments, both his plate and the baking dish were clean. And Thrayle was sitting there, sucking at his stained teeth, thinking, breathing and very much *not* choking, dying or dead.

How had this happened? What had gone wrong?

Candice wondered if, somehow, she'd unconsciously set aside the stones. But she told herself she couldn't have – she would've remembered. Besides, they would *be* somewhere: by the sink or the stove… in the trash. The truth could only be that Thrayle, in his gorging, had eaten them – a dozen stones from a dozen peaches – and swallowed them whole.

She looked at him.

Drawing a hand across his mouth – sitting like an old emperor – he finally spoke.

'Make me another,' he said.

And with that, he got up, went out of the kitchen, locked the door and left.

Initially, Candice was simply stunned. How *could* she have missed with this trick? She went and found a tray of Thrayle's peaches in the pantry and cut one open – just to be sure that its stone was there. Which it was: woody and – in colour – somewhat bloody. Yet Thrayle was now wandering the house with a dozen of them – rattling – inside him. What's more, in the manner of a bad-guy gunfighter in a Western, who'd been holed with a whole belt of bullets, the old buzzard was still hungry – and coming back for 'dessert'.

She baked a second tart, which, to her astonishment, Thrayle devoured, just like the first. Afterwards, he rose silently, clumped out of the kitchen and locked the door.

Lord Almighty, Candice thought to herself. Twenty-four stones. The man was a freak!

That night, a storm of a great and strange kind gripped the house and estate. Not a tropical cyclone of the type that sometimes surged in over the South, this one seemed to Candice to be rooted right there, at the mansion. Through the windows of the kitchen, she saw the trees writhing in their groves. Torrents of rain turned the ground between them into rivers, then mud baths. The downpour beat on the old, dry creeper, which, perhaps for the first time in years, sprouted shoots and leaves. The plant seemed to tighten its grasp of the mansion – the grizzled vines turning, squeezing… *alive* – energised by the storm. The house creaked, groaned, *moaned* around Candice. The howling wind, the hammering rain all seeming part of some elemental lament.

And there were other, strange wails – that *may* have been human.

Candice sat quietly in the kitchen rocker, tilting to and fro.

Come morning, the storm had blown itself out. A curtain with a pink blush hung across the sky. Through the gaps in the vines that wreathed the kitchen windows, Candice caught sight of the battered peach groves. Numerous trees had been split asunder, limbs either sheared or hanging broken, like so many ugly scarecrows.

The house was quiet around her.

She slid up the hatch on the dumbwaiter and called to Thrayle.

He made no answer.

She tried the door of the kitchen – and found it locked, as before. She beat on it and called Thrayle's name.

But still the house was silent.

Having had more than her fill of confinement, she rifled the drawers of the kitchen and found a meat cleaver. She brought its blade down on the door, then stood and listened. Nothing stirred in the house. So she went at the wood again and again, hacking around the lock and handle, till the door came free.

Having obtained her liberty, she began to wander – her right hand tight on the cleaver.

Since Thrayle's voice had always come to her from up above, she made her way to the grand staircase and began to climb. Its faded red carpet was thick with dust. On the walls, Thrayle's forebears seemed – deliberately – *not* to eye her from their portraits as she climbed – as if they deemed her unworthy.

Stepping onto a landing, Candice wondered what she might find: the skeleton of Momma Thrayle springing – like some awful cuckoo – from the case of a grandfather clock?

Out of curiosity, she pushed at a door.

It opened with a creak, like a pussycat's miaow.

A room revealed itself – the contents covered with sheets. These she chose not to lift… out of concern at what they might conceal: Poppa Thrayle, perhaps: stiff as a board, seated in an armchair where he'd been sitting since Gettysburg.

The next chamber was similarly shrouded but had book-lined walls. A gust – a vestige of the storm – caused a vine from the creeper outside to whip against a window, in a way that briefly spooked her.

In the next room, there were signs of life: an old four-poster bed: its linen and pillows tangled and scrunched, as if its occupant had suffered a disturbed night. Unless she was mistaken, she seemed to smell Thrayle: the collision of high-end tailoring and low-down cunning that was the mark of men like him.

He wasn't there, though – and neither was his walker.

From somewhere along the landing, its cause perhaps the last gasps of the cyclone, came the sound of a door, clattering, repeatedly, against its jamb.

Candice's hand tightened on the cleaver.

She walked towards the noise.

At the end of the landing, she caught sight of it… the door: opening, swinging shut, then opening again.

She continued towards it. 'Thrayle,' she called out, '… are you there?'

Suddenly, in a room whose door was open to her right, a bunch of crows took flight from a window that was broken and part-covered with planks.

The abruptness of their action made her spin. She dropped the cleaver to the carpet.

Meanwhile, the clatter kept on from the door at the end of the landing.

Eyes fixed on its swinging and shutting panels, she half crouched and felt for the cleaver. Her fingertips danced over its blade on the carpet, found its handle, picked it back up.

'Thrayle,' she called again, '… if you're in there, I want you to come on out.'

Still there was no sound – save the clatter of the door and, so it seemed, the hammer of her heart.

And now she was a yard from it… within touching distance of its old, black wood.

She raised the cleaver above her head.

She pushed the door with her free hand.

It opened, with a long, high creak.

Thrayle sat in front of her – on the john of a bathroom, his walker before him, his linen pants at his ankles… enthroned.

His back and head were slumped against the downpipe; his eyes looking heavenwards, to the rusty, iron cistern.

On his ancient face: a horrible, pained grimace.

The man was dead.

Stone cold.

A firm of undertakers from the town came for his body later that morning.

The next day a man who identified himself as being from the Coroner's Office called at the house.

Sherman Travis was middle-aged, carrying some weight, losing his hair and seemingly in need of new razor blades. He said his inquiries were routine but necessary in a case of 'sudden death' like Seymour Thrayle's.

'Sudden?' said Candice, on the porch, as Travis showed her his badge. 'The man was ninety-eight.'

'Ninety-seven, I believe, ma'am. Yet to celebrate his birthday – but you'll know that.'

She let him in.

'Case like this, we just have to make sure everythin's how it oughtta be. You'll understand, ma'am. Man of Mr Thrayle's fortune and years… gentleman like that… there's always a risk that someone will want to take advantage.'

He swung his eyes around the vestibule, then over her, scarcely concealing that he was computing the age gap between her and her late husband – seventy years, to be sure.

She registered the smirk on his face but chose not to react.

At his request, she took him to Thrayle's bedroom.

While claiming he had no wish to be needlessly intrusive, he asked – all the same – if she and her *husband* – he paused before uttering the word (in what seemed a clear attempt at mockery) – had shared the four-poster that stood there. To which she said No, they slept apart. After this, he had her take him to the bathroom at the end of the landing. He stood there for a moment, shook his head and pulled the chain.

Going back down the staircase, she thought a little hospitality might not go amiss. 'May I offer you something, Officer Travis?' she asked.

He stopped and looked at her, at the foot of the stairs, in a way that she felt was more than a little loaded.

'Thank you, ma'am, but I've already eaten,' he said.

'Oh, I was thinking a glass of lemonade, that's all. Warm day like this.'

'Oh, that's mighty kind of you, but I really do have to get back. Maybe I'll take you up on your offer some other time.'

'Yes, indeed,' said Candice.

Travis's second visit came two days later. Candice was cutting back the vines of the creeper when she caught sight of a car coming up the drive.

'Officer Travis,' she said, when he closed the door of his auto and walked over to where she was pruning. 'I'm surprised to see you here again.'

He gave her a look of a kind she didn't like: sneery, 'lookin' down on her' (as she felt him to be).

'Well, you see, ma'am,' he said. 'That's all on account of the circumstances.'

'Circumstances?'

'Some folks in this county and elsewhere for that matter… they might think the death of a man, like that of Mr Thrayle, to be… *strange*.'

'*Strange*? I don't follow you.'

'With twenty peach stones up his ass.'

She looked at him and closed the blades of the cutters she'd been using. They were old and not particularly sharp, and came together with a scrape.

'Steady, officer. Some manners if you, please. That's my late your husband you're talkin' about.'

'Beggin' your pardon. Up his… *rectum*, Miss Canyons.'

'And there I have to correct you again, Officer Travis. It's *Mrs* Thrayle – as you should well know.'

Earlier, on account of the heat, she'd loosened her shirt, and she became conscious that a number of its upper buttons were undone… that Travis (while sneering) was trying to catch sight of anything that might be on show for free. She did up two of the buttons with the fingers of her right hand in a way that she hoped seemed casual.

Having watched her fingers, Travis continued: 'Some folks – who sit on juries and the like – might find a thing like that – all those peach stones, I mean – rather… puzzlin'. I mean, *one* might be understandable: an accident. But twenty? Well, that might look to some like a case of forced feedin'.'

'Well, on that score let me put your mind at ease,' Candice began. 'My husband always used to say—'

'Would that have been during your *forty-eight hours* of marriage?' Travis cut in on her.

'My husband,' she continued (ignoring him), 'loved his peaches. Fact of the matter is that peaches were his obsession. Lifelong. There's plenty of evidence of that pretty much anywhere you'd care to look: yearbooks, newspapers, county fairs. He was famous for it. I'm surprised you didn't know that, Mr Travis.'

'And he was a rich man, too. One of the richest, by all accounts.'

'I *don't* see what that has to do with anythin' – unless there's somethin' on your mind that you're not tellin' me.'

'Oh I've a few things on my mind, Miss Canyons – I mean, *Mrs*… Thrayle.'

'Well, that's as maybe. But as you can see, I have work to be gettin' on with here. My husband – like many a man – liked his peaches. That's really all there is to it. Now, if you don't mind, I'll bid you good day, officer. I really do need to get on.'

She turned away from him and opened and closed her cutters on a vine.

'Those cutters look a little… *stiff*, ma'am, if you don't mind me sayin',' said Travis.

'Well, I expect that's because they're gettin' on. Must've spent a hundred years cuttin' vines 'n peach stalks hereabouts. There's life left in 'em, though,' she countered. 'They'll do the job, officer. Don't you worry about that.'

For the next week, Candice busied herself with tasks. She cut back as much of the vine as she was able, swept the leaves from the vestibule, replaced boards where they were missing from broken windows, and cleaned out sinks, bathtubs and toilets. Something told her she hadn't seen the last of Officer Sherman Travis, and – amid her other work – she made preparations to 'receive' him.

When the old Bakelite phone that sat in one of the reception rooms rang on an evening of rainless, rumbling thunder, Candice knew the caller would be Travis.

'I just wanted to make sure you were home,' he said.

'Why, this is an irregular hour to be callin',' she answered. 'What did you have in mind?'

'Oh, just to take down a few things,' he said (sounding less than sober). 'You'll know what I mean by *that*… Candice.'

'Well, if you're intent on comin', you'd better make your way. Where are you now.'

'Edge of town.'

'Well, I'll see you in forty-five minutes, I guess. Mind how you drive.'

She hurried upstairs and put on the dress she'd picked of Momma Thrayle's – a scarlet, satin number of the traditional kind she'd found in a wardrobe on a rack dutifully preserved by her son Seymour (save for where moths and mice had got at them and spiders had spun their webs).

Beneath the gown, she put on some hosiery, brought with her from her trailer, of the kind she sometimes wore in her acts, together with a pair of heels. Finally, in an old mirror, she put up her hair.

Through the sash window she'd raised (never mind the storm that was threatening: the night was sultry and short on cool air), she heard a car.

Glancing down the drive, she saw headlights.

Taking one last look at herself in the mirror ('Quite the Southern Belle'), she made her way downstairs.

Standing at the foot of the staircase, she listened as an engine cut out, quickly followed by the slamming of a door.

'Lights, camera, action,' she whispered to herself, and waited.

Travis didn't knock. He just pushed open the door and walked (after a fashion) right into the vestibule – his gait possessing a visible sway.

'Why, Officer Travis,' Candice began, standing by the newel post of the staircase, in a script straight out of Blue Rooster, her scarlet gown hitched for the apparent adjustment of a garter, 'I do believe you've taken me unawares.'

Beyond the house, there was a fresh rumble of thunder. The electric light of the chandelier dimmed, then restored.

He seemed unsettled by this but staggered on.

'I know what you did to your husband,' he said. 'I know what you *are*.'

'Why, officer,' she continued, 'what *do* you mean?'

Travis took a bottle from his jacket… swigged.

'You got the right dress for it. I'll give you that,' he said.

'Give me what?' she answered. 'I *don't* understand.'

'Oh, you'll understand, all right – when *I've* finished with you!'

He lunged for her.

She stepped aside.

He crashed against the newel post.

'Couldn't we do this a little differently?' she asked, as he straightened himself. 'Unless I'm mistaken, you appear to be… *packin'* somethin'.'

'Oh, I am… *Missy*, you can be sure of that.'

'Well, why don't—'

On your knees, woman!'

'What?'

'On your knees!'

He unzipped himself. 'Now, *get* on with it!'

She knelt, spreading her gown, so that it looked like a great red lily pad on the floor of the vestibule.

Amid another distant rumble of thunder, the chandelier again dimmed.

She took hold of him… and sensed him shudder.

'Do it woman!' he barked. 'I'm waitin'!'

'And so am I,' her voice came back.

Drunk as he was, Travis was puzzled how she could be doing what she was supposed to be doing – with something sharp and tooth-like at his groin – and yet be speaking, at the same time.

As the light of the chandelier restored, he looked down… and saw the vine-cutter in her hands, its blades (from their hiding place on her garter) seizing him – where few men would want to be seized with cold steel.

'I advise you not to move, Officer Travis,' she said, looking up. 'I suggest you stand v-e-r-y still, just like that stair post behind you, and hear what I have to say. Do I have your attention?' Travis managed a horrified nod. Candice continued: 'Good. Now, it obviously hasn't escaped your attention that this – in the main – is a peach farm. But, believe you me, I am not opposed to lowerin' a pair of over-ripe cherries, should I need to. And, if you know what's good for you, you'll clear out of here, leave me alone and never come back. What's more, Officer *Dibble*, you've been caught on camera.

You've made it pretty plain that you know all about my past. Well, it so happens that I've put my expertise to use. And your comin's and goin's, especially tonight, have all been recorded. Frankly, I think they'll make a nice few frames for the next big release from Blue Rooster. Are you married, officer? Is your boss a church-goer? Southern Baptist perhaps? Maybe your wife? Or her parents? I really think you've underestimated who you've been dealin' with, mister. And now, if I were you, I'd get out of here – and scram!'

Travis paled, as if her were about to puke.

He nodded. 'Lemme go,' he said.

She withdrew the cutters, rising to her feet. At the same time, she held them out at him, blades open, ready – in case he was fool enough to come at her.

He scurried to the front door, hurried down the steps, jumped in his car and drove.

Two days later, Seymour Thrayle's corpse was returned to her in a casket, to do with it whatever she liked – no questions asked – as his widow and rightful heir.

Feeling she owed Thrayle a favour, she buried the old buzzard on the estate – in a plot in a peach-tree grove (whose particular fruit, since then, she's never picked, allowing it to fall on him, the soil sucking-up its juices, till the storms wash away the wasp-blown waste).

She's the farmer of that land now and the lawful mistress of the Thrayle House, which, in her hands, has been largely restored, as well as its estate.

On the vine, so to speak, she's heard that a certain local officer has long since transferred, at his own request.

Although her life is now mostly given over to the land, she occasionally drives to town and – for the sake of old times – shows her face (and no more than that) at the Southern Peaches Go-Go… afterwards, heading home – hood down – in the old, cream Lincoln.

For the past three years – just like Momma Thrayle's once did – her peach tart has been voted 'best in class' at the district festival. While no one says as much (of course), the judges seem to think it would be unwise to award her daughter-in-law anything less.

The Picnic

Never mind the 'Keep Off the Grass' sign, the man in uniform marched across the lawn to the bench where Harold and Enid were sitting.

He stepped sternly from the turf and onto the gravelled path of the Winding Rose Walk.

'You'll have to put all of that away,' he said, with what seemed to Harold and Enid a distinct lack of civility.

'What?' said Harold. 'I don't—'

'*That!*' said the man, pointing to the small picnic – fishpaste sandwiches, a pork pie cut in two and a tomato each – that, together with a tartan-patterned cylindrical flask of tea and a couple of fondant fancies (for dessert), they'd laid on a towel between them on the bench.

The man seemed to lean over them as he spoke: '*No picnicking!*'

Harold saw a badge on his jacket lapel that bore the words 'Duty Manager'.

'But we've always picnicked here,' said Harold.

'Always,' echoed Enid.

'Well, the place is under new management. And that's the rule.'

'"New management"?' said Harold. 'What d'you mean? This is Lord Tyckmere's house, isn't it? I presume he's still with us?'

'And a very nice man, too,' said Enid. 'We had a conversation with him once about his roses, not five yards from this seat.'

'Nobody's denying that. But there's a new... structure... in place, and things have changed. Rules are rules. And picnicking isn't permitted.'

'But why?' asked Harold.

'We're not doing any harm,' said Enid.

'Fully-licensed catering and hospitality is available on-site,' said the man. 'Doubtless you'll have seen the signs. You'll find a range of meals in the restaurant, and teas in the marquee.'

'"Fully licensed?". We don't drink,' said Enid. 'Besides, we're ordinary folk. Have you seen what they serve? Not to mention the prices.'

'I'm fully aware of the menus and tariffs, madam.'

'Salmon mouse and salad at ten pounds a throw,' said Enid.

'Mousse,' corrected Harold.

'Strawberries and cream at six ninety-nine,' she continued. 'That's not *our* food. We're pensioners. We can't afford that.'

'I'm sorry but—'

'No, you're *not* sorry. You're just saying that,' said Enid. 'Striding over here... badgering us about our sandwiches. I've never heard anything so—'

'So you want us to stop eating, then?' asked Harold.

'Yes,' said the man.

'But we've *always* picnicked,' said Enid. 'All our lives. We've rambled... camped... climbed... hunter-gathered... used our resources. I was a Brown Owl. My husband here was an Akela. In his case, thirty-six years of service to Scouting. Doesn't that count for something?'

'Look. I haven't got time to argue. You'll just have to pack up and...'

'Go? Is that it?' said Harold. 'You mean that you're really going to throw us out over a pork pie and a couple of fishpaste sandwiches?'

'Well for one thing there are the pests.'

'Pests?' asked Enid.

'Yes. Pigeons, crows, gulls and God knows what else this sort of thing brings in. Rats, squirrels.'

'Squirrels? What's wrong with squirrels? I like squirrels,' said Enid.

'Vermin,' said the man. 'Look, are you going to—'

'Yes, we're leaving,' said Harold. 'Come on, Enid. We'll find somewhere else.'

'Well, I…' began Enid. 'Words fail me. Fifty years we've been coming here. Since before *you* were born,' she told the man.

'Come on now, love,' said Harold. 'Let's leave it lie.'

'No, we *won't* leave it lie,' said Enid. 'This fellow needs putting in his place!'

'If you've any complaint you're welcome to send an e-mail to customer services. You'll find the address on our website. Alternatively, you can download the app.'

'E-mails? Rules? Pests? I've never heard such rubbish in my life. I feel sorry for you. D'you hear me? Having to enforce such… nonsense!'

She began packing the picnic into her husband's knapsack.

'Madam, I'm simply doing my duty.'

'Oh don't give me that. You don't know the meaning of the word. We've done ours – to God *and* the Queen, like it said in our oaths. My husband had letters of commendation from three separate Chief Scouts. And you're bickering about us eating a pork pie? Well, as far as I'm concerned, you can jolly well get knotted.'

They walked to the exit. The man watched them from the end of an avenue.

Enid saw him eyeing them as they passed through the gatehouse. 'Treating us like that,' she said. 'He wouldn't know a sheepshank from a half hitch. Who *does* he think he is?'

Later, in the manner of a couple who'd forgotten something that perhaps one had brought to the attention of the other in a discussion on the lower deck, Harold and Enid alighted from the No.28 bus which was bound for town. Having done so, they crossed over the road and waited for the outgoing service, in a shelter on the other side.

Later still, at an hour when the castle and gardens had long been locked and anyone wandering the grounds could only have been doing so by virtue of having become lost, or perhaps having concealed themselves within the maze, such souls (though there were, in fact, no witnesses) might have heard – in the sweet-scented gloaming and above the whine of gnats and the late buzzing of bees – the sounds of various muffled protests, followed by some scuffling and hammering.

When, the next morning, staff arrived before breakfast to ready the house and grounds for the public, they found the teas marquee in a state of collapse and, after that, a sight so very odd that their eyes and minds found it difficult to digest.

On the main lawn – in the pink, early light – beneath the feet and bills of gulls, the darts and scampers of squirrels and the advances and retreats of sundry magpies and crows, there seemed to be a man – and maybe, by now, merely the *body* of a man – tied between tent pegs… where he'd been left to lie, by persons unknown.

Uncorked

'So, what appears to be the problem?' asked Doctor Julian Pound, who, rather than looking at his video-link screen, was busy drying his hands with a paper towel (having dealt with the day's first 'problem').

He opened a bin with the toe of his tanned, leather half-brogue, and dropped the dampened towel, and then the bin's lid.

In the absence of a reply to his question, he stepped over to his computer and pressed a button.

A giant, grey-white blob suddenly filled his screen. It did so with such shocking enormity that Pound found himself stepping back in his consulting room.

The blob – by virtue of its colour and its odd compression within the rectangular frame of the screen – looked, Pound thought, like nothing so much as one of those curios of human and farmyard anatomy, pickled in glass jars, that – due to distortions caused by confinement, the nature of the glass, the preservative and the light – weirdly exaggerated some aspect or feature and even made it seem as if the corked and jarred exhibit was alive… and about to break free.

To one side of the screen, Pound now saw – in a panel – the note that had been written by Mandy, on reception: 'Mrs Skyrme-Beggs and her son Tyler. (Something "personal".)'

The huge, near-lifeless blob – which Pound deduced to be the face of Tyler Skyrme-Beggs (into whose all-encompassing whale-blubber any distinguishing features had, by the looks of him, long disappeared) – was shoved, unceremoniously, out of camera shot.

The marginally smaller face of Mrs Kylie Skyrme-Beggs – her countenance visibly red, hypertensive and having a fur to it that made Pound wonder if its growth wasn't a by-product of something steroidal – took her son's place.

'Er… yes?' said Pound.

'It's our Tyler,' announced Mrs Skyrme-Beggs, in the short of breath way of the obesely overweight. 'He's got a problem. Something personal.'

'Yes?' said Pound, remembering from previous in-person consultations the foulness of her breath and the gag-provoking nature of her body odour. (He again thought how very wise the company that owned his practice – in which he was a not insignificant shareholder – had been to institute this system of remote consultations with patients.)

'He's constant-painted,' said Mrs Skyrme-Beggs.

'I'm sorry?' said Pound, his attention now drifting back to Tyler's malaise.

'Constant-painted,' said Mrs Skyrme-Beggs. 'You know. He canna go.'

'I see,' said Pound. 'Well, what's his diet like? He seems quite a… *big* young lad.' As he asked this, Pound wondered what his wife Arabella would be cooking for dinner that evening – the wine he might have to pick up at the off-licence on his way home. It occurred to him that he might have to phone ahead – in case she was doing fish. He pictured their wine rack in the kitchen: some Malbecs and perhaps a Shiraz, neither of which would do. He might try to get something 'New World', or maybe a bottle of the Calfician Burino Oro he'd seen when he'd last been in the store: a snip at just under twenty quid.

'Diet?' asked Kylie Skyrme-Beggs, drawing Pound's thoughts back to the boy-mammoth lurking beside her, the camera at their end too small to capture both Madonna and Child, never mind their use of any wide-angle lens. Her facial expression and vocal tone betrayed her consternation at Pound's use of such a word with reference to the titanic young Tyler.

'Uh, yes, Mrs Skyrme-Beggs,' Pound ventured to her video image. 'What's he been eating... recently?' (He wondered how long it might take to chill the Burino Oro.)

'The usual,' Kylie Skyrme-Beggs responded.

'Which is?'

'Burgers... like most young lads his age.'

Pound's ears detected her wounded offence, her busy barbed wiring of her defences against what she sensed was coming next.

'*Just* burgers?' he asked.

'Mainly... yes,' harrumphed Kylie Skyrme-Beggs.

'How many does he get through... typically,' queried Pound, judging it best to sound interested in a technical aspect. He needed no reminding how Mrs KSB had once put the surgery in a rather unpleasant spot – a complaint to her councillor and then her MP about 'the imposabillity' of getting to see a doctor. There'd been a fuss for a while about her nasty little letter. True to form, the affair, such as it was, had fizzled out – Pound, in fact, signing the MP off sick after the launch of a probe into the politico's expenses.

'Three or four,' Kylie Skyrme-Beggs answered after a moment (seeming to have some difficulty computing the sum).

'What?! Every day?' Pound responded, with genuine surprise.

'Oh no,' said Kylie Skyrme-Beggs. 'Every meal.'

'What?!' said Pound again. 'So he's eating a dozen of these things every day??'

'About that,' Kylie Skyrme-Beggs answered, in a tone that to Pound's ears sounded an attempt at insouciance.

'Are there never any greens? What about salad?' Pound continued, doing his best not to splutter.

'Oh yes. Lettuce, peppers, tomatoes. But he generally takes all of that out. Sometimes they don't put it in for him. It depends which restaurant he goes to.'

'Restaurant?' For a moment, Pound pondered her meaning. To him, the word meant white tablecloths, leather-bound menus, wine waiters, petits fours. If he and Arabella were on holiday abroad, the meaning might well extend to a trattoria, taverna or sushi bar. Suddenly, Pound realised that his interlocutor meant establishments that – to his senses – were of the gaudy, plasticky kind, lit-up like carousels and Christmas trees. He'd never entered one but had reliably been informed that cutlery didn't even exist and 'meals' – if that was what they could be called – were identified not by any name but by a number or barcode, the dishes having prefixes such as 'Gigantic', 'Nuclear' and 'Extreme'.

'So when did he last have a movement?' Pound now asked.

'I'm sorry?' said Kylie Skyrme-Beggs, blank-faced at the use of a word that seemed to suggest activity on the part of her son.

'Tyler. When did he last have a movement… a *bowel* movement?'

Kylie Skyrme-Beggs's blank and soundless stare remained on the screen.

'A shit, Mrs Skyrme-Beggs,' Pound felt provoked – eventually – to say. 'When did Tyler last have a shit?'

'Oh,' said Kylie Skyrme-Beggs.

Pound watched as she swung heavily to one side to confer with her off-camera offspring. He heard some whispering and muttering of a muffled kind over the speaker.

As all of this went on, Pound wondered about the proliferation of the Skyrme-Beggses of this world… the extent of their existence. Apart from formerly at the surgery, and now on his computer screen, he seldom saw such people. The only near connection came outside his car, when he saw them on the pavement, if he happened to have been held up at a set of lights.

'Six weeks,' said Kylie Skyrme-Beggs, eventually.

'I beg your pardon?' responded Pound.

'I said "six weeks",' said Kylie Skyrme-Beggs, in a louder voice. And then, in a slightly quieter one: 'Or maybe seven… or eight.'

Good grief, thought Pound. Could such a thing be possible? He wondered what to say.

For a moment, he just sat there… staring at the screen: at Kylie Skyrme-Beggs, who was staring back at him.

'Can you give him some anthill-biotics?' came her voice, eventually.

'What?' said Pound, still stunned.

'Anthill-biotics? For our Tyler? Can you give him some?' asked Kylie Skyrme-Beggs.

'Oh, *they'll* be no good. This isn't a case for them,' said Pound, coming to his senses.

'Pills then? Or medicine? Something from the farmsee?'

'No,' said Pound. 'Tyler is going to have to come to see me.'

'What?! In person?'

'Yes, I'm afraid he's going to have to undergo a procedure.'

'A procedure?!' replied Kylie Skyrme-Beggs, who, to Pound, now looked and sounded genuinely anxious. 'D'you mean surgery?'

'There's no alternative, I'm afraid, Mrs Skyrme-Beggs.'

'Is it gonna hurt?'

'On the matter of pain, I will be honest with you and say that I can make no guarantees.'

'What you gonna do? He might look big, but my Ty's a sensitive lad, you know.'

Pound leant away from the screen for a moment, and then leant back.

In his right hand he held – in clear view of his monitor – the large rubber plunger with which he'd extracted a toy fire engine from the U-bend in the patients' WC prior to the commencement of his consultations – said 'comfort' vehicle having become lodged there after being dropped in the toilet bowl by an infant due for vaccination jabs with Nurse Burns.

Suddenly, a splatter, that had the colour and density of estuarial mud, flung itself against the picture on Pound's screen. And, after it, came further, more powerful splatters that, in the manner of an incoming tide, or a wall that was being pebble dashed, filled – to the point of obliteration – Julian Pound's portal to the temporarily unblocked burger world of Kylie and Tyler Skyrme-Beggs.

He clicked the 'Leave' button on his software.

In a voice already weary, he called into his computer's microphone: 'Next!'

Oh, how he was looking forward to getting home and uncorking that Burino Oro.

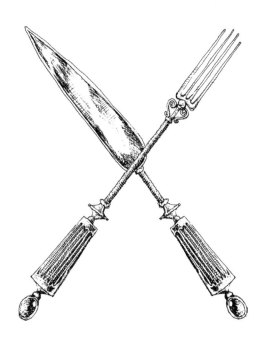

Thanks

Matthew G. Rees expresses his thanks to many; on this occasion, particularly: David Yates for his art; Paul Murgatroyd for reading the manuscript and finding it worthy of endorsement; Sally Spedding for her encouragement throughout.

Matthew G. Rees

Matthew G. Rees grew up in the border country between England and Wales known as the Marches. He trained as a journalist and worked on newspapers for ten years. He is the author of the story collections *Keyhole* and *Smoke House & Other Stories*. He has also written plays. His employment in a varied life has included time as a teacher and as a night-shift taxi driver. He has a PhD from the University of Swansea. For more about Matthew G. Rees please visit www.matthewgrees.com

Praise for Matthew G. Rees's other story collections

Smoke House & Other Stories
(Periodde Press)
Tales of the liminal and the uncanny with
photographs by the author

'*Matthew G. Rees oxygenates language and playfully conjures up the oddest things and happenings while making them seem casual, almost everyday events as he mesmerises the reader, holding our attention in a velveteen vice… a writer at the top of his game and then some.*'

Jon Gower

'*Rees has crafted a superb "smorgasbord" of weird, unusual and often terrifying characters and events which make up this unique collection of short stories. "Unputdownable" is often an overused adjective, but never has it been so appropriate.*'

Sally Spedding

'*We have no hesitation in recommending this collection to anyone with a taste for the macabre and bizarre or indeed anyone who appreciates exquisite story telling.*'

AmeriCymru

'*By turns bawdy, hilarious, thrilling, breathtakingly inventive – effortlessly exploding imaginative horizons… such beautifully-crafted work. With Rees, you never know what's lurking around the next page.*'

Keith Davies

Printed in Great Britain
by Amazon

85767150R00164